Shadow Rescue

REBECCA DEEL

Copyright © 2018 Rebecca Deel

All rights reserved.

ISBN-13: 9781726764544

DEDICATION

To my amazing husband. I love you.

ACKNOWLEDGMENTS

Cover design by Melody Simmons.

CHAPTER ONE

A bullet slammed into the wall an inch from Sam Coleman's head followed by a barrage of gunfire. Small pieces of brick peppered her cheek. While her brain screamed at her to move or the next bullet would slam into her, Sam's body stood rooted in place, sweat beading under her uniform on this hot, sultry July night in Nashville.

A second later, she was falling. A hard-muscled teammate took the brunt of the hit with the ground, then flipped their positions and covered her body with his. Joe Gray quartered the area with a Sig in his hand, his expression grim.

Through Sam's ear piece, her team leader demanded a sit rep.

"Sniper shot at Sam," Joe snapped. "Trace, you have a bead on this clown?"

"Negative. You could stick your head up so the shooter fires a few shots for me to pinpoint his location."

"East quadrant near the rock wall," Ben Martin, Shadow's EOD man, said, his voice ice cold. "Caught the muzzle fire."

"Ben, circle around to the east. I'll take the west. Capture if possible," Nico said. As always, Shadow's leader was calm under fire. Unlike Sam. Not anymore.

"Copy."

"Sam, Joe, check the principal."

"Come on. We need to move." Joe rose and crouched, placing his body between Sam and the shooter.

Furious with herself and terrified for Joe, Sam scrambled to her feet and ran toward the corner of the house with Joe on her heels, covering her back. The gunfire should have alerted the principal to trouble but the woman hadn't checked the area.

Praying the shooter didn't focus his scope on Joe's back, Sam vaulted over the low fence. She winced at the jarring pain in her chest when she landed on the other side.

Ignoring the discomfort, she raced to the back door. Light spilled from the kitchen window, the beam illuminating part of the patio. Sam avoided the patch of light and turned the knob. Locked.

So much for a simple grab-and-go. Sam thrust her hand into a cargo pocket and pulled out her lock picks. She noticed the fresh scratches around the lock and frowned. Not good. Within seconds, the tumbler shifted and she twisted the knob.

Sam palmed her Sig and stepped into the silent house. She glanced around the kitchen quickly. Nothing looked out of place. Not wanting to be a well-lit target if the shooter managed to slip past her teammates, Sam turned off the overhead light, leaving a low-watt bulb burning over the stove.

Joe entered the kitchen with silent steps and closed the door. "Anything?" he whispered.

She shook her head. The place was quiet as a tomb.

"Take the bedrooms. I'll start in the living room and meet you back here."

Sam scowled. Joe would be in the line of fire if the shooter remained in place. Knowing him, that was the reason he'd chosen to search for their principal in the front part of the house.

She sighed, frustrated with herself. One of the best-trained operatives she'd ever worked with, Joe wasn't careless or reckless. As alpha as he was, Joe would be angry if he knew she worried about his safety. Talk about insulting the man's ego.

Despite chaotic emotions rioting through her, Sam nodded and turned to the darkened hallway. Joe grabbed her hand and squeezed gently before heading for the living room.

Sam's heart rate skyrocketed, this time for a different reason than fear. Joe had been doing that since she'd been shot 12 weeks, 5 days, 3 hours, and 20 minutes ago. Just touching her, the contact unfailingly gentle. But what did it mean? Did he still see her as a friend?

Dragging her attention back to the task at hand, Sam entered the hallway, gaze searching the darkened spaces as she approached the first door. Ignoring the beads of sweat trickling down her back, she pushed the door open. A bathroom, shower curtain pulled back. Empty.

Sam returned to the hall, scanning for changes in the narrow corridor. Nothing. Drawing in a calming breath, she moved toward the second door, this room on the front side of the house.

She pressed her back to the wall and opened the door, expecting more gunfire but heard silence. A quick glance inside revealed a guest bedroom. The closet door stood open. Empty.

Sam hurried past the open doorway and headed for the two remaining rooms. Praying the shooter had been apprehended by Nico or Ben, Sam pushed open the partially closed door of the room to the left and peered inside. Home office. No closet or principal.

She eyed the remaining room. Had to be the master bedroom. Weapon raised and ready, she moved into the room on silent feet, tracking with her Sig. A suitcase filled with folded clothes lay open on the queen-size bed along with a carry-on bag and purse.

Sam's attention shifted to the closed bathroom door. If the Shadow unit had arrived in time to thwart an attack on their principal, Sam was about to embarrass the woman. Joe had tasked her with finding Janine Hollingbrook. The woman would be mortified if Shadow's spotter walked into the bathroom while she was in the shower. Sam knew that wasn't the case. Something was wrong.

Sig by her side, she went to the bathroom door, grasped the cold metal knob, and twisted. Sam pressed her back against the wall, pushed against the door, and met resistance.

Pushing harder, Sam opened the door wide enough to see jeans-clad legs, sneakered feet, and a pool of blood.

Oh, man. Her medic training kicked in. Sam holstered her weapon and shoved her way into the bathroom. One look and she knew Shadow unit had arrived too late.

CHAPTER TWO

Joe walked into the living area, Sig up and tracking as he quartered the room. Empty. That left the garage, laundry room, and basement. As skittish as Sam had been since the shooting three months ago, he refused to send her into a dank basement to search for their principal or an intruder.

His mouth curved. If she knew he deliberately gave her soft duty, the feisty medic would hand Joe his head on a silver platter. The smile faded as he remembered the moment Sam froze after the shooter's bullets whacked into Janine's house near her head. Although Sam insisted she was ready for duty, his partner was still working through the aftermath of her near-death experience.

He opened the basement door and shined his small, powerful flashlight around the interior. Memories of Sam on a bathroom floor, bleeding out from a bullet wound to the chest, flooded his mind. He'd never been more terrified in his life as he held her in his arms while a teammate drove to the nearest hospital. Afraid every shallow breath would be her last, Joe had begged God to spare her life and pleaded with Sam not to leave him.

Now, she was almost healed and on her first mission with Shadow since the shooting. An easy grab-and-go mission, according to Fortress Security's CEO, Brent Maddox. Joe snorted. Right. No such thing as an easy mission for his unit.

"Joe."

He started to ask if Sam had located Janine. Her grim expression told Joe the other woman was dead. If the principal had been injured, Sam wouldn't have left her alone. "Show me."

She led him to the master bathroom and moved to the side. Joe's stomach knotted. As a former SWAT officer, he thought he'd seen everything. This was a whole new level of viciousness. What information had Mike Hollingbrook withheld? "You know what this is?"

She slid him a look. "A slit throat. I haven't been sidelined that long."

"It's a Columbian necktie. Someone wanted to send a clear message to her father."

Sam grimaced. "They succeeded."

Joe's gaze returned to their dead principal. "How long has she been dead?"

"A few minutes. The body is still warm."

He growled. Fortress had dispatched them to retrieve Janine thirty minutes ago. Her father had received the threat six hours earlier and delayed contacting Fortress. The delay cost Janine her life.

"We should take pictures of the scene and leave. The cops need to be notified." Joe activated his comm system. "Nico, we located the principal. She's dead."

"Copy. Shooter's in the wind. I'll contact the boss. He'll handle the next of kin notification as well as the police contact."

"Two minutes."

His partner slid her phone away a minute later. "Finished."

"Let's go. We can't be here when the cops arrive." His lip curled. "We'll be the first suspects. Did you touch anything?"

"Only with gloves on."

Relief loosened his muscles. The need to whisk Sam from the house rode him hard. They returned to the SUVs where their teammates waited.

As he and Sam climbed into Nico's vehicle, sirens sounded in the distance. Joe twisted in the shotgun seat to keep Sam in his peripheral vision. He didn't like her pallor. His hand clenched. Was the reaction from the brutality of Janine's death or Sam's near-death experience outside the principal's house?

Although he hadn't said anything, Joe was worried about her. He was no stranger to PTSD. With his experiences in the Army plus his years as a cop, he understood as did every member of Shadow. The horrors of war and the situations they encountered in their quest to stop human trafficking took a high toll from them all and caused Maddox to keep a close watch on the unit.

When Joe was alone with Sam, he intended to broach the subject of another counseling session. She had to deal with the memories before she or someone else was hurt.

"What happened to Ms. Hollingbrook?" Nico asked as he merged into Interstate 65 traffic.

Between them, Joe and Sam gave a detailed accounting of the scene inside the pretty house, a house now marred by the death of the owner.

"Any evidence of the intruder inside the house?"

Joe frowned. "Aside from the dead body, no. I wish we'd had more time in the house."

"We'll ask Zane to hack the police computers to see what they discover. How did the perp enter the house?"

"The back door had fresh scratches," Sam said. "The person who killed her picked the lock, slit her throat, and locked the door on the way out."

"A child could have broken in that house." Janine had installed an adequate alarm system with low quality locks. While Sam was a top-notch medic sought after by Fortress units, she wasn't the best or fastest lock picker. That dubious distinction belonged to Joe. Leftovers from his misspent youth. "Hollingbrook should have insisted his daughter install a better alarm system."

"Wouldn't matter if the system wasn't armed." Nico passed a slow-moving motorist and eyed Sam in the rearview mirror. "You okay, Sam?"

"I'm fine."

"Have anything to tell me?"

Sam turned away from Nico's scrutiny. "No."

Shadow's leader glanced at Joe, his eyebrow raised. Not going there, especially with Sam in earshot. He gave a slight head shake. Joe would speak to Nico later. Maybe. He wanted Sam by his side if she wasn't a danger to herself or a teammate. He'd worked with Rio Kincaid and Jake Davenport over the past twelve weeks while Sam recuperated. They were good but they weren't Sam.

Nico activated his Bluetooth system.

"Maddox." Their boss's deep voice filled the interior of the SUV.

"It's Nico. We're on the way back from Hollingbrook place. We were too late, Brent."

"What happened?" After a summary of events from the operatives, Maddox said, "Be here as soon as you can. Her father is in the conference room. He'll want details."

Joe spoke up. "Boss, he doesn't need them. No father should have that information in his head."

"That bad?"

"Columbian necktie."

Maddox growled. "All right. It's enough for him to know her throat was cut. After Hollingbrook leaves, I want every detail."

The rest of the trip to Fortress headquarters passed with silence in the SUV. After Nico parked in the underground garage, Joe hopped out and opened Sam's door. His brows knitted at Sam's careful movements as she exited the vehicle. Concerned, Joe stopped her with a hand on her arm and looked at Nico. "We'll be right behind you."

"Don't take long." Nico strode to the elevator with the remaining members of Shadow.

As soon as the silver doors closed behind Nico, Ben, and Trace, Joe swung around to face Sam. "Did I hurt you?"

She frowned. "Why do you ask?"

He moved closer. "Sam, you don't have to put on a front for me. I know you're in pain. Did I hurt you when I tackled you?"

Sam shrugged and flinched.

Oh, man. He had hurt her. That was the last thing he wanted to do. All Joe could think about at the time was getting Sam out of the line of fire. "I'm sorry. I didn't intend to hurt you."

"Stop it," she hissed. "I'm not an invalid, Joe. Doc Sorenson cleared me for duty."

A decision Joe didn't agree with. He'd seen her fight through recovery and, because he studied all things Sam, knew almost every nuance of her body language. "I didn't say you weren't able to do your job. I just hate that I hurt you."

"You saved my life. I won't complain over a little soreness. Besides, you took the brunt of the hit with the ground."

"Your upper body is not in pre-injury condition. You're the one who insisted I give my body a chance to heal when I was shot in the chest two years ago. Cut yourself some slack."

He stared into her beautiful face, longing to draw Sam into his arms and kiss her. He'd dreamed of kissing Shadow's medic for years. Fear had held him back. No more. Her close call three months ago convinced him he couldn't wait any longer. He had to find out if she would consider a different relationship with him. "Tell me the truth. How bad is the pain?"

She dropped her gaze, refusing to answer.

Unable to help himself, Joe cupped her chin and raised her face to his. Her eyes widened in surprise. "Talk to me," he murmured. "Please."

"It's improving," she hedged.

"But?"

"I need over-the-counter pain meds," she admitted. "I'm okay. If I wasn't, I'd tell you."

He brushed his thumb lightly over her bottom lip. What he wouldn't give to kiss Sam's perfect mouth right now. Too fast, he reminded himself. Wasn't it? "I'll hold you to that." Joe released her and turned toward the elevator. "Come on. Maddox will be pacing the conference room by now."

The elevator ride was silent. When the car stopped, Joe laid his hand against Sam's lower back. She gave him a sideways glance but said nothing. He counted the fact she didn't move away from his touch as a victory. Sam was prickly about people touching her. One day he hoped she would share the reason with him.

Their teammates, Maddox, and Zane Murphy, Fortress's communications guru, turned to look at them when he and Sam walked into the conference room. Maddox motioned toward two empty chairs across from his seat. "Need anything before we begin?"

Joe glanced at the side table where the staff usually kept a supply of water. No bottles. Good. "Water for both of us." Joe pulled out Sam's chair for her. "I'll get some from the breakroom. Anyone else want water?"

Nico stood. "I'll go with you. We'll bring enough for everyone."

Joe strode from the room with his team leader on his heels.

As soon as they were away from the conference room occupants, Nico asked, "What happened with Sam at Hollingbrook's place?"

"What do you mean?"

The other operative turned to face Joe, frowning. "Come on, man. I'm not Maddox. You know I have your back and Sam's. I can't help if I don't know what's going on."

Joe pushed past Nico and continued to the breakroom. Once inside the room, he shut them inside to avoid the possibility of being overheard. "She froze, okay? It's not a big deal. She'll be fine."

"PTSD?"

"Yeah. Which one of us doesn't have issues with that?"

"The rest of us didn't freeze in the line of fire. If you hadn't tackled her, she would have taken a bullet in the next second. She was lucky, Joe."

"You think I don't know that?" he snapped. "I'll be the one with nightmares tonight. I thought I would lose her." Again.

"She shouldn't be on mission rotation yet."

Joe snorted. "You try telling her that. Sorensen cleared her for duty."

"The doc evaluated her physical condition, not her mental state."

"Back off, Nico."

"I can't. Our lives depend on Sam's ability to do her job. It's my responsibility to get every member of my team home in one piece."

"She'll work through it and come out stronger. You'll see. I have her back. You know I won't let anything happen to her."

Nico studied him a moment, then gave a slow nod. "All right. I'm depending on you to keep me apprised of any progress she makes. I need to know if she's incapable of doing her job, preferably before she takes another bullet."

"Understood."

"Let's go. Maddox will come after us himself if we don't return to the conference room."

Joe went to the wall of cabinets and found a packet of Sam's preferred OTC pain meds, then grabbed several bottles of water. He followed Nico who also carried several bottles of water.

"About time." Maddox scowled at them. "Pass out the water and start talking, Nico."

While Shadow's leader began his summary of events, Joe pressed the packet of painkillers into Sam's hand under cover of the table. She flashed him a smile and swallowed the pills while everyone's attention was centered on Nico.

When Nico finished, Maddox pointed at Joe. "You're next."

Beside him, Sam stiffened. Did she think he would throw her under the bus? As Joe began his report, he wrapped his hand around hers and squeezed. Not wanting to push too hard, he loosened his grip. Sam entwined their fingers.

Surprised, he stumbled over a couple words, cleared his throat, and plunged ahead. Despite the distraction, Joe chose his words with care, glossing over Sam's momentary lapse.

After he finished and Maddox moved on to Trace, Sam didn't release Joe's hand. Nice. He could get used to that.

Finally, Maddox turned to Sam. "Your turn."

Her recitation was nearly identical to Joe's with the exception of the additional medical information.

"Did you talk to her father?" Nico asked.

"He's devastated. Mike lost his wife five years ago. Janine was an only child and they were close."

"Why didn't he report the threat sooner?" Trace frowned. "We could have rescued her before someone broke in."

Ben set aside his empty water bottle. "Might have been two of them involved in her death."

"I agree." Nico dragged a hand down his face. "One to break in and slit Janine's throat, one to keep watch with the rifle."

"Evidence to back up that assumption?" Maddox asked.

"Gut only," Joe said. "We didn't have time to analyze the scene." He'd been more interested in getting Sam out of the house.

"I'll look into the police reports," Zane said. "Cal might also be able to find out the information. He still has a lot of contacts inside the Metro Nashville Police Department."

Cal Taylor had resigned as a homicide detective with MNPD the month before and was currently at PSI training for his first mission with Fortress. A SEAL teammate of Maddox, he was as tough as they came. Any team would be lucky to have him.

"I'll contact him." The Fortress CEO handed out five folders. "Shadow's new assignment."

Joe's eyebrows rose when he saw a picture of a Hollingbrook cruise ship. "You're sending us on a cruise? Why?"

"A few female passengers aboard this particular cruise ship have gone sightseeing and disappeared."

"Same port each time?" Nico asked.

Maddox shook his head.

Ben scowled. "How many women are we talking about?"

"Seven to date."

"Why haven't we heard about it on the news?"

A snort. "Hollingbrook kept the information off the media's radar. Didn't want bad publicity. This cruise has experienced a long run of bad luck."

"Didn't the families make inquiries?" Trace asked.

"They were told the women voluntarily left the ship and didn't return in time to board. The cruise line gave the families contact information for the local police departments. So far, none of the women has been seen or heard from again."

"Are we posing as workers?" Sam asked.

"Trace and Ben will be working as security. They'll have easy access to areas the rest of Shadow won't. You and Joe are posing as newlyweds."

CHAPTER THREE

Sam's mouth gaped. "Newlyweds?" She glanced at Nico before returning her attention to Maddox. "Nico and Mercy are real newlyweds. No pretense required. Why not use them for the role?"

"Mercy isn't a trained operative. More important, I have another role for her and Nico. She will be an artist in residence on the cruise ship. Nico is going along as her besotted husband."

A slow grin curved Nico's mouth. "Not a hard role because that is the absolute truth. I adore my wife."

"What happens if the team has to leave the ship?" Joe asked. "Mercy shouldn't be without protection."

"Curt Jackson is going as Mercy's assistant. He refused to act as a waiter. Claims he'll cost the cruise line money in broken dishes. He'll tote her supplies and prevent people from harassing Mercy while she works. If Shadow leaves the ship, Curt will stay with Mercy. I considered asking him to work security as well, but he wouldn't have an excuse to stay with Mercy if Shadow chases a lead off the ship."

At least they didn't have to worry about the safety of Nico's new wife. No one would get through that tough Marine to nab the artist.

"What about the rest of Shadow?" Sam asked. "We'll need them if we leave the ship."

"Ben and Trace will work security without being in the official rotation. They'll keep an eye on you and Joe as well as Mercy and Nico on board ship. Hollingbrook launched an internal investigation into the disappearance of the women. Not long after that, Janine started having accidents. The longer Mike persisted in looking into the disappearances, the more serious the threats became until ultimately someone killed her."

"Will he stop the investigation now?" Trace asked.

"He'll never stop until he makes them pay for taking his daughter from him. That's Shadow's new mission. Find the men who killed Janine Hollingbrook. Second, unmask the people behind the disappearing passengers and dismantle the organization. The people responsible for Janine's death may also be responsible for the missing women."

"When do we leave and where are we going?"

"The jet will be ready to leave John C. Tune airport in two hours. The cruise liner sails from Vancouver to San Francisco, San Diego, down the pacific side of Mexico through the Panama Canal to Fort Lauderdale. You're joining the ship in San Diego. By the time you board the jet, I'll have more information from Hollingbrook. He's arranging your accommodations aboard ship."

Trace paled. "Oh, man. You better stock up on motion-sickness patches, Sam."

She smiled, sympathy in her eyes. "I'll be ready."

Joe's eyebrows rose. "How long is this cruise?"

"Twenty-three days."

"Have there been passenger disappearances from other Hollingbrook cruise routes?"

"There's a shorter Mexican cruise that departs from San Diego with one disappearance, but the other six missing women were on this cruise."

"I want more details." Nico stood. "Ports of call, contacts we have in the areas, our contact person aboard ship. We'll travel heavy, Brent. Our hardware will prevent us from boarding."

"Hollingbrook cleared it," Maddox said. "You won't have trouble boarding."

"If I think Mercy is a target, I'll send her here with Curt. I want him, Eli Wolfe, and Jon Smith assigned to her protection detail until I return."

"If Wolfe and Smith aren't available, I'll watch over her myself. We'll protect your wife."

Nico turned to Shadow. "Pack your gear. I'll meet you at the airport." He strode from the room, phone in his hand.

As the remaining members of Shadow prepared to stand, Maddox said, "Joe, Sam, stay behind a moment."

Sam's hand tightened around Joe's. He glanced at her and winked. Joe always had her back as she did his. They were partners and friends. Thinking about their linked hands, she wondered if there was a chance for a deeper connection. Sam focused on their boss as the conference room door closed behind Ben.

"How do you feel, Sam?" Maddox asked. His piercing gaze missed nothing. "You took medicine a few minutes ago."

"Over-the-counter pain meds. I'm a little sore." She smiled. "Joe hits like a linebacker." From the corner of her eye, she saw Joe wince.

"I'm not surprised. He played football in high school. Any problems with flashbacks?"

How did he know? Sam's teammates had been careful in their word choices, especially Joe. Yet Maddox somehow knew she had a problem when the shooter fired a volley of bullets her direction. "Flashbacks?"

Maddox leaned on the conference table with his folded arms. "I've been shot before. I know how it works. Some of the toughest SEALs I worked with had problems in the field after a close call. You almost died. I'd be surprised if you didn't experience a flashback in the field."

She glanced at Joe who squeezed her hand and gave a small nod. She might as well tell Maddox the truth. He suspected anyway. Would he pull her off duty?

Sam swallowed hard. She hoped not. The walls of her house were closing in on her. Never one for crafts or just staying home, she had read books and magazines and watched movies with Joe and by herself while she recuperated. Now she itched to return to work. She wanted to stay on the job. How else would she get past the reaction to gunfire? On orders from Marcus Lang, her Fortress-appointed counselor, she'd blown through boxes of ammunition in the past month. Taking live fire was a different animal and Sam couldn't imagine how much worse she would have been if not for following Lang's advice.

"I froze," she admitted.

"For a split second," Joe added.

"And that's why you tackled her."

"Yes, sir."

"Are you mentally ready for a mission, Sam?"

"I am. This is my first time under live-fire conditions since I was shot. I'll do better next time, sir."

"You talked to one of our counselors?"

"Marcus Lang."

"Talk to him again on the flight to San Diego. Be honest with yourself and me. If you're not ready, take yourself off the assignment. I want you alive and healthy. While I value your skills as well as your friendship, your life isn't the only one at stake. So is Joe's and the lives of your teammates."

Like she would forget that. Sam literally held four lives in the palms of her hands every time she went out on a mission with Shadow. "I'll be fine, boss."

"If you decide you need a little more time, contact me. I'll pull Shadow and assign Adam Walker's team to this mission. Adam and Veronica or Remy and Lily Doucet would be good substitutes for the two of you." The buzz-cut blond stood. "Don't wait too long to make the call." Maddox glanced at Zane and left the room.

Sam sighed. "Brent doesn't pull any punches."

"Not when the consequences of playing nice are deadly." Zane wheeled to Sam's side, maneuvering his wheelchair with ease, and laid a fake marriage license on the table by her hand. "Want me to contact Marcus and set up a video chat during the flight? You can use the jet's bedroom to talk to him without disturbing your teammates or baring your soul in their hearing."

"Thanks, Zane."

"Sure." He started to leave and paused. "For what it's worth, we've all been there. The only way you fail is if you give up." With a quick smile, he zoomed from the conference room.

Joe tugged Sam to her feet. "We need to get moving. I'll drive you home, go to my place, then pick you up on the way to the airport."

"Sounds good." Joe had moved to a house a few blocks from hers last year. Joe said he liked her neighborhood, but she thought it was odd that he chose to leave the apartment he raved about to buy a fixer-upper house. While magic with weapons, her partner was all thumbs with home repairs.

In her bedroom, Sam perused her wardrobe, puzzled about what to pack. Her preference was black fatigues, black t-shirts, and combat boots. She scowled. Guess a bride wouldn't wear all black on her honeymoon cruise. Since she had to pack for every eventuality, including pursuit of the people responsible for the missing women, she packed her Fortress gear as well as two one-piece bathing suits with thin wraps to cover the evidence of her gunshot wound, capris, jeans, and tops.

No shorts. If Shadow had to chase a perp on the ship, capris would at least protect her legs. Sam had enough scars without adding more by tackling a suspect with bare legs.

After adding tennis shoes and the rest of her clothes and toiletries, Sam checked her medical supplies, restocking and adding more supplies her unit needed in jungle settings. She hoped the precaution was unnecessary.

Trace was going to be miserable the entire time they were on board the ship. The tough sniper fought a losing battle with seasickness. Sam dove back into her medical supplies stash and grabbed every anti-nausea patch she had. If Shadow was still on board ship in ten days, she would have to obtain more patches. Otherwise, Trace would be sick as a dog and useless as a bodyguard.

By the time Joe knocked on her door, Sam had her bags packed and in the entryway. "Ready?" he asked.

Sam grabbed her mike bag. "All set."

"I'll take the rest of your gear to the SUV while you set the alarm."

After setting her alarm, she joined Joe in the vehicle. "Anything new from Maddox?"

"Hollingbrook gave us a suite. The rest of Shadow and Curt are in rooms close to ours."

Sam stared. "A suite?"

He glanced at her with a grin. "The Honeymoon suite."

"Why not house the whole team in there?"

"Can't. That would blow our cover." Another glance. "Are you nervous?"

"Why would I be?" Just because marrying Joe Gray and honeymooning in a suite anywhere with him was a dream of hers.

"Is there another reason why your hands have a death grip on the seat?"

Sam looked down. Joe was right. Good grief. She loosened her grip and relaxed in the seat. "I'm okay with it."

"I'm not overwhelmed with your reassurance."

She smacked him lightly on the shoulder with her palm, making him grin.

At the airport, Joe parked in the lot designated for Fortress Security and circled to the cargo area for their gear. "Anyone who sees inside the bags will never believe we're on our honeymoon." His lips curved. "Looks like we're going to war."

"We're prepared for it." Sam hoisted her mike bag and reached for one of her duffel bags.

"I've got it. I'll carry it to the jet with my gear."

She considered arguing but knew the effort was futile. Besides, her chest still ached from Joe's tackle, not that she'd tell him. He already felt bad. No need to heighten his guilt. "Thanks."

Sam crossed the tarmac to the jet and climbed the stairs into the cabin where she was greeted by her teammates, Curt Jackson, and Nico's wife, Mercy.

"Where's Joe?" Nico asked.

"Right behind me."

"Pilots are ready. We'll leave as soon as you're settled."

"Yes, sir."

Joe entered the cabin, stored their gear, and held out his hand for Sam's mike bag. Since the plane had an accessible mike bag on board, she handed the spotter hers to store.

When she and Joe were seated, the jet taxied down the runway, gathering speed until it lifted into the air. Once they were at cruising height, Sam received a message from her counselor that he was available and waiting for her to contact him.

Joe looked over. "Marcus?" he asked, voice low.

"He's available to talk now."

"Want company?"

She didn't have anything to hide. Joe had been by her side for months after the shooting. Although he tried to act as though her choice didn't bother him, Sam knew her partner's body language. He wanted to be in that room with her. "Yes."

He stood back and motioned for her to go ahead of him to the bedroom at the back of the jet.

Sam paused as she reached Nico and Mercy. "I have a conference call with Marcus Lang. Maddox's orders."

"Understood."

Mercy smiled. "Tell Marcus hello for me."

With a nod, she continued down the aisle with Joe at her back. Inside the room, she sat at the small table in the corner of the room and contacted Marcus. No point putting this off. The sooner she moved past the PTSD, the safer Joe and her teammates would be. She'd rather take a bullet herself than cause any of them harm.

Marcus Lang's smiling face appeared on her phone screen a moment later. "Hello, Sam. Ready to begin?"

Not really. "I am. Thanks for talking to me on such short notice."

"No problem." The counselor's gaze shifted. "Joe. Good to see you, buddy. Are you staying for our session?"

"Yes, sir." Joe reached for Sam's hand and linked their fingers together. "I'm here for moral support. I promise to remain silent unless you direct a question to me."

"I want him to stay," Sam added. "I assume that's okay."

"Whatever you're comfortable with. I understand you had some difficulty today. Tell me what happened and we'll go from there."

She drew in a deep breath and started to talk.

CHAPTER FOUR

By the time Sam finished her session with Lang, she felt as though she'd bared her soul and then some. The one thing Sam didn't want was for Joe to think of her as the weak link in the unit, especially in their partnership.

Joe tugged Sam to her feet. Instead of releasing her and heading for the door, he moved closer and wrapped his arms around her.

For a moment, she froze, shocked at the full body contact, then Sam melted against him, soaking up the comfort he offered in silence. For several minutes, Joe rubbed her back with gentle strokes, finally settling one hand at her lower back, the other cradling the back of her head.

What was it about this one man that brought down her barriers and made her comfortable with his touch? She trusted every member of Shadow. Yet Joe's touch was the only one she didn't fight herself to allow.

"Tough session." Joe eased back enough to see Sam's face. "You okay?"

"I will be. Just need a few minutes to settle."

His gaze dropped to her mouth, then shifted to her eyes again. "Do you want a few minutes to yourself?"

"I've been inside my own head for the past 90 minutes. I'd rather not keep myself company right now."

"What do you need from me?"

A kiss. Sweet, scorching, or something in between. She didn't care as long as he kissed her. Sam just couldn't bring herself to ask for the kiss. "This," she whispered and snuggled closer.

Joe's hold tightened. "A real hardship," he teased. "Holding a beautiful woman is a tough job."

Sam lifted her head from his chest to stare at him, eyes wide. "Beautiful?"

He tilted his head, studying her. "Hmm. Wrong word."

Her heart sank. "Oh."

"Gorgeous is the right word. Drop-dead gorgeous. Yeah, I'm really suffering here."

Just like that, her emotions soared as did her confusion. Where was the teammate who had been so reluctant to get involved with her for the past five years? No question Sam was thrilled at the change in Joe, but what did the shift mean? "You're turning on the charm today."

Joe sobered. "I'm being honest." He used the pads of his thumbs to brush away the remnants of tears from her cheeks. "We should go back. Nico will have more information from Maddox and Zane by now."

She released him and reached for the door knob. Joe covered her hand with his to still her movements. When she turned to ask him what was wrong, her partner moved into her, captured her chin in his hand and pressed a light, gentle, lingering kiss on her lips, nibbling from one corner of her mouth to the other.

Her knees weakened and she would have gone down if not for his secure hold. When he eased back, Sam's breath stuttered out. "What does that mean?"

A slow smile curved his mouth. "If you have to ask, I'm out of practice." His gaze dropped to her mouth. "Maybe I should try again."

Oh, yeah. Good plan. "Maybe you should."

Joe took his time bending down to kiss her. He cupped the back of her neck and squeezed gently. "You planning to tell me to stop?"

As if. "I'm not stupid."

With a soft laugh, he closed the gap between them and captured her lips with his. Gone was the gentle exploration. Joe took control of the kiss from the first touch. Where earlier his lips brushed across Sam's mouth with a touch as light as a butterfly, now his touch was possessive and hot. His lips caught and explored her own with a thoroughness that stole her breath and made her moan. He lifted his head to stare at her with glittering eyes.

Sam shivered as goosebumps surged across her skin. "Where did you learn how to do that?" She held up her hand. "Wait. Scratch that. I don't want to know. I'll assume you were born with a gift for dynamite kisses."

Joe laughed and reached around her to open the door.

Sam made her back way up the aisle in a daze.

Nico motioned to Sam and Joe from the conference table. "Join us. Zane sent more information. We have copies of the emailed threats Hollingbrook received and a list of the accidents Janine suffered along with the police reports from the disappearances of the women."

Ben's hand hovered near a carafe. "Coffee?" he asked.

Sam's stomach rebelled at the idea. Normally as much of a caffeine junkie as the rest of her unit, today she couldn't handle the buzz. "Not for me."

"None for me, either." Joe opened the small refrigerator and pulled out two decaffeinated soft drinks. He handed one to Sam.

Joe Gray had good instincts. After being shot at and her long session with Marcus, Sam's stomach was unsettled. Joe's kiss had butterflies dive-bombing inside her stomach. Somehow, he knew and hadn't made a big deal out of it. Still protecting her, she realized.

Nico tapped a few keys on the keyboard and projected a document on the screen. Sam scanned the contents as she sipped her soft drink and frowned. "Is this the first threat Hollingbrook received?"

"It has the earliest date."

Trace whistled. "He should have reported this immediately, whether to us or the cops."

"That threat is specific." Joe laid his arm across the back of Sam's chair, the warmth of his skin seeping into her own. "Mentioning Janine's school is a deliberate shot across the bow, warning her father that they knew how to get to her."

"At the very least, Hollingbrook should have assigned her a bodyguard." Curt rubbed his jaw. "We could have prevented her death if we'd been called in sooner."

"Her father knows," Sam said. "He'll have to live with that on his conscience for the rest of his life."

Joe motioned to the screen. "Put up the next one, Nico. Side by side if possible."

More keystrokes. Eight documents popped up on the screen. As Sam read each one, her frown deepened. "Do we have a timeline of the development of Hollingbrook's investigation?"

"Zane thought we might want to see the overlay." A moment later, Nico brought up a new image on the screen, thumbnail prints of the threats with lines drawn from each email to specific points on the timeline.

Each time Hollingbrook made more inquiries into the disappearances of the women and the possibility of connecting an employee with the women, the threats ramped up, all centered on Hollingbrook and the cruise line. Janine's death seemed to be a way to hurt her father. She didn't appear to be the target of the terror campaign.

"What about Janine's accidents?" Joe's brows knitted. "Did Z add those to the diagram?"

The screen morphed again, this time including Janine's accidents.

"After the first couple of accidents, Hollingbrook should have sent Janine for a long vacation out of the reach of these clowns." Trace folded his arms across his chest. "There are only a couple of days, three at most, between the new threat and Janine's next accident."

"Does Hollingbrook have any idea who targeted Janine?" Sam asked. She didn't hold out much hope that he'd suspected one person or group in particular. If he had, Hollingbrook would probably have gone after them himself.

"He doesn't, no."

Curt's eyebrow rose. "But we do?"

"Not confirmed. Maddox has been hearing rumors of a human trafficking organization targeting vacationing women, especially women traveling alone. If the woman is beautiful enough, they will try to capture her anyway."

Sam closed her eyes briefly. That was the reason Shadow had been assigned this mission. Their unit specialized in freeing victims from human traffickers.

"But we don't have confirmation." Joe turned slightly, his thigh pressing against Sam's. "The human trafficking group might not have anything to do with the missing women." He angled his head toward the wall screen. "Most of the threats are focused on Hollingbrook and his cruise line. Maddox said his business has been under attack, especially this cruise route. Someone wants to take down Hollingbrook and his company. Who has it out for him?"

CHAPTER FIVE

"Excellent question." Nico tapped on another key and brought up pictures of three men and one woman.

Joe studied the pictures. "Who are they?"

"Mike Hollingbrook's confidants. They are executives in Hollingbrook Cruise Lines. Each of these four people are friends, some closer than others. They know the best ways to hurt him and the business. As a whole, Hollingbrook stays in the background and out of the media spotlight. The average person on the street wouldn't have a clue where to strike to hurt him the most. These four have that knowledge."

"Trouble in paradise?" Ben asked.

"That's what we're going to find out." Nico shut down the projection screen. "The four executives are already on board the Pacific Star. Hollingbrook was scheduled to go. Their plan was to combine planning meetings with enjoying the cruise. They were supposed to fly back to Nashville from Puerto Caldero. With all the trouble plaguing this cruise, Hollingbrook hoped to see for himself what was happening. With the death of Janine, his part in the plan changed."

"But the other four went on the cruise anyway?"

"He told them to go and come up with plans for the next year. He'll review the plans when they return and schedule a meeting to discuss them. The cruise planning sessions are a yearly tradition. They usually meet for two or three hours, then knock off for the rest of the day, enjoying the cruise experience for themselves."

Joe thought about what Nico said and what he hadn't. "There are problems behind the scenes."

Shadow's leader nodded. "Aside from the missing women, the cruise has been plagued with mishaps and deliberate sabotage, all minor to this point."

"At least one person on board is involved in the campaign to discredit the cruise line." Trace poured more coffee into his mug. "Maybe more. Does Hollingbrook think his executives might be connected to the sabotage?"

"That's what we need to determine. Zane sent files on each of the executives to your email. Familiarize yourselves with them. We'll be interacting with the four of them on board the ship. Charlaine Bennett is a fan of Mercy's art work as is Colt Riley. Dax Alexander is all about mechanics while Lance Farraday is obsessed with tree houses. Learn everything you can about each of them. Zane's information was thorough, as usual. We'll land in San Diego in four hours. We don't have long to become experts on these executives. In the meantime, Maddox and Zane are digging into the human trafficking angle. Maybe we'll get lucky and nail down one of these problems before the cruise is finished."

Trace grunted. "We need a list of employees who worked this cruise since the sabotage and threats started."

Nico stood. "I'll send the request to Zane. We should receive new information soon. Joe and Sam focus on Dax and Lance. Mercy and I will dig into Charlaine and Colt. Ben and Trace, start on Hollingbrook's background. Even though he didn't mention a relative with motive, that doesn't mean there isn't at least one. People tend to be blind to motives of those they love. Curt, focus on the security people. They have access to everything on board ship. Everyone be looking for the employee information from Zane."

Joe followed Sam to their seats and grabbed his laptop. "Dax first?"

"Sure. Dax loves machines and Lance loves building." Sam eyed him. "I know Maddox assigned Shadow because of the possible human trafficking angle. Other teams could have handled the job as well."

"Yeah, except for the interest in art, mechanics, and tree houses. No other team will connect with the executives as well as we will." He gave a short, soft laugh. "The boss always has more than one reason for his choices. Never thought of my knowledge of mechanics as a strength."

"No one would ever think of my tree-house hobby as an advantage."

"At least building tree houses is an interesting conversational piece. Backyard mechanics are plentiful. Do you have pictures of your work?"

"On my phone."

"Good. We'll use the pictures as a way to draw Lance in."

"What about you and Dax?"

He smiled. "I have a lot of pictures to flash. Who doesn't love talking about classic cars?"

"The sweet 1957 Corvette?"

Joe narrowed his eyes. "Sweet? That 'Vette is a piece of art. The term 'sweet' doesn't do it justice."

Sam rolled her eyes. "If you say so. Boot up your laptop. Nico is glaring our direction."

He glanced over. Shadow's leader was looking at them with that intense stare of his, the one that said quit goofing off and get busy. Joe saluted and booted up his computer. A moment later, he angled the computer so his partner could see the screen as well, then settled in to read.

Dax had worked at Hollingbrook Cruise Lines for twenty years, joining the company as soon as he graduated from college. He'd worked his way up the ladder in the finance department until he'd been promoted to vice president of the company. He was reputed to be Hollingbrook's best friend. Married and divorced four times, he was currently on wife number five. Two children, a girl from the first wife and a boy from the fourth. There was a fifteen-year gap between his children. Dax's son had just turned five. His daughter was a sophomore at Vanderbilt, studying to be a doctor.

The finance VP made good money, an excellent thing since Dax also had a weakness for classic cars. Joe whistled softly as he read the list of vehicles Dax had acquired. Absolutely amazing. He'd love to see Dax's collection. The pictures Zane had embedded in the file wouldn't do justice to the beauty of the cars.

"Can you estimate on how much money he spent collecting those?"

"Easily four million. He also has maintenance and upkeep plus the insurance on each of the vehicles."

"Sounds like a black hole for money."

"It can be. That's why I restore and sell the classics. I enjoy fixing them, making a tidy profit, and sending the restored beauties off to a new home."

"Except for the Corvette?"

He was never selling that baby. The 'Vette was special and he loved driving that car. "Except that one. She's mine." The Corvette was his first restoration project on his own. The ones before that had been finished working in tandem with his father. Heath Gray loved vintage cars and trucks and passed his passion on to Joe. The rest of Joe's brothers hadn't been interested in their father's hobby.

"Will you let me ride in her?"

He slid her a look. "Maybe. You'll have to offer a top-of-the-line bribe to convince me." He'd planned to sweet talk Sam into a date using the car as an incentive. Didn't mean Joe couldn't take advantage of her interest.

Sam frowned. "Like what?"

"Don't know yet. I'm still thinking about the price for a ride in a work of art."

"Let me know when you figure it out." Her eyes sparkled. "If you're lucky, I'll be willing to pay up."

That smart-aleck response surprised a laugh out of him. Courting Samantha Coleman was going to be a lot of fun. He loved a woman with a sense of humor. Joe sobered. If Sam gave him a chance. Based on her response to his kiss, they had serious chemistry going between them and she was attracted to him. That didn't mean Sam would be willing to lower her protective barriers and allow him to occupy more than a friend's role.

She placed her hands on the keyboard and called up the next file on Lance Farraday.

They read the file in silence. "Your boy Lance is a player," Joe muttered. Until the past year, Lance never dated a woman more than a handful of times before moving on to someone else. He didn't like Sam cozying up to this guy. Yeah, it was necessary to connect with the man. Still didn't make him happy. Her startled question after the counseling session with Marcus indicated Sam didn't view herself as attractive, but she would catch the interest of Farraday.

Some men didn't make a distinction between married and unmarried women. Guess they'd find out soon if the PR director respected wedding vows. Wish Maddox had given Joe a wedding band to place on Sam's finger. Wouldn't newlyweds have rings?

"Did you see this?" Sam pointed at the screen.

Joe jerked his attention back on task and read the paragraph she mentioned. His eyebrows winged up. Interesting. "He's been seeing Charlaine Bennett for a year even though the relationship is unacknowledged by either of them. He's also a new father. He has a daughter who is four months old."

"And Charlaine just came back from maternity leave."

"He's well paid. Hollingbrook is a generous employer." According to Zane, Farraday started building tree houses when he was a teenager and kept up the skill by building for friends, family, and by referral. The tree houses looked sturdy, but they didn't hold a candle to Sam's creations. Farraday's tree houses were simple cabins and houses. Sam's work was more creative. Joe couldn't wait to see the other man's face when he looked at Sam's photographs.

"Look at the date he joined the company."

Huh. The same month and year as Charlaine. Newbies at the same time. Made Joe consider whether the two rookies had cemented a friendship during those early years and it had grown from there.

They spent long minutes reviewing the files of Dax and Lance, branching out into further research on the two men and their interests, families, and backgrounds.

Thirty minutes before the jet was scheduled to land in San Diego, Nico spoke up. "Zane just sent the list of employees who worked the cruise route from the time of the first accidents and disappearance. He'll send preliminary background on each soon. In the meantime, have you noticed something you want to share with the class?"

"Charlaine Bennett and Lance Farraday joined Hollingbrook Cruise Lines during the same month and year." Joe's brow furrowed. They were the same age. Was it possible they knew each other before they started working for the company? "Farraday and Charlaine Bennett have been an item for a year but their relationship isn't one that's acknowledged by either."

Nico nodded. "Charlaine and Lance are parents of a four-month old girl."

"The baby is gorgeous," Mercy said.

"Anything to add, Sam?" Nico asked.

"Dax is all about machines and collects classic cars. He's also on wife number five."

Ben's jaw dropped. "Holy cow."

"Hate to know how much he pays in alimony," Trace said.

Joe huffed out a laugh. "And child support. He has two children by different mothers. The oldest is a sophomore at Vanderbilt."

"Lance also builds tree houses in his spare time," Sam said.

A text chime signaled and Nico grabbed his phone. He scowled. "Hollingbrook just received another threat. This one is specific to the Pacific Star."

CHAPTER SIX

Joe studied the emailed threat to the ship Zane had forwarded to the members of Shadow and Curt. He sighed and glanced at his fellow operatives on the other side of the conference table. "This threat isn't specific enough to help us avert the next attack."

"I don't like the wording." Ben frowned. "Got a feeling this round of sabotage might be more serious than ruined desserts, lack of hot water, or spray-painted graffiti. The reference to an explosive surprise makes me wonder if there's a bomb on board the ship."

Nico stiffened and glanced at Mercy. "Maybe I should send you back home with Curt."

"I'll be fine." The artist laid her hand on her husband's arm and kissed him. "Shadow will figure out what the threat means and deal with it before anyone is hurt."

"I don't like it." On the table, his hand fisted. "I don't want you anywhere near this ship if there is a bomb on board."

"If there is a problem, Shadow will find it."

Trace blew out a breath. "While we appreciate your faith in us, that ship is a floating city."

"Too many nooks and crannies in which to hide a package." Ben shoved a hand through his hair. "A bomb would be easy to miss."

"But you said the cruise ship is large. Wouldn't a large bomb be needed?"

"Too hard to smuggle a large bomb aboard," Nico explained. "A small explosive device in the right place would do a lot of damage."

"The point might not be to sink the ship," Curt said.

"So, what would be the point?" Mercy asked.

"Terror. Chances are the saboteur is aboard ship. Sure, he or she could take down the ship, but why bother if terrorizing passengers causes catastrophic economic fallout for the cruise line? Simple can be effective. And bonus? The saboteur won't die as a suicide bomber."

Mercy stared at the operative. "I can't say I'm reassured here, Curt."

He held up his hands. "I'm not good at reassurance. I'm a facts and statistics man."

"We need the ship's schematics," Ben said. "We don't know there's a bomb on board, but we should be able to narrow down the areas where one might be hidden."

Sam stared. "How?"

"Cruise passengers are awake at all hours of the day and night. Employee-only access areas are the most likely target to plant a bomb, especially if a crew member or one of the executives is involved in the problems attacking this particular cruise. Less chance of the bomb being discovered and a smaller likelihood of someone seeing you plant it."

"Best place is the engine room," Joe said. "Sabotage the engine or the propulsion system and that ship's going nowhere."

"Do we have direct contact in ship security?" Ben asked.

Nico shook his head. "I'll call Maddox and get you the information on security and the schematics as soon as possible." He paused when the pilot announced the jet was on final approach. "Strap in. We'll find out what we're facing soon."

Joe followed Sam to their seats. "Nothing like coming off three months of medical leave to face a possible bomb on board a cruise ship."

"No kidding. I considered taking a cruise later in the year. I'm seriously rethinking that vacation plan."

"Cruise ships are soft targets with minimal protection. A small boat loaded with explosives could sink a ship or injure a number of passengers. Those ships have up to 5,000 people aboard."

Sam blew out a breath. "Oh, yeah. Definitely changing my plans. I think I'll go skiing instead."

"Sounds like fun. Have you been skiing before?"

"Two years ago. I'm definitely not an expert, but I manage to stay on my skis."

Joe would love to see Sam on the slopes. With her natural athleticism, she would be a pleasure to watch. Right. Who was he kidding? To him, Sam was always a pleasure to watch. No excuse needed. Man, he had it bad for the woman at his side.

After the jet taxied to a stop, the operatives gathered their gear and headed for the large SUVs waiting for them. They loaded their equipment quickly and drove toward the Port of San Diego.

Joe checked his email and found more information from Zane. "Z sent the schematics for the ship."

"Zane's quick," Mercy commented from the shotgun seat.

"We have thirty minutes before we reach the port," Nico said. "Download the schematics and familiarize yourself with the layout of the ship. If Ben's right, we'll need every minute to find that bomb."

While Shadow's leader weaved through traffic, Joe and Sam studied the ship's layout.

A cell phone rang. Nico grabbed his phone and tapped the speaker button. "Go, Ben."

"Bart Winestock, head of security on the Pacific Star, called me. His people are beginning a search of the public areas. Passengers are boarding the ship so there's a lot of chaos. Winestock's hoping the heightened security activity will go unnoticed. Doesn't want to tip off the wrong people and trigger an early detonation."

"If there is anything to detonate. I still wish we knew exactly what we were up against."

"What about the employee areas, especially the engine room?" Joe asked.

"Two of his people have been assigned to employee-only areas. Winestock is searching the engine room himself."

"Will he recognize a bomb if he sees it?" Curt asked.

"Probably. He's a military vet."

"EOD experience?"

"Unfortunately not. He knows to secure the area and make sure no one stumbles into the danger zone. Otherwise, he's to do nothing. His people will be told to follow the same procedure."

"Copy that," Nico said. "We'll be at the port in five minutes. Unless one of Winestock's people has located a bomb elsewhere, you and Joe head for the engine room. The rest of us will search areas not being covered by the security people." He slid a pointed glance to his wife. "Mercy will stay close to where we board the ship in case of trouble."

"Yes, sir," Ben said. "Where should we store our gear?"

"Leave it with Mercy."

"I'll keep an eye on everything," she said. "What should I do if there is an explosion, Nico?"

"Get off the ship. Our gear can be replaced. You can't."

"I can't replace you, either. Keep that in mind while you're saving the world."

He smiled. "I hear you, sweetheart."

Within minutes, the Fortress operatives were unloading the SUVs and walking toward the B Street cruise ship terminal. "I hope Hollingbrook cleared the way for us to bring our gear on board the Pacific Star," Trace said. "Otherwise, security is likely to think we're the threat."

"That sniper rifle of yours will raise a few eyebrows," Joe said.

His friend glanced over his shoulder, one corner of his mouth curled. "And yours won't?"

Joe grinned.

Despite the concern, as soon as Nico talked to the security officer screening passengers for boarding, he waved the six operatives through the checkpoint. "Good luck," the security guy murmured as Joe passed him.

Hopefully, they had attached more significance to the threat than was warranted. The way things usually worked in their world, though, that hope was likely to be dashed. Joe prayed one of the Fortress operatives found the surprise before a passenger stumbled on it or before the ship headed out to sea again. He didn't want to fight off a bunch of circling sharks.

As they boarded the ship, they were greeted by a perky cruise line employee who asked for their names to direct them to their cabins. "Later," Ben said. "We need Winestock. Tell him Ben is on board. He's looking for me."

She looked puzzled but grabbed her phone and turned away to make a quick call. When the worker turned back, alarm filled her eyes. "Mr. Winestock is outside the engine room. He said to hurry."

Joe's gut tightened. Not a good sign.

Curt and Trace took Ben and Joe's duffel bags, leaving them to carry their Go bags with all their equipment.

"The engine room is...."

Ben cut off the woman's spiel. "We know where it is." He glanced over his shoulder at Joe, hoisted his Go bag higher on his shoulder and set off at a fast clip. Joe squeezed Sam's hand briefly and followed on his teammate's heels.

Once they were out of the main flow of foot traffic, Joe and Ben picked up the pace to a jog. They traveled into the bowels of the ship until they reached a long corridor. Turning right, they spotted a tall, muscle-bound, dark-skinned man standing in front of a red door. His attention zeroed in on the operatives.

"Ben Martin?"

Ben nodded. "This is my teammate, Joe Gray. What have we got?"

"Something out of my worst nightmare. I hope you're as good as you say you are."

"Show us."

Winestock unlocked the door and led the way into the interior of the engine room. Machines hummed and the scent of oil filled the heated room. As Joe feared, the chief of security led him and Ben straight to the engine. On the back side of the engine in a darkened section someone had attached C4 and the timer had just ticked down to five minutes.

Ben blew out a breath, a scowl on his face as he slid his Go bag off his shoulder and unzipped it. "Not enough time to evacuate passengers."

"Let's just hope there isn't another surprise package somewhere else on the ship," Joe murmured.

"Can you defuse that thing?" Winestock demanded.

Ben found the tools he needed to work on the bomb. "I can defuse it. Call the bomb squad, though. Once I dismantle this thing, the components will have to be disposed of safely."

The security chief winced. "Mr. Hollingbrook isn't going to be happy about that."

"Tough." Joe shined the beam of his flashlight on the bomb for Ben. "A few hours' delay in leaving the port is better than risking people's lives."

"What do you mean by a few hours' delay? We have a schedule to keep."

"The bomb squad will want to search the ship for more possible explosive devices," Ben said as he slid into the narrow space to begin his work. "They won't take no for an answer." Ben talked Joe step-by-step through the procedure he was following and why. "This is like the bombs we dismantled two weeks ago."

Joe drew in a deep breath. Not so bad, then. Didn't matter. As long as Ben was available, Joe's EOD skills wouldn't be needed.

"I am so getting fired for this," Winestock muttered.

"Our boss will talk to Hollingbrook on your behalf. Can't do anything about the cops and their procedure for dealing with this. Might as well be prepared, Winestock. My guess is the feds will get involved, too."

The other man groaned.

Joe's cell phone signaled a text. He checked the screen and his stomach knotted. "Oh, man."

Ben glanced at him before returning to his task. "Problem?"

"Sam found another one. Winestock, hold the flashlight for Ben."

"Can you handle it?" his teammate asked.

"I have to. The second one is timed to explode at the same time as this one."

CHAPTER SEVEN

Sam's heart beat in time to the relentless countdown of the digital timer attached to the bomb. She had hustled the staff from the kitchen amid loud protests and returned alone to keep vigil.

She prayed Ben could defuse the bomb before it exploded. Sam didn't want to end up in the hospital again from shrapnel wounds or on a slab in the morgue.

She turned when she heard someone running toward her. Joe rushed into the kitchen. Oh, no. Not Joe. Yes, his job with Fortress was dangerous. But Joe usually worked behind a scope, not face-to-face with an explosive device. "Where's Ben?"

"Defusing a bomb in the engine room. Where's this one?" Joe shrugged off his Go bag and pulled out what he needed to work on the bomb.

"In here." She led him to an oversized pantry and pointed to the bottom shelf. "The bomb is attached at the back on the underside of the shelf."

"Get your flashlight." Joe shoved aside the supplies stacked on the floor, got on his back and wiggled underneath the shelf.

Sam dropped to Joe's left side and aimed the light toward the ticking clock and the housing filled with C-4. "Do you have enough time to defuse it, Joe?"

"Yeah. Barely. Guess it's a good thing I badgered Ben into training me."

"I suppose." She hadn't been thrilled with the idea of Joe handling explosives when he'd mentioned the dual training although she didn't tell him as much. Sam thought it prudent to keep her misgivings to herself. No need to poke her partner's ego by questioning his need or ability to handle bombs. Obviously, she'd been wrong. Turned out Shadow needed a backup EOD man.

"Move that light a little to the right. Perfect. You worried?"

"Why would I be?" she asked, tone tart. "You have two minutes or less to defuse a bomb with enough C-4 to blow a hole in the side of the ship and kill both of us. What do I have to worry about?"

He chuckled. "There's that spark I've been looking for since you were shot. Nice to have the real Samantha Coleman back in action."

"You can say that after I froze earlier tonight?"

"A one-time occurrence," he assured her.

"I hope you're right."

"Trust me. I know you. You won't freeze up again."

Sam appreciated Joe's utter faith in her abilities and prayed it was warranted. "How do you know?"

"You're rock steady right now. Most people would be running from this thing as fast as possible by this point."

"Yeah? I might be holding still to help you but I'm running away screaming on the inside."

Another laugh from her partner. "I'm almost there. Have any trouble with the kitchen staff?"

"You could say that. They weren't happy to be kicked out of here when meal preparation should be in full swing."

"I bet." Joe was silent for several seconds, then blew out a breath. "Got it. Let me dismantle the pieces and we'll contact Nico." A moment later, he scooted out from under the pantry shelf and sat up.

"Are you going to pull out the components?"

He shook his head. "The cops will want to examine it in place. It's enough that I took apart the pieces to prevent the countdown from restarting. They will transport the C-4 in a secure container and bag up the rest for evidence."

"What about the kitchen staff?"

"We can't let them back in here until it's been cleared by law enforcement." Joe called Nico and reported that the bomb had been dismantled. After he ended the call, he turned to Sam. "We're to stay in place until one of the security people arrives."

When they informed the chef and his staff that the kitchen was still off limits, she and Joe were the recipients of a tirade of epic proportions. They left the kitchen after one of Winestock's staff arrived to ensure no one entered the area, including the irate chef and his minions. Sam gladly handed off the explanations to Pacific Star's security.

They joined Mercy, Curt, Ben, and Trace as law enforcement teams arrived, many accompanied by what Sam assumed were dogs trained in detecting explosives. Passengers watched the new arrivals with growing alarm.

"The captain needs to make some kind of announcement," Curt said. "The last thing we need is a panic."

Nico walked up at that moment. He crouched beside his wife. "You okay?" When she nodded, he stood and turned to the operatives. "Captain Nelson will be informing the passengers soon that the crew found a suspicious package on board and that it's been dealt with by law enforcement. The search teams are looking for more packages."

"Where did they find so many teams?" Ben asked.

"Local police, highway patrol, FBI, ATF, and I think the military contributed a couple teams as well."

"It's still going to take a while to search the ship." Trace frowned at a couple of men edging closer to the Fortress group, probably hoping to eavesdrop and find out what was going on. "It's a big area to cover even with all these teams on board." One of the men blanched under Trace's scrutiny, grabbed his buddy by the arm, and steered him in the opposite direction.

"The passengers will want food before long." Mercy turned toward Nico. "Any chance the kitchen will be operational soon?"

"Doubt it."

At that moment, the captain's voice sounded over the speaker. "Attention Pacific Star passengers. This is your captain. Cruise line personnel discovered a suspicious package aboard the ship. That package has been handed over to law enforcement authorities. You'll notice that we have several search teams aboard. They will search the Pacific Star out of an abundance of caution. The search will delay our departure from San Diego by at least six hours. Because part of the search area includes the kitchen and dining facilities, our culinary staff will not be able to prepare meals as scheduled. Please disembark and go to the terminal. Although the terminal does have dining facilities, we arranged for area restaurants to bring food into the terminal as well. We apologize for the inconvenience but feel the precaution is necessary for the safety of our passengers and crew members. When it's safe to return to the ship, an announcement will be made inside the terminal. We'll give instructions on the procedure to board the ship at that time."

Within a few minutes, passengers began to leave the ship. A few griped about the necessity for finding food in the terminal. Most took it as a minor inconvenience in light of heightened safety concerns. A group of women who passed the Fortress group debated whether or not they would have any luck seeing SEALs in training in the terminal.

Sam and Mercy glanced at each other and burst into laughter.

Joe stared at Sam. "What's so funny?"

"Did you hear what those women were talking about?"

He shook his head.

She moved closer. "They were talking about their chances of spotting SEALs in the terminal."

A scowl from Shadow's spotter. "What's wrong with soldiers?"

"Sore spot?"

"Didn't it bother you when you were enlisted?"

"The Special Forces teams were more interested in me being female than anything else. My medic skills didn't matter unless they needed patching up."

A member of the security staff approached. "You're the Fortress group?"

Nico stepped forward. "That's right."

"The captain would like to speak with you and your team."

The operatives grabbed their gear and followed the employee. Mercy walked beside Nico, carrying her art supplies.

The security worker led them off the ship to a conference room in the terminal and knocked on the door. He opened it for the operatives, then left.

A dark-haired man at the head of a long table stood and motioned toward the empty chairs. "Have a seat. I'm Captain Jerry Greer."

Nico held out his hand. "Nico Rivera. My wife, Mercy."

A smile bloomed on the captain's face. "The resident artist."

"That's right. I paint under the name MJ Powers. Thank you for allowing me to share my love of art with your passengers."

"The pleasure is ours, I assure you. Did you bring paintings to sell?"

Mercy shook her head. "Too difficult to travel with my inventory. I have a slide show that continuously scrolls through my complete catalog of work. I brought business cards with my website listed. The website showcases my available work and provides purchasing options."

"I'll have to visit your website. My wife is a fan of your work." He turned his attention to Nico. "Introduce me to your team."

Nico pointed to each team member in turn. "Sam, Joe, Ben, Trace, and Curt."

Greer's eyebrows rose. "No last names?"

"I'm protecting my team. We're on an undercover assignment although our role in today's events makes keeping our cover intact more difficult."

The captain looked skeptical. "I don't know if you will blend in with the Pacific Star's passengers."

"As long as the employees who know about us keep quiet, we'll be able to proceed as planned."

"How much can you tell me about the bombs?"

Nico inclined his head toward Ben and Joe. "They defused the devices."

"Simple construction," Ben said. "Timer along with enough C-4 to do serious damage to your ship. The bomb in the engine room was placed on the engine."

"The bomb in the kitchen was in the pantry attached to the underside of a shelf against an outside wall," Joe said. "The blast would have blown a hole in the hull. Both devices were timed to explode at the same time."

Greer dragged a hand down his face. "Law enforcement insisted the passengers and crew leave the ship while the dog teams are searching for more bombs."

"Standard procedure," Nico said. "We'll be close and available to answer law enforcement questions."

"You're familiar with law enforcement procedures. Have you worked in the field?"

"Joe was SWAT before he joined Fortress. We work with law enforcement on many missions inside US borders."

"Although our passengers won't know what you did, thank you for handling this dangerous situation. You saved many lives by your selfless actions."

"Glad we could help."

"I know you have protocols to follow, but I want updates on any progress or discoveries you make while you're on board my ship."

Nico helped Mercy stand. "We'll tell you what we can."

The captain smiled slightly. "But it won't be as much as I want? Fine. I'll take what I can get."

After a nod at Greer, Shadow's leader led his team from the room. He approached the security employee standing a few feet from the door, keeping watch.

From his alert stance, Sam wondered if the man was protecting the captain. If so, Winestock was wise. Since the bombs hadn't detonated, the next obvious target was the Pacific Star's commander.

If the saboteur hadn't planted other unpleasant surprises.

CHAPTER EIGHT

Shadow, Curt, and Mercy followed the security member's directions to the terminal employee dining room where they were to meet Winestock. Joe dropped into a chair beside Sam, gear at his feet. "Who is buying food for everybody?" he asked Nico.

"Not you or Ben. The police will want to talk to you."

Trace glanced at Curt. "That leaves us since Nico's running this operation. The cops will want to interview Sam as well. Anyone have a problem with burgers and fries?" When no one protested, Trace and Curt left.

Ben grinned at Mercy. "You should have specified what size burger you wanted. Those two have appetites of teenage boys."

Nico chuckled. "Like you're any different."

"Just thought Mercy should be prepared for a serious meal, not her usual child-size portion."

Bart Winestock entered the dining room followed closely by two men in suits. Joe's lip curled. At least one of them was a fed. He shifted his chair closer to Sam's.

The security chief nodded at Joe. "Good job with the second bomb."

"Thanks."

He glanced around the table. "I'm Bart Winestock, Pacific Star's security chief."

Nico held out his hand. "Nico Rivera. This is my wife, Mercy." He introduced the rest of the Fortress operatives. "Two more team members will be here soon."

"First, I'm sure Captain Greer expressed his gratitude for your service but I want to add mine as well. Second, local and federal police want to interview those directly involved in discovering and defusing the bombs."

"Sam discovered the explosive device in the kitchen. Ben and Joe defused the bombs."

"Then those are the three we need to interview." The six-foot blond-haired man spoke for the first time. "The rest need to join the other passengers and crew."

Nico stared at the cop. "We'll stay."

A scowl from the blond and the scarecrow thin man with a scar running from his temple to his ear. "If you stay, you'll keep your mouth shut," Scarecrow insisted. "If you don't, we'll boot you out."

"We're on the same side."

Joe flinched. Although Nico's tone was mild, a storm brewed in their team leader's eyes.

Blondie snorted. "You aren't on anyone's side but your own. You're a mercenary."

Winestock sighed. "Can we get on with this? Pump up your ego on your own time, Brock. Nico, this is Special Agent Travis Brock and Detective Ray Mathis with the San Diego Police Department."

Nico motioned to the empty chairs around their table. "Have a seat, gentlemen. I assume we'll be here a while."

"Which one of you is Sam?" Brock asked.

"I am."

The two law enforcement officers frowned. "You know what a bomb looks like?" Brock asked, a sneer on his face.

Joe scowled, his temper ratcheting up several levels at the implied disrespect from the man.

"I spent six years in the Army."

"What was your job?" Mathis opened his notebook and grabbed a pen from his pocket.

"Medic."

The detective glanced up, respect in his eyes. "Tough job."

"It can be."

"You answered in the present tense. Are you a paramedic now?"

"I'm a medic with Fortress Security."

A soft whistle. "I've heard of your company. Hard to get a job there."

Brock snorted. "Tell us what happened from the time you boarded the ship until now. Don't leave anything out. We'll decide what's important."

Joe bit back a growl at the patronizing way they treated Sam. They acted as though she wasn't as trained as the rest of the Shadow team. Nothing could be further from the truth. In some ways, her training was more extensive. She had completed the same training regimen as the rest of them plus all the ongoing medical training.

He remained silent during her recitation of events. Not much to question her over in Joe's opinion.

Eyes narrowed, Brock asked, "How did you know where to look, Sam?"

"I didn't. The kitchen and dining facilities were my assigned area."

"Why did you contact Joe?" The agent glanced up from his notes. "Is he your team leader?"

"I texted Joe because he was with our explosives expert in the engine room."

"Why not contact the expert directly?"

Sam smiled. "Never a good idea to startle a bomb tech when he has his hands on a bomb."

"You knew about the bomb in the engine room?" Brock's stare made Joe's hands clench under the table.

"Winestock was in contact with Ben while we drove to the ship. He knew about Ben's training and suspected there was a bomb in the engine room. With the timer ticking, I contacted Joe."

"Why?"

Enough. Joe knew the men had to ask questions, but they were hounding Sam. "I've been training with Ben between missions."

"Is there a reason for that?" Mathis asked.

"The rest of our unit knows something about bombs, but it seemed wise for Ben to have backup."

Brock's eyebrows soared. "Your team sent a rookie to handle a bomb that could have killed hundreds of people and damaged the ship?"

"I dismantled bombs like this before under Ben's tutelage. If I had waited for the bomb squad, that device would have gone off before they arrived."

"You're lucky."

"How about well-trained? I had a good teacher."

Ben saluted him.

"Your turn." Brock gestured to Ben.

He explained where the bomb was located, it's components, and the procedure for dismantling the device.

By the time the cops had finished questioning Ben, Joe, and Sam, Trace and Curt returned, arms full of takeout bags and cardboard drink carriers from a restaurant in the terminal.

Brock and Mathis stood, shoving notebooks and pens in their jacket pockets. "How can we contact you if we have more questions?" Mathis asked.

"Call Fortress Security's main number."

The FBI agent frowned. "I want a cell phone number. You already mentioned texting each other so we know you have phones."

Shadow's leader smiled. "We do have phones. We don't, however, pass out the number. Security reasons. We'll contact you if you leave a message with Fortress."

"You better or you'll see me on your doorstep with an arrest warrant for obstructing justice." The agent eyed Winestock. "You coming?"

He shook his head. "My people know how to reach me. I'll be along in a few minutes."

Curt and Trace dug into the bags and pulled out a mountain of hamburgers and fries. They handed out drinks. "You want to join us, Winestock?" Curt asked. "We bought plenty."

The security chief glanced at the logo on the bags. "Thanks. Those hamburgers are my favorite food in the terminal." He dropped into a chair beside Nico. "Those cops are only the first of many who want to talk with you and your team. Eat while you have the chance."

Nico glanced at Joe who nodded. "He's right. The Coast Guard will want in on this along with the alphabet agencies."

Shadow's leader turned back to Winestock. "Since we don't want our cover blown, we'll stay here until it's time to board the ship. Direct the agents to us. Trace, Curt, once you finish eating, join the crowd in the terminal. I want eyes on our targets."

As Winestock swallowed the last of his meal, his cell phone rang. He glanced at the screen and rose. "Captain Greer wants to visit with passengers in the terminal." He gathered his trash. "I'll send the law enforcement agencies here." The security chief slid Nico a business card. "Call if you need me. Otherwise, I'll see you on the ship." After dropping his trash in the garbage, Winestock left.

Soon afterward, Curt and Trace joined the terminal crowd.

Over the next few hours, various law enforcement agencies came in and out of the dining room. Amazing how similar their questions were. They left the interviews frustrated that the Fortress operatives didn't know more.

When the door closed behind the last of the agents, Joe scrubbed his face with his hands. "Well, that was fun."

"As much fun as having a bone set without anesthesia." Sam stood and stretched, wincing as she lowered her arms.

Nico pulled out his phone. "I'll update Maddox and let him know to expect multiple contacts from law enforcement." Before he could initiate a call, his cell phone rang. "It's Curt."

He tapped the screen. "You're on speaker with our unit."

"We've got trouble. Greer was attacked. We need Sam."

CHAPTER NINE

Sam grabbed her mike bag. "Where?" she asked Curt as she hoisted the bag to her shoulder. Weren't paramedics on site?

"Conference room. He insisted Winestock take him there so the passengers wouldn't panic."

Joe stood. "I'll go with you. You might need another pair of hands." He grabbed his bags and her duffel.

"Trace and Curt's hands work fine."

He winked at her. "Not as well as mine. Besides, they need to keep tabs on our targets." He glanced at Nico. "Find out if the four of them were together when the captain was attacked."

"I'll look into it." Nico turned to Mercy. "You want a tour of the terminal, sweetheart?"

"Looking forward to spending time with you in a crowd of impatient cruise passengers who want to get on with their vacations in the next minute." She grinned at her husband. "Where did you say the body armor was?"

With a laugh, he planted a quick kiss on her mouth.

Their easy manner and obvious love for each other was fun to watch. Maybe one day she would have the same kind of relationship with Joe. She turned to the man in question. "I'm ready."

"I'll hold off on reporting to Maddox until you update me on the captain's condition," Nico said.

"Yes, sir." Joe pressed his hand to Sam's lower back, urging her forward.

They retraced their steps to the conference room. One of Winestock's people glowered at them as they approached. He pulled back his jacket, revealing the weapon he wore holstered at his waist.

"I'm Sam, the medic Winestock asked to treat Captain Greer."

The man indicated Joe with his chin. "Who's he?"

"My partner." She didn't elaborate on the fact Joe wasn't a medic. All Fortress operatives had basic training in field medicine in case they had to assist teammates or treat themselves in the field. "Confirm it with Winestock or get out of the way."

The door behind the security man opened. Winestock stood in the opening. "Good. You're here. This way."

When Sam entered the room, her gaze tracked immediately to Jerry Greer. He was seated at the table with Trace at his side, pressing his hand against the captain's bloody sleeve.

"What do we have?" She slid her mike bag from her shoulder and sat in the chair Joe moved next to the captain for her.

"Knife wound. Looks like it needs stitches."

"Let's have a look." Trace removed his hand and blood spilled from Greer's wound. Sam whistled softly. "Oh, yeah. You need stitches. Do you want a paramedic to treat this for you?"

The captain shook his head. "Trace says you're a crackerjack medic. Would you take care of it, please? The passengers are already upset. I don't want to make matters worse by scaring them, too."

"I can, but I'm not approved to work as a paramedic in California."

Greer waved her protest away. "I need you to do this for me, Sam. Bart, find me a long-sleeved shirt to hide the bandage. I can't walk around the terminal in a bloody shirt."

"I'll take care of it, sir."

Sam pulled out her suture kit, lidocaine, and hypodermic needle and set them on the table for easy access. She hurried to the nearby sink and washed her hands. While Joe washed his, she slipped on a pair of gloves, then handed him a pair. "Trace, you can return to your assignment. Joe and I will handle this."

She sat in front of the captain again. "I'm going to clean the wound and numb your arm, then stitch the cut."

Greer glanced at his arm and grimaced. "You can't just tape it together?"

Sam shook her head. "With a wound this deep and in this location, it's better to use stitches."

"Trust Sam's judgment. She knows what she's talking about." Joe ripped open a packet of alcohol wipes and cleaned the captain's arm. "You sent for her instead of your ship's doctor."

"All right. Let's get this done. I need to be out in the terminal."

Sam filled the hypodermic with lidocaine. "This will numb your arm. You'll feel the tugging as I stitch the wound, but that's all."

Greer hissed when she inserted the needle in his arm.

"Is your tetanus vaccination up to date?"

"Yes. The ship's doctor keeps a close eye on the crew's vaccinations."

"Smart." Sam dropped the needle in the hard container she used to store used hypodermics until she could dispose of them safely.

"How did you get cut?" Joe asked.

"I was visiting different areas in the terminal, talking with our cruise passengers. As you can imagine, it's crowded in there. I found myself in a large group of people. There was a lot of jostling around. I felt something tug on my sleeve and didn't think anything of it until my arm started to burn. I looked down and saw blood."

"Your security team didn't see anything or anyone acting suspicious?"

"We were surrounded by at least thirty people. The security team couldn't have known one of them had a knife."

Sam exchanged a glance with Joe and saw the same knowledge in his eyes. The Pacific Star's security people should have been more aware. How much training did they have? This might be a good opportunity for Maddox to suggest sending the Hollingbrook security personnel through Personal Security International, Fortress's bodyguard training arm based in Otter Creek, Tennessee. PSI was run by two of the best teams Shadow had worked with on missions, the teams Maddox called on for the toughest missions because they always got the job done.

Those teams plus Shadow, Zoo Crew, and Adam Walker's team, based in Nashville, were deployed frequently. That was the reason Maddox had recruited the Texas team and was in the process of forming more teams. Shadow had been close to burnout. Sam wasn't sure about the other teams, but she knew the mental wellbeing of his teams was as important to Maddox as their physical safety.

Winestock returned, a bag in his hand. "Found a long-sleeved t-shirt with the Pacific Star's name on it, sir."

"Perfect. Thanks, Bart. What's the latest from our employees?"

Sam and Joe listened to the update on the ship's crew without commenting. When the security chief finished, Sam pinched Greer's arm near the injury. "Do you feel that?"

"Just pressure."

"Excellent. Winestock, sit across the table from Captain Greer and talk to him about your new security plan while I work on his arm."

A frown. "How did you know I'm making changes?"

"The plan in place at the moment needs adjustment. Whoever set the bombs knows ways around the procedures you're following at the moment. It's logical you would make changes to prevent a repeat of events." She inclined her head toward the captain. "Talk to him." Hopefully, she would finish her work before Winestock completed his report.

The security chief shifted his attention to Greer. "She's right, sir. Our procedures obviously have holes in them."

"Tell me how you plan to close them."

As the two men discussed options, Sam stitched Greer's wound. Joe held the edges of the wound together, making the stitching process easier and faster.

When she finished, Sam covered the wound with gauze and tape. "Are you allergic to any medications?" she asked the captain.

He shook his head.

She handed Greer two packets of pill. "The capsules are antibiotics. Take one twice a day. The white pills are mild pain killers. Take one every six hours as needed. Have the ship's doctor check your arm and change your bandage tomorrow. You'll be sore for a few days, Captain." She told him a list of things to watch for that indicated the wound was infected.

"Thank you, Sam. I appreciate it."

"Glad I could help, sir." She and Joe cleaned up the medical debris and left the conference room with Greer and Winestock deep in conversation.

"Nice work." Joe glanced at her. "How do you feel?"

"Fine."

"Sam."

Maybe having a partner so attentive to her wasn't such a great idea. "I'll be fine, Joe. I'm a little sore, but it's not bad. How did you know?"

"You winced when you stretched a few minutes ago in the employee dining room. Take something to dull the pain."

She stopped in her tracks and stared at him, eyes narrowed at the command in his voice.

"Please," he added, his tone softer.

With a nod, Sam resumed walking toward the dining room where they met the rest of their teammates.

"How is Greer?" Nico asked.

"He has a cut on his arm that required twelve stitches."

"I want to know how the captain was injured and so will Maddox." Nico called their boss who picked up on the first ring.

"Talk to me, Nico."

"You're on speaker with our team and Mercy. We had trouble brewing before we arrived on the ship." He went on to explain about the bombs on board the Pacific Star. Joe and Ben explained the steps taken to dismantle the explosive devices and the interviews with the various law enforcement agencies.

"I'll warn the communications people to expect an influx of phone calls with follow-up questions for the three of you. I assume you're still in port?"

"Yes, sir," Nico confirmed. "We're in the terminal, waiting for law enforcement teams with bomb-sniffing dogs to clear the ship. An hour ago, Jerry Greer, the Pacific Star's captain, was attacked while visiting with cruise passengers."

"Not what I wanted to hear. What happened?"

Joe summarized the incident and Sam chimed in with her treatment of Greer's wound.

"What about the four executives?"

"All of them were eating together at the time of the captain's attack," Trace said. "They were more than three hundred feet away."

"One of them could still be involved in planning the attack on the ship and the captain. How can I help?"

"Find out what the feds know," Nico said. "Local law enforcement and the Coast Guard are also in the mix. Everybody is cutting us out of the loop. I don't like working in the dark."

"I'll see what I can do. Anything else?"

Nico glanced at his team members and his wife. No one spoke up. "Not right now. Tell Zane to keep digging into the backgrounds of the four executives and Hollingbrook's relatives. Someone is out to hurt Hollingbrook and his business."

CHAPTER TEN

Twelve hours later, the announcement finally came over the terminal's loud speakers for the passengers to begin boarding the Pacific Star by decks. Joe stood, held out his hand to Sam, and helped her to her feet as his teammates grabbed their own gear. "Can't say I'm sorry to see the last of this dining room. I'm ready to change clothes." And take a shower. He'd gone longer between showers and fresh clothes on missions. Didn't mean he liked it.

Nico paused in the doorway and shoved his hand into his pocket. "Forgot to give you these." He placed two gold wedding bands on Joe's palm. "You and Sam are now on stage and will be every minute you're outside of the suite. Zane set up a cover story that Mercy and I are longtime friends of you and Sam."

Joe stared at the rings a moment while the rest of his team left the room. This marriage was fake despite the license in his duffel that said otherwise. He raised his gaze to Sam. She looked uncertain.

Wouldn't be easier if he waited. Joe lifted Sam's left hand and slid the smaller gold band on her finger, then handed her the larger one and held out his left hand.

Fingers trembling, the medic slid the wedding ring on his finger.

"Are you okay with this?"

That brought her eyes back to his. "Why do you ask?"

"Your body language says you don't want to do this, that you'd rather be anywhere else than here." With anyone other than him. And that caused a sharp pain in his chest. "We can form another plan."

"It's too late. We board the ship any minute."

"I don't want you uncomfortable with me, Sam."

"I'm comfortable with you," she protested.

"Not like this. We have to act like we're on our honeymoon. That means me touching you. A lot. People will notice if newlyweds don't even hold hands." And, man, did he want to do more than hold her hand.

Sam moved close enough to lay her hand over his heart. Her light touch branded him.

"I can handle it as long as you are the one touching me."

He studied her for a moment, then nodded. "If I do something to make you uneasy, tell me."

"It's not a problem. Besides, the relationship isn't real."

Joe framed her face with his hands. "The piece of paper isn't real. I wouldn't say everything else is fake."

Sam's eyes widened, confusion clouding their depths. "Joe?"

He kissed her, his touch feather-light and filled with a glimpse of what was in his heart. When he drew back, Joe dropped one hand from her face and let the other slide down her arm to clasp her hand. Breathing room. He had to back off or risk losing his chance with Sam. "We need to go. They just called the name of our deck for boarding."

While they walked, he saw Sam glancing at the wedding band several times. Joe's lips curved. His ring felt like it weighed several pounds. Guess the weight bothered him because he didn't wear any jewelry. Never seemed prudent to wear a ring when he was likely to end up in hand-to-hand combat while on a mission. If the ring signified a real marriage, he would adjust and wear the band proudly. Not gold, though, he decided. Maybe cobalt to absorb light instead of reflect it.

They breezed through security again with the security personnel glancing at their IDs and waving them through without checking their bags. This time when Casey, the perky employee, took them through the check-in procedures and offered to direct them to their cabins, they accepted her assistance.

Casey glanced at the cabin listing for their names and beamed at them. "Aww! You're in the honeymoon suite. Congratulations."

Joe lightly rested his arm across Sam's shoulders. "Thanks." She stiffened for a second, then deliberately relaxed against his side and smiled at Casey.

"Enjoy your cruise. If we can do anything to make your stay with us more enjoyable, please let us know."

With a nod, Joe urged Sam forward. "Let's go so we can change clothes," he murmured. "We are a tad conspicuous in all black."

"Oh, yeah. Passengers are beginning to stare."

They hurried toward their cabin, arriving in time to see Nico and Mercy unlocking the door next to theirs.

"Curt, Trace, and Ben have already dumped their gear in the cabins and left. They're keeping eyes on the foursome."

"Six," Mercy corrected.

"The client is here?" Sam asked.

"Charlaine is traveling with her daughter and nanny."

Sam's face softened. To Joe, she was always beautiful but he'd never seen this expression on her face before. Would she look like this as she held her own child? His child? He turned to Nico, afraid Sam she would catch a glimpse of the naked longing that lived inside his heart. "Orders?"

"Mingle with the passengers and crew as newlyweds. Mercy and I will do the same. People talk. Hopefully, they'll say something useful."

Based on the conversations he overheard in the security line, Joe wouldn't bet on that. He glanced at Sam and noticed she looked tired. Although Dr. Sorensen cleared her for duty, Sam wasn't at full strength. "Any time in your schedule for a nap? I need my beauty rest."

Shadow's leader snorted. "Won't help your ugly mug. You're right, though. We need sleep. We'll mingle until lunch, then take shifts. Mercy has a drawing seminar this evening. The whole team is on duty during her session."

Nice. Joe loved watching Mercy work. "We'll walk the decks soon to learn the ship's layout." Joe unlocked the door. Because several couples were in the corridor, he scooped Sam into his arms, carried her over the threshold, and kicked the door shut behind them. The action startled Sam but made the right impression based on broad smiles from the men and envious looks from the women who witnessed his behavior.

He set her down and placed their bags inside the bedroom near the door for easy access.

She set the mike bag beside her Go bag and duffel. "We should change clothes."

"We have time. Take a shower if you want. I'll wait in the living room and take mine when you're finished."

Joe returned to the living area and drew in a deep breath. This was harder than he thought it would be. He wanted everything to be easy and natural for Sam's sake. But this felt real to him. He glanced at the wedding band on his finger and grimaced. He wasn't helping himself.

Joe moved across the room. Wouldn't do for Sam to think he was a stalker. She'd find out soon enough he was nuts about her, had been for the past five years. He couldn't stay near the door where he'd hear the shower run and his imagination would drive him crazy.

Looking out the glass balcony doors, Joe scanned the activity on the dock and noticed one man watching passengers board the ship from the terminal. He stayed in the shadows and leaned against a nearby building. No threatening moves, but the man looked out of place among the excited crowd. The man raised his cell phone and took a picture.

Joe swung his gaze toward the area the stranger had photographed. His gut tightened. A group of young, beautiful women. Maybe he enjoyed looking at beautiful women. What man didn't? But this man set off Joe's trouble meter. Joe snapped a picture of him with his phone, hoping Z could ID him.

The man took another picture of a different group of women, turned around, and walked away.

Joe sent his photo to Zane and called his friend. "It's Joe."

"Heard you defused the second bomb. Nice work."

"Thanks."

"I know you're a crack shot with a rifle. Why didn't I know about your second skill set?"

He smiled as he watched people boarding the ship. "I thought my sparkling personality was my second skill set."

Zane gave a bark of laughter. "No one but Sam Coleman thinks you have a sparkling personality, buddy, and that woman is biased."

"Maybe."

"When did you learn to defuse bombs?"

"I'm still a rookie compared to Ben. I've been training with him on weekends for months. My first chance to use the new skill was on the South American mission two weeks ago. The bombs on the Pacific Star were similar. Ben talked me through what he was doing before Sam contacted me about the second bomb. They were set to detonate at the same time. Made sense to split the work."

"Your new skill came in handy. Since chatting is not in your arsenal of skills, you must need something. How can I help?"

"I just sent you a photograph. Quality isn't good but I need an ID on the man. He was taking pictures of female passengers as they boarded the ship."

"I'll do what I can and get back to you."

"Thanks, Z." He ended the call.

A door opened behind him. "Everything okay?"

"I don't know." He continued to watch the passengers streaming onto the ship in case the suspicious man returned.

"What do you see?"

"Nothing at the moment." He brought up the picture he'd taken and turned his screen toward Sam. "This guy was photographing female passengers as they boarded the ship."

Sam studied the photo. "I don't recognize him. Is it possible he took pictures of friends or family members going on the cruise?"

"If he watched one woman or group of women, I'd consider that possibility. He took pictures of several groups of women and left."

"And you don't like it."

He shook his head. "This guy is trouble."

CHAPTER ELEVEN

Joe's words reverberated in Sam's head long after he'd left the living room to shower and change clothes. She studied the photo, her stomach twisting into a knot. The stranger's stalker-like behavior made Sam worry about the women blissfully unaware of the potential danger.

From this angle, Joe couldn't take pictures of the women to identify and warn them. Sam had noticed cameras as she and her teammates passed through security. She and Joe might be able to match the time stamp from Joe's picture to the security feed and identify the women.

Sam kept her attention riveted to the dock in case the stranger returned. While she maintained her vigil, she considered the turnaround in Joe's attitude toward her in the past three months.

Her shooting scared him. She understood. The close call scared her, too. When the bullet had slammed into her, Sam thought she would bleed out on that bathroom floor before her teammates found her. Worse, she'd failed in her role as Mercy's bodyguard. Nico had almost lost the woman he later married.

On the heel of those thoughts came the sweet, dim memory of Joe carrying her to the SUV, holding her tight in his strong arms and begging her to stay with him as a teammate drove her to the hospital. After she woke from the haze of anesthesia, Sam found Joe at her bedside, holding her hand tight in his. He stayed by her side for the next month, sleeping on her couch in case she needed him after she was released from the hospital.

During that month, she grew comfortable with Joe's company and ached for him when he and the rest of Shadow deployed with a substitute medic. While he was gone, Joe texted and called often. The contact helped. Not enough, though. A phone call was a poor substitute for seeing his face and feeling the gentle touches she'd come to crave as much as her next breath.

She was in so much trouble and in serious danger of losing her heart to the handsome spotter. What if he didn't feel the same?

Sam rolled her eyes. She needed to get a grip. If he didn't return her feelings, Sam would move on. Whether she could work on the same team with Joe was another consideration. She loved her team and their working rhythm. Maddox would transfer her to another unit if necessary, but she didn't want to change teams. They were adults. If she and Joe dated and the relationship didn't work, they would figure out how to work together. Sam didn't want to lose his friendship or her team.

The bedroom door opened. "Did he return?"

The sound of Joe's voice sent goosebumps surging over Sam's skin. She would give almost anything to have the right to touch him. "Not that I've seen."

She turned from the window. Joe looked amazing. Her gaze skimmed over his short-sleeved polo, jeans, and combat boots. Sam smiled. "No running shoes today?"

He shrugged one shoulder. "I'm more comfortable in boots. Hiding my knives is easier with them."

She gestured to her own jeans and boots. "Same here. After what happened earlier, I feel better with more weapons." Annoyed at her trembling fingers, Sam clenched her hands into fists. What was wrong with her? This was Joe, not some stranger Maddox paired her with for this mission. She trusted him.

"You're nervous."

Joe never missed anything, a quality that made him such a great spotter and an annoying friend. "A little."

He remained silent a moment. "Come here, Sam."

She raised her head, her gaze locked with his. She crossed the expanse between them, stopping inches from his body.

Joe cupped her nape and tugged her forward, closing the remaining gap. "Maybe this will help," he murmured and lowered his head. His mouth captured hers in another soft, tender kiss that went on and on until her body melted against his, knees weak and shaking.

Sam needed air but refused to stop the magic of his touch. Who needed to breathe?

Joe lifted his head long enough to allow them to drag in a much-needed breath. "Again." His lips slanted over hers, this time with more pressure and heat. He would ruin her for another man's kiss. Who was she kidding? No other man would hold a candle to Joe.

His tongue brushing over her bottom lip made her gasp. Joe took advantage of her response to deepen the kiss.

Sam heard a soft moan, a woman's moan. Hers. That's when she became aware her arms were locked around his neck and she stood on her tiptoes to be as close as possible to this man.

She should step back. But having Joe in her arms was a dream come true. She reminded herself this relationship wasn't real. They weren't in public, though. Did he care about her as more than a friend? Man, she hoped so.

Joe lifted his mouth and pressed his forehead against hers, breath ragged. "Give me a minute and we'll go explore the ship." He tightened his hold. "Good grief, woman, that nearly got out of hand." He paused a second, then whispered in her ear, "I can't wait to do it again."

Sam laughed, glad she wasn't the only one blown away by their chemistry.

Finally, Joe dropped a light kiss on her mouth and released her. "We have to leave the suite before I cross a line, Sparky."

Her eyebrows rose. "Sparky?"

"Oh, yeah. You light me up like a firecracker, Samantha Coleman."

"Fire burns, you know."

A slow smile spread. "I'm counting on it." After a kiss to her knuckles, Joe ushered her from the cabin to the upper decks. His arm wrapped lightly around her waist, keeping Sam close without hindering her ability to maneuver.

They found places at the rail with the rest of the crowd as the Pacific Star got under way. A large man moved to the rail beside Sam, too close for comfort. She edged away, but the only place to go was closer to Joe.

He noticed her dilemma and stepped back to move her in front of him. He placed his hands on the rail beside of hers, preventing anyone from encroaching on her space and fulfilling the role Maddox had assigned.

"Better?" he murmured in her ear.

She nodded. "Thanks."

"Relax, Mrs. Gray. I have your back."

Sam marveled that one minute her concentration centered on the stranger too close to her only to shift to the man protecting her back and sides. Her heart was in so much danger.

Focus on the job. They were supposed to be newlyweds. Hard to carry off that role if Sam was stiff as a board. She deliberately leaned her back against his chest, nestling her head against his shoulder.

"I could get used to that." He kissed her temple.

Once the ship sailed far enough from San Diego that passengers lost interest in waving at friends and family wishing them a good journey, the crowd thinned and Sam could breathe again. "We need to find Trace."
"Why?"
"Patch."
Joe sucked in a breath. "I forgot about his seasickness."
"By this point, he's starting to feel it."
"We better go. He'll stand out if he starts puking on the deck."
They found their teammate down two decks, standing near a wall, looking a little green. Relief filled his eyes when he saw Sam.
"Please tell me you brought my supply of patches," he muttered.
She glanced around. Coast was clear. "Bend down." When he complied, Sam ripped open the packet she'd slid into her pocket before leaving the bedroom and applied the patch behind his ear. "You'll feel better soon."
"You're a lifesaver, Sam." He bussed the top of her head with a light kiss.
Joe stiffened.
Sam stared at him. He had a problem with Trace kissing the top of her head as though they were siblings? She noted the icy stare sent Trace's way. Whoa. Not good. Of all people, these two members of Shadow depended on each other to survive more than the rest of them. Joe was Trace's spotter. They had to have each other's backs. Bad blood between the two could be deadly for one or both of them.
She deliberately moved in front of Joe and laid her hand over his heart. "Stop."
Joe's gaze remained fixed on the sniper.
"Dial it back, buddy," Trace said, amusement coloring his voice. "I don't have designs on your wife."

Those words appeared to snap Joe back into focus. "Sorry."

"We should keep moving." Sam looked at Trace over her shoulder. "Let me know when the symptoms return and I'll give you another patch."

"Yes, ma'am."

Sam wanted to ask Joe about the death glare he'd lobbed at Trace but this wasn't the time or place. When they returned to the suite, she'd talk to him. It was time she figured out what changed between her and Joe.

She and Joe made appearances at various populated spots around the ship. By the time they finished, Sam was ready for a nap, too tired to launch into a serious discussion. Their talk would have to wait a little longer.

"Are you hungry?"

"I'm too tired to eat."

"All right. We'll eat when you wake." He clasped her hand as they walked to their suite. Inside, he nudged her toward the bedroom. "I know Nico wants Shadow on duty during Mercy's seminar. Listen to your body, Sparky. If you need more time to sleep, take it. We aren't far from the dining room. If Shadow needs us, we'll be on hand in two minutes or less. I can tell Nico we need to be off duty for this evening."

She wanted to be angry with him for suggesting she couldn't pull her weight but Sam was feeling the results of the flight and the long stay in the employee dining room at the terminal. "I'll see how I feel when I wake up."

Joe trailed the backs of his fingers down her cheek. "I'll be here. I have your back. Let yourself sleep." He brushed his thumb over her bottom lip, then dropped his hand from her face and stepped back.

Sam closed the bedroom door and leaned against it. Joe Gray was addictive. She sighed. Daydreaming about the handsome spotter wouldn't help her obtain the sleep she desperately needed.

She untied her boots, toed them off, and set her weapons within easy reach. With a soft groan, Sam reclined on the bed. She fell asleep within seconds of closing her eyes.

Waking sometime later, she was disoriented. The light from the window was dim and the sun was in a different position. She padded into the bathroom and splashed water on her face to help sweep the cobwebs from her brain. After brushing her hair, tying on her boots, and strapping on her weapons, Sam opened the bedroom door.

Joe looked up from the sofa where he was working on his laptop. "Feel better?"

"Much. Did you sleep?"

"A few hours." He closed the computer lid, set it aside, and stood. "Ready to eat now?"

She nodded. "Are we too late to help with Mercy's demonstration?"

"We'll be on time if we leave now." He walked to her side. "Nico sent a text ten minutes ago. He and Mercy saved us seats at their table."

When he reached for the knob, Sam laid her hand on his arm. "Wait."

"What is it?"

"When we were with Trace earlier, you pinned him with the 1,000-yard stare. Why?"

CHAPTER TWELVE

Joe froze, his heartbeat accelerating. She wanted to do this now? Fine. He prayed she could handle the answer and still carry off the charade necessary for their assignment. "You know why."

Her eyes narrowed. "Don't do that. I don't want cryptic statements from you. Help me understand what's going on."

Joe turned then and wrapped his arms around her. "You're an observant woman. You know what's happening between us."

"Spell it out for me."

"I don't want another man kissing you."

She blinked. "We're teammates and he's one of your best friends."

"He's a man and single."

"This marriage isn't real, Joe. We're playing a role."

"The license isn't real. Everything else is."

Sam growled at him. "Explain that or we'll miss dinner."

"The chemistry between us is real. How I feel about you is real. I don't share, Sparky."

"You don't share what?"

"You."

Her eyes widened.

"This isn't a charade to me, Sam. The license is fake. The rest is pure truth." He dropped a quick kiss on her mouth and broke his hold. "Come on. We need to go."

"But...."

"Just think about what I said and consider giving us a chance." Joe opened the door to the corridor, forestalling further questions. He didn't want to push her tonight. Their relationship had shifted. Whether the shift was a positive or negative was up to her. But it was taking every ounce of willpower he had not to fall on his knees and beg her to give him a chance.

He entwined their fingers and led her to an upper deck. The buzz of conversation and laughter, scent of food, and clink of glasses and silverware greeted them as they walked into the dining room.

Joe scanned the room and lifted his chin to Nico. He and Sam threaded their way through the crowded tables to their teammates. Seated at the table were Captain Greer, Nico and Mercy, and the four executives from Hollingbrook Cruise Lines.

He seated Sam, then sat in the chair beside hers. "Sorry we're late. We got distracted."

Sam's face flamed as the others at the table smiled at them, some winking or giving them a sly grin. Mercy squeezed Sam's hand. "We explained to our tablemates about you and Joe being newlyweds." She introduced the captain and Hollingbrook executives.

"Congratulations," Charlaine Bennett said. Longing filled her eyes as her gaze shifted to Lance Farraday who looked anywhere but at Charlaine.

The lack of interaction between the two puzzled Joe. Had Farraday and Bennett had a falling out since their daughter was born? "Thanks."

Joe turned his attention to the plate full of food the waiter had placed in front of him. As he ate, Joe scanned the room for the exits and located Ben and Trace. Twenty feet from the captain's table was a raised platform with a tall stool, a microphone, and an easel with Mercy's pens and paper.

"What do you do for a living, Gray?" Dax Alexander asked.

Joe went with the story he and his teammates had decided was the easiest to maintain because it had been true for both him and Sam earlier in their careers. "Army. Sam, too."

Colt Riley's eyebrows rose. "Wow. Will Uncle Sam keep you assigned to the same place?"

"We're not due for reassignment for a while. When the time comes, we'll request to be posted to the same base."

"What are your jobs?" Charlaine asked.

"I'm an MP." A true job description before he joined his Ranger unit as a sharpshooter. "Sam is a medic."

Lance Farraday spoke up. "Thanks to both of you for your service to our country."

Greer set down his glass. "What are you drawing tonight, Mercy?"

"A lighthouse on a jut of land on a stormy night seemed most appropriate."

"I hope we don't run into a storm." Charlaine glanced toward the dining room's entrance.

The captain put down his fork. "Don't worry, Charlaine. The long-range forecast is clear but if we know a storm is brewing in the Pacific, we take measures to safeguard the passengers and ship."

Lance's grip tightened on his fork but he remained silent.

Interesting. Was he worried about himself, Charlaine, their daughter? Maybe Lance wasn't as unaffected as he tried to appear. Joe glanced at Sam and noticed she was watching the father as well.

"Is Kayla settling in all right?" Mercy asked the female executive.

Charlaine beamed. "She's the sweetest baby ever. Nothing seems to faze her. Even the time we spent in the terminal didn't seem to bother her at all. She only cried when she needed a diaper change or a bottle."

"We'd love to see her, wouldn't we, Sam?"

"Absolutely. I love kids."

"What about you and Joe? Are you planning to have children?" Charlaine asked.

"Not for a while yet." Sam leaned her head against Joe's shoulder causing his heart to go into overdrive. "I want Joe all to myself right now."

He raised her hand to his lips and kissed her knuckles. Feeling her shiver made him smile. Good to know she was as affected by their chemistry. "Having kids is more challenging with our careers. We'll work it out, but for now I want to enjoy our time together. When we're ready, we'll make decisions about our jobs. We'll handle it together." Having children would be a challenge as Fortress operatives.

His gut clenched. When had he gone from wanting to date Sam to thinking about raising a family with her?

Charlaine turned to Mercy and Nico. "What about you two?"

"We've only been married two months." Mercy smiled at Nico. "We're still in the honeymoon phase, too. What about the rest of you?" Mercy directed her question to the other men at the table. "Are you married? Have children?"

Colt Riley grinned. "Sorry, Mercy. No woman or kids. I'm a footloose and fancy-free bachelor. If Joe hadn't seen Sam first, I might have been tempted to leave my partying ways."

Joe forced a smile to his lips when he felt like punching Riley in the face. "Too late."

"Four ex-wives, one current wife, and two kids for me," Dax said with a grimace.

"No wife," Lance said curtly. He said nothing about children.

"I need to check on my daughter," Charlaine said and rose. The men of the table stood until she left. Lance stared after her before dragging his gaze back to his meal. As soon as conversation around the table restarted, he started steadily wolfing down his meal.

Wouldn't surprise Joe if Lance cut short his evening. He couldn't figure out was why Lance and Charlaine weren't a couple in public. Zane's research indicated they were still seeing each other.

Greer reached for his fork and grimaced.

"How are you feeling, Captain?" Sam asked.

"Sore, like you said."

Dax looked from Greer to Sam and back. "Are you sick, Greer?"

"Not like you mean. I cut my arm in the terminal and Sam was kind enough to treat it for me."

"Handy to have a medic around."

"The terminal was such a madhouse I couldn't find our ship's doctor for him to take care of the injury." He looked at Sam. "What do you and Joe do in your spare time for fun?"

"I restore classic cars." Joe nodded at Sam. "My wife builds tree houses."

Dax's eyes brightened as he stared at Joe. Lance pulled his attention away from his plate. "Tree houses?"

"That's right." Sam smiled.

"Don't you live on a base?"

"Some with families want their own space. I build tree houses for those living off base. Since military personnel are reassigned all the time, new families move into the area.

Word gets around and I have more tree house requests than I can fill."

"Do you have pictures?"

Sam palmed her phone and tapped the photos app. She slid the phone across the table.

Lance's jaw dropped as he scrolled through the images of the structures she'd built over the years. "These are miniature works of art. I build tree houses, too, but nothing like these. How did you become interested in them?"

Because Joe's thigh rested against hers, he felt her muscles tense. Not sure what caused the reaction, he laid his left hand on her knee as he scanned the room for trouble.

Ben caught his eye, eyebrow raised in silent inquiry.

Joe gave a slight shake of his head. He didn't see a direct threat to their safety.

Sam laid her fork on her plate and, underneath the table, gripped Joe's hand, hard. "Tree houses were my refuge as a kid. They were safe places. I want to provide that same refuge for other children."

Joe kept his face impassive while inside his thoughts whirled and spun in chaotic fashion. Sam's voice told Joe the words she spoke were the truth and convinced him her childhood had been difficult. He longed to go back in time and protect her. The idea that someone would hurt this woman sliced deep into his heart. What he wouldn't give to have the right to protect her from pain and hurt.

Because he knew her, Joe shifted the conversation back to Lance. "When did you start building tree houses?"

"A friend took me to a charity homebuilding project for a low-income family. I loved the process and volunteered for more home builds. The next summer, a neighbor asked for help building a tree house. Seeing results that fast was satisfying and fun. I've built tree houses for five years."

A small commotion at the entrance to the dining room caught Joe's attention. Trace had stopped a frantic Charlaine at the threshold, his hands resting on the woman's shoulders while she gestured toward the captain's table with one hand and held the baby against her with the other arm.

A moment later, Shadow's sniper glanced at Joe, then Sam, and gave a subtle hand signal. Nico stood along with Sam and Joe. "We'll be back," Joe said. They followed Nico into the corridor.

Charlaine grabbed one of Sam's hands. "Please help my daughter."

CHAPTER THIRTEEN

Sam looked at the infant who appeared to be sound asleep against her mother's shoulder. "What's wrong with her?"

"It's time for her to eat and I can't wake her."

"Did you or your nanny notice anything unusual about Kayla before dinner? A fever or inconsolable crying like she was in pain?" Sam was out of her depth. She worked with adults, not babies.

Charlaine shook her head. "When I checked on Kayla a few minutes ago, Bianca was gone and I couldn't rouse my daughter."

Footsteps hurried toward them. Sam glanced back to see Lance moving their direction, worry in the eyes he'd focused on the baby.

"What's going on?" he asked, voice low. "Is the baby all right?"

"She won't wake up," Charlaine said, tears streaking down her face. "I can't find Bianca."

Lance scowled. "She left Kayla alone? If she doesn't have a rock-solid reason for leaving the baby, she'll be looking for another job."

A telling statement. Would Lance have been as free with his words and feelings if the other executives from Hollingbrook were near?

"What do you need, Sam?" Joe asked.

"A quiet place to check the baby and my mike bag." She didn't have supplies to treat an infant's ailment but she could check Kayla's vitals.

"I'll be back in a minute." Joe spun and ran.

"There's a lounge at the other end of the corridor," Nico said. "It should be deserted. Will that work?"

"Lead the way." As the group walked away from the dining room, Sam sent Joe a message, letting him know where to bring her bag. When they entered the lounge, they discovered the area was deserted.

Charlaine hurried to the closest couch. Lance spread the baby's blanket over a cushion and stepped aside for Charlaine to place Kayla on the makeshift bed. Although he didn't touch the mother, he stayed close.

"May I undress your daughter to see if she has a rash on her torso or marks on her skin?" It would also give her a chance to check Kayla's temperature.

"It's fine. Please, just help her."

Charlaine's heartfelt plea tugged at Sam's heartstrings. She'd felt the same utter terror when Joe had been shot in the chest on a mission. Yeah, she understood how desperate Kayla's mother felt. Sam had worked feverishly to save Joe's life and stayed by his side during the nightmare flight to safety and Dr. Sorensen's clinic. Like Joe had done for her not so long ago, Sam had stayed with the spotter while he recuperated.

Joe raced into the lounge with Sam's mike bag slung over his shoulder. He shrugged it off and set it beside the couch. "Any change?"

She shook her head as she unsnapped Kayla's sleeper. She eased the baby's arms and legs from the outfit and checked her skin. No rash on the front. With a glance at the mother, Sam gently turned Kayla to her stomach. Still no rash. No odd marks, either. As she examined the baby, Sam talked to her, pausing to gently tap her cheek or the bottom of a tiny foot, hoping for a response. Nothing.

Joe crouched beside her. "What do you need?"

"Stethoscope and digital thermometer. I want to check her heart rate and temperature."

A moment later, he laid the instruments in Sam's hand.

She listened to Kayla's heart. The beat was too slow for a baby her age. Sam checked pupil reaction, then used the thermometer. When she finished, Sam turned to Charlaine. "I'm not an expert on babies and children, but I think your daughter has been drugged."

Charlaine clamped a hand over her mouth, her eyes wide. Lance cursed. "Can you treat her?" he asked.

Sam shook her head. If they'd been on a mission outside of the US with no access to doctors, she would have done what she could to help. This wasn't a war zone and a qualified medical staff was available. "You should take Kayla to the infirmary. The doctor will treat her. Charlaine, do you mind if Joe and I search your cabin? The doctor needs to know what Kayla might have been given."

The distraught mother shoved her hand in her pants pocket, yanked out her key card, and thrust it toward Sam. "Cabin 2347. Hurry."

"I'll escort Charlaine and Lance to the infirmary with Kayla," Nico said. "Joe, go with Sam." He urged the parents to follow him with their daughter.

Joe scooped up the mike bag and clasped Sam's hand. They jogged to the stairs. Three decks down, Sam slid the key card in the lock on Charlaine's door. She surveyed the cabin. "I'll take the bedrooms. You start with the bathroom."

"Gloves first." He glanced at her. "In case foul play is involved in the nanny's disappearance." Joe set Sam's mike bag on the floor and opened it. "We don't want to contaminate evidence if law enforcement needs to step in. Making ourselves a target of their interest would be a waste of time and resources."

Sam handed Joe gloves before tugging on a pair herself. She moved into the room and began to search. The room included a bed and luggage of one of the women. Shoving aside her qualms about invading the woman's privacy, she rifled through Bianca's belongings and didn't find medicine aside from birth control pills. She passed through the bathroom to the second bedroom and shifted her search to the next set of luggage on the far side of the bed. Charlaine's luggage was a set Sam recognized from an Internet search into vacations and luggage during a lazy, boring afternoon while she recuperated and Joe was out of the country with Shadow. This set of luggage was one Sam admired and marked off her list of possible purchases because she felt the price too steep to pay for something she might use a handful of times.

Hoping she wouldn't find evidence incriminating the mother, Sam searched through the Hollingbrook executive's luggage. Nothing except over-the-counter pain meds. Caplets, nothing that could be easily given to an infant.

"Sam." Joe stood in the doorway to the bathroom, two small bottles on his palm.

She rushed across the cabin and took the bottles from his hand. Children's allergy medicine and pain reliever. Sam scowled. The bottles were empty. This had to be what they were looking for unless the nanny or someone else brought meds to drug the baby. "Let's go."

Joe slung her mike bag over his shoulder and they ran to the infirmary. Nico turned as they raced inside. "Find anything?"

"Maybe." Sam extended her hand, bottles on her palm. "Charlaine, did you bring these on the ship?"

She frowned. "I always travel with these in case Kayla needs them."

"Were the bottles new, partially used, nearly empty?" The doctor glanced away from Kayla for a moment. His gaze locked on Sam. "What was in the bottles?"

"Pain reliever and allergy meds. The bottles are empty."

Charlaine gasped. "That can't be. Each bottle was at least a quarter full."

"I don't understand." Lance frowned. "Why would Bianca want to hurt a baby?"

"If she gave Kayla the meds, she didn't intend to hurt her." Sam bagged the bottles, then handed the empty containers to the doctor. "I think the intent was to make sure Kayla slept for a while."

Lance cursed. "Bianca will be looking for another job."

"If she's guilty." Charlaine's attention shifted to her daughter. "Bianca came highly recommended and she's never done anything to suggest she would do something like this."

"Kayla was left alone in the cabin for at least 40 minutes. I want to talk to the ship's security chief. I want Bianca found and questioned."

"Did you bring any other medication for Kayla?" Sam asked.

The baby's mother shook her head. "She's been healthy except for a mild cold last month. Her pediatrician recommended I bring the allergy medication and pain reliever just in case Kayla came down with another cold while we were on the ship."

"I'll talk to Winestock," Nico said. "He'll want to examine Charlaine's cabin and Bianca's."

"I don't care if he tears the place apart. I just want answers." Charlaine turned toward the doctor. "Can you help my baby?"

The man nodded. "We'll be here a while. You should get comfortable."

Nico signaled Sam and Joe to follow him to the corridor. Lance followed on their heels.

"I want to know anything you find out about Bianca or the baby," he demanded, his voice low.

Shadow's leader folded his arms across his chest. "Why do you think we will know anything?"

Lance snorted. "Please. I'm not stupid. You may not work for Hollingbrook but you work in some type of security profession. My brother is a cop. I recognize the awareness of everything and everyone around you." His gaze swung to Joe and Sam. "Military training might explain the same awareness in the two of you. I'm not convinced that's all it is. There's something about the way you carry yourselves that says you're more than Army grunts."

"We'll tell you what we can."

"Next to nothing, in other words." Lance frowned. "I can get what I need from Winestock. I'd rather get it from you. I'm betting your curiosity won't let you drop this until you find Bianca. Weird things have been happening on this cruise route and I want to get to the bottom of it, especially since Kayla and Charlaine are involved. I won't let anything happen to them."

"What's your interest in them?" Joe asked.

The other man swallowed hard and glanced toward the room where his daughter and lover waited. Lance turned toward them, dragging a hand down his face. "Kayla is my daughter. You can't say anything to anyone about this or Charlaine and I will be fired."

"Why?" Sam asked.

"Hollingbrook Cruise Lines has a no fraternization policy. If anyone finds out, our careers there are toast."

Sam stared, glad Maddox didn't have the same rule. At least two Fortress couples she knew were married and suspected a few of her other friends were interested in dating another operative. She knew office romances could be messy but wouldn't it be better to allow the relationships than make a blanket declaration that workplace romances were off limits?

She looked at Joe and found him watching her, eyes filled with intense emotion. Sam didn't want to imagine having to choose between Joe and her job. At least at Fortress, if she couldn't work on the same team with Joe, she'd have the option of working with another team. It wouldn't be the same, though. Shadow was her family. Losing them or Joe would savage her.

Lance returned to the infirmary, closing the door softly behind him.

The Fortress operatives looked at each other a moment before Nico said, "We need to tell Winestock about Charlaine's nanny. I'm afraid if we don't find Bianca soon, we'll be too late."

CHAPTER FOURTEEN

Winestock met the Fortress operatives at Charlaine's cabin. "What's this about a missing woman?"

Joe shoved the key card in the lock and opened the door. "It's Bianca White, Charlaine Bennett's nanny for her daughter. Charlaine came to Sam for help because Kayla wouldn't wake up to eat."

The security chief turned to stare at Joe like he'd lost his mind. "Maybe the kid's tired. Ms. White might have gone for a walk." Winestock scowled at the operatives. "If the child is sleeping, maybe the nanny stepped out for some fresh air."

"For more than an hour? I'm not buying it. Besides, Kayla is four months old."

Winestock's mouth gaped. "Four months?"

Sam gestured to the baby clothes and supplies scattered around the cabin. "She's too young to be left alone. Charlaine's daughter takes a bottle frequently and doesn't vary her feedings by more than thirty minutes. Joe and I found two empty vials of over-the-counter medicine for babies in the trash. Kayla isn't sick and the vials had at least a quarter of the medicine still in them when she left for dinner. When she returned to feed her daughter, Charlaine found Kayla alone and couldn't rouse her."

Winestock scowled. "The nanny drugged that baby?"

"We want to find her and ask," Nico said.

"My team may not find anything useful," the security chief warned. "Cabin stewards clean between occupants but they don't obliterate all the fingerprints. Besides, you searched the place less than an hour ago. Your prints will be in here as well."

"Only on the knob. We used rubber gloves to search." Joe folded his arms across his chest. "I haven't been away from police work that long."

Nico signaled Joe to back off. Joe locked down his emotions with a tight grip. Winestock didn't know anything about him or the other Fortress operatives aside from their ability to deal with bombs. He had no inkling of the skill sets Shadow brought to this investigation. Still, the security chief knew Joe used to be a cop. Ticked him off that Winestock believed he would be so careless as to obliterate evidence at a possible crime scene.

"Does your team have the proper equipment to handle a crime scene?" Nico asked.

"We have the basics." With that statement, he walked into the cabin and made a call, his voice hushed.

"The security chief won't share the results of his investigation," Sam said.

"If necessary, we'll request Hollingbrook encourage Winestock to cooperate." Nico scanned the corridor. He stared at the domed shape on the ceiling 100 feet away. "Security camera. Maybe Winestock won't mind if we look at security footage."

"Would we be able to access the security footage of passengers boarding the ship as well?" Sam asked.

"Probably. Why?"

Joe explained about the man taking photos of women as they boarded, then leaving. "I sent the photo to Zane. It's not a great shot, Nico. I'm not holding out much hope."

"Z has been known to work wonders with bad photography."

Winestock rejoined them. "My team will be here in a few minutes. I'll secure the scene until they arrive."

In other words, shove off. Joe's lip curled. Guess Winestock was territorial. No problem. Joe and his teammates would work around him to get what they needed. If all else failed, they'd go to Hollingbrook.

"Charlaine will need access to her baby's supplies and formula," Sam said.

"I'll take care of it."

"We'd like to check some security footage." Nico inclined his head toward the dark-colored dome on the corridor ceiling.

"I'll alert the men in the security office. No taking footage from the office and I want to know everything you see."

"Deal."

"Need directions?"

Nico shook his head.

"If you find Bianca White, hold her until one of my security team arrives to take charge of her."

"No problem."

When the Fortress operatives were far enough away from the connected cabins to avoid being overheard, Nico said, "After we talk to her."

Joe chuckled.

The operatives walked to the security office and went inside. A dark-haired, stocky man in a security uniform sat at a desk. "Help you?"

"Chief Winestock cleared us to view security footage. I'm Nico. This is Sam and Joe."

"You're with Fortress." His shoulders relaxed. "Name's Caleb. I met your teammates a few hours ago. Good guys. We owe you for defusing those bombs. Anything you need, you let us know."

Nice. This is the attitude Joe had expected from the security chief. "We appreciate your cooperation."

Caleb pushed away from the desk and led them to the next room. Another security employee twisted in his seat to stare at the newcomers. "Chip, this is Nico, Sam, and Joe. They're part of the Fortress team."

Chip stood and extended his hand. "You guys saved our skins yesterday. Which one of you is Joe?"

"That's me." Why single him out?

"Ben told me you were the second half of the duo to defuse the bombs. How long have you been doing that job?"

Joe didn't figure Chip should know this was his first solo job. "Not long."

"Where did you train?"

"Fortress. We have a training facility in Otter Creek, Tennessee where we train bodyguards and operatives. We have world-class snipers, EOD and communications experts, computer techs, and more. We have some of the best trainers in the world at PSI." Not that Joe had used PSI for his EOD training. No, that training had come courtesy of Ben and a desperate need for Joe to get out of the house on weekends instead of wishing he was with Sam. He'd almost driven himself crazy walking around the house in a daze like a lovesick puppy.

Caleb and Chip exchanged glances. "Sounds like training we could use," Caleb muttered. "Don't tell Winestock I said this, but our security training is barely adequate and we're understaffed. We're a soft target with thousands of potential hostages or victims on board every time we leave port. We need to be better prepared for terrorist attacks."

"We can help," Nico said. "Convince Winestock and Hollingbrook it's necessary for the protection of passengers."

"We'll definitely run the idea past them." Caleb folded his arms across his chest. "Now, what security feeds do you want to see? We also need an approximate time."

"We have two locations. The corridor outside cabins 2345 and 2347 from 5:30 to 6:30 tonight and the security line for passengers boarding the ship. Joe, what's the time you're interested in?"

"Let's try 4:30 to 5:00 this afternoon." That range of time surrounded his time-stamped photo by fifteen minutes on either side. Hopefully, their security cams had good enough definition to enable identification of the women of interest to the clown at the dock. If security kept a digital picture of each passenger, the identification process would be faster. The sooner they identified the women, the better.

Chip swung around to the bank of monitors and the computer on the desk. "Which location first?"

"The cabins," Nico said. "We have a missing woman and a four-month-old baby who was drugged to keep her quiet."

Both security men scowled at that information. Chip's fingers flew over the keyboard and one of the blank monitors to his right flickered to life.

"Set it to fast forward." Joe nudged Sam to the empty chair in front of the monitor as the time stamp at the foot of the screen started running. Various passengers passed by the cabins without stopping on the way to dinner. About twenty minutes before Joe had escorted Sam to the dining room, Charlaine left the cabin. For twenty minutes more, the traffic pattern outside the cabins remained the same.

At the forty-minute mark, a man dressed in a cabin steward's uniform walked into view with his head down, face averted from the camera. He pushed a large dinner cart with a white cloth draped over top and approached the cabin. He knocked. Seconds later, the door opened to reveal a fresh-faced young woman in jeans and a short-sleeved shirt.

She smiled, seeming surprised by the cart. After a moment of conversation, Bianca stepped back and allowed the man to push the cart into the cabin. The door closed behind him.

Joe kept an eye on the time stamp. Fifteen minutes had passed when the cabin door opened again. The steward pushed the cart from the cabin, closed the door behind himself, and continued toward the elevator. "Back up the footage by twenty minutes and play it again at regular speed."

They watched the footage again. When the steward pushed the cart down the corridor, Joe said, "Freeze it." He tapped the screen and glanced at Nico. "Do you see the anomalies?"

"The covered dishes are still in exactly the same place. I doubt Bianca wolfed down her food with the steward standing over her. What else am I missing?"

He turned to Sam. "Do you see it?"

She was silent a moment as she studied the screen. "He never looks toward the camera. The steward knew where the security cam was located and kept his face turned away."

"Anything else?" He glanced at the two security employees who shrugged in response to his question.

"The steward didn't have difficulty pushing the cart to the cabin. When he came out again, he put his back into pushing that cart down the hallway."

Nico frowned. "There was more weight in the cart coming out than when it went in."

"Wait." Caleb held up a hand. "You're saying this guy shoved the woman under the cart and took off with her without the lady making a fuss. How would that work?"

"Easy." Sam glanced at him. "Knock out Bianca, hogtie her, shove her under the cart on her side, whip the tablecloth down to conceal the unconscious woman, and take off."

Joe leaned a hip against the desk. "If you're worried about your extra cargo falling off, you secure her to the cart."

Chip shook his head. "Too risky."

"I don't think so. Most of the passengers are in the dining room. If he didn't call attention to himself, the few people who did see him would only see a steward taking dinner to a passenger who doesn't want to eat in the dining room."

"I'm still not sold on the idea. Let's say you're right and this clown stuffed the woman under the cart and took off with her. Where did he take her? She's been gone for more than two hours. Where is she?"

"Track his movements with the security feeds," Nico said.

"Easier said than done," Caleb muttered. "We have cameras all over the ship except in the cabins. He could have dumped the woman in one of the unoccupied cabins and left her."

"Easy enough to find out," Sam said. "If the security footage doesn't tell us what we need to know, your people can check the unoccupied cabins."

"Mark this security footage and the timing we've pinpointed," Joe said. "We need to find Bianca soon."

Sam twisted in her seat to look at him. "Gut?"

He nodded. Kayla's nanny was in trouble.

Chip's fingers flew on the keyboard again. This time the security footage showed an elevator. A couple minutes after the time stamp began to move forward, the steward pushed the large dinner cart into the car and punched a button with one finger. The whole time he was in the elevator, the man averted his face from the camera.

Nico growled. "He knows where every camera is located on his route."

"An inside job." Joe's hands tightened on the back of Sam's chair. "That's how it looks to me."

Caleb's jaw dropped. "You think one of us did this?"

"Makes the most sense. Think about it. Wouldn't you or one of the other security personnel have noticed if a passenger walked around the ship noting the security cameras on a particular route?"

"I guess." He sounded disgruntled at Joe's logic.

Nico motioned toward the screen. "Where does he go from the elevator?" he asked Chip.

"Deck 2, port side. Take a look at this." The security guard restarted the security footage.

The steward pushed the cart to the laundry facility door after a covert glance around, still with his head lowered to hide his face from the camera. Once he'd determined the coast was clear, he shoved the cart inside and closed the door. He reappeared five minutes later sans the cart. Head down, he headed in the opposite direction.

Joe frowned. "Where did he go from there?"

"Haven't been able to find him yet," Chip muttered.

Nico turned to Joe. "You and Sam go to the laundry room. I'll stay here and help track our steward. Let me know what you find."

"Yes, sir." He escorted Sam from the security office and nodded toward the elevator. "We'll conserve energy and retrace our suspect's route on the elevator."

"I'm not an invalid," she protested.

"Never said you were. We know where he went with the cart and time isn't on our side or Bianca's."

"Fine. If we're trapped in that thing when a terrorist strikes, I'll never let you live that decision down."

"Noted." After a short elevator ride, they turned toward the laundry facility. At the door, Joe stopped Sam and said softly, "Gloves. Just in case." No need to derail an investigation by introducing their fingerprints. After they covered their hands and had their weapons held down at their sides, Joe opened the door to a darkened room.

Joe frowned and signaled for Sam to step to the side while he located the light switch. A moment later, light flooded the room. Multiple washers and dryers gleamed in the overhead lights. Two machines were washing loads of clothes. Two dryers were also running. No one was in the large room.

"No exit other than this door," Sam said.

He glanced around, dread growing in his gut when he spotted the serving cart against the far wall. "Bianca is here somewhere. Take this side of the room. I'll start at the back and work my way to you."

As he approached the serving cart, the scent of food grew stronger. He raised the side of the white cloth and peered under the cart. Empty aside from a long strand of dark hair twined around a screw. The same color and length of Bianca's hair. Jaw tightening, he turned toward the row of dryers.

Joe climbed on the closest machine and checked behind the row in case the steward had dumped her back there. Nothing but a few wads of lint and dust bunnies. He glanced over his shoulder in time to see Sam doing the same with the bank of washing machines. When she hopped down, he figured she hadn't found anything.

He walked to the farthest dryer and began checking inside them. Halfway through the line, he opened a dryer door to see white material similar to the material covering the serving cart.

Gut knotting, he stuck his hand inside the machine. Instead of a large load of sheets or tablecloths, Joe's hand wrapped around a slender arm.

CHAPTER FIFTEEN

"Sam."

The tone in Joe's voice had Sam twisting to look at him. The grim expression on his face told her he'd found Bianca. Sam hurried to the dryer and peered inside. The woman who had looked surprised to see the steward bringing her dinner two hours before had been stuffed inside the dryer with a load of white cloth.

She reached in and pressed her fingertips to the side of Bianca's neck. No pulse and her skin was cooler than normal. Sam blinked back the sting of tears, frustrated that she and Joe found her too late.

Sam pulled out her flashlight and aimed the beam at the body. Bianca's hands and feet were no longer bound, but a sticky residue remained on the wrist Sam touched and her skin was red. The steward might have used duct tape.

She focused the light on the nanny's neck and frowned. Nothing on the neck to indicate she'd been strangled and no petechial hemorrhaging in Bianca's eyes.

Sam noticed a small puncture mark. Drugged? "Can we get her out of the dryer?" Determining cause of death would be easier if she was able to examine the body out of the cramped enclosure. Leaving Bianca there also seemed wrong.

Joe ran a gentle hand down Sam's back. "I want her out of there, too, but it's better if we don't. We have to let Winestock and his personnel collect what evidence they can with their limited resources. If we move her, we'll disturb evidence and reduce the likelihood of Winestock figuring out the identity of the creep who did this to Bianca."

"If they find him. I'm not holding out much hope." She leaned into his touch, unashamed to take a moment to settle before doing what was needed. "We need to contact Nico. He'll have to break the bad news to Winestock."

"Better him than me. Winestock rubs me the wrong way. The sooner this place is processed, the better the chance of finding something to help identify the killer. The security chief needs someone at the door to keep the public from this room. I imagine the laundry room will be a popular place after dinner is over."

Sam called Shadow's leader. "We found her. She's dead, Nico. We need Winestock and his crime techs."

"How did she die?"

"She was stuffed in a dryer. Examining her is problematic without disturbing the scene. I don't see signs of strangulation, but I discovered a puncture mark on her neck. If her cause of death is some kind of drug or poison, the ship's doctor or a medical examiner will have to identify the substance. The tests need to be completed soon. Some drugs disappear after a certain time."

"Understood. Expect Winestock soon."

She grimaced. The Pacific Star's security chief would not be happy when he arrived. Ten minutes later, Winestock strode into the laundry room with a team of two people trailing behind him, his face set in grim lines. The team members carried small black bags.

"Where is she?"

"This way." Joe led him to the dryer in the middle of the gleaming row of machines.

Winestock crouched to peer into the interior. He glanced at Sam. "You checked her?"

"Enough to determine she was beyond my help."

"Do you know what caused her death?"

"Hard to say with her still in the dryer. The ship's doctor might be able to determine Bianca's cause of death when he examines her. Have him check the puncture mark on her neck. Looks like Bianca was drugged."

Winestock stood. "No question this is foul play?"

"No way." Joe folded his arms across his chest. "Chip and Caleb helped us track the movements of a man dressed in a steward's uniform." He pointed at the dinner cart at the other end of the room. "The steward pushed that cart to Charlaine's door and knocked. He gained entrance by using the food. Fifteen minutes later, the man left with the cart. The food dishes were in exactly the same place on the surface of the cart and the cart was much heavier than when he brought it to the cabin. You can see all of this on the security footage Chip marked for you."

"We have a murderer on board the ship."

"Yes, sir, we do."

"Do I need your prints to eliminate you and Sam?"

Sam held up her gloved hands as did Joe.

"Would it do any good to ask you to volunteer your prints anyway?"

Joe smiled. "No."

Winestock frowned. "Your people are that good?"

"The best you would get is our names and a few facts. The military scrubbed my missions. Fortress did the rest and blocked access to Sam's background as well. Our company protects the identities of its operatives."

The security chief froze. "Wait. You were Special Forces?"

"Yes, sir."

A soft whistle, then he pulled out his phone. "I need to inform the captain that we have a suspicious death on board and a possible suspect among the crew."

"You can't think it's one of us. Maybe this fake steward is a civilian who stole one of our uniforms," one of Winestock's employees said.

"Check the security feed before you decide," Joe said. "This man knew where the security cameras were located. It's possible the killer is a civilian, but wouldn't someone notice a stranger in restricted areas? More important, how would he learn where every security camera was located without calling attention to himself?"

The chief's face hardened. "I'll look at the security feed after I notify the captain and help my team with Ms. White." He turned to his two employees. "Start processing the scene. I'll let the ship's doctor know, but his priority is the four-month-old baby he's treating."

"Yes, sir."

Winestock looked at Sam and Joe. "Stay available in case I have more questions." He hesitated, then sighed. "Look, I'm short-staffed right now with two crime scenes. Do you mind helping my people look for this steward?"

"We planned to offer our assistance," Sam said. "We'll do what we can to help but your people will probably be the ones to track this man down. You know the ship far better than we do."

"I appreciate your assistance. Keep me posted on your progress. If you find this man, hold him for me to interrogate."

With a nod, Joe grabbed Sam's mike bag and escorted her from the laundry center. When they were far enough away, Joe said, "Our unit should call Maddox from the suite. He needs to warn Hollingbrook to expect more fallout."

"Do you think this is connected to his daughter's death?"

He slanted her a look. "Do you believe anyone would have this much bad luck in the space of two days? Someone is out to hurt Hollingbrook from every side."

"Personal or professional motive?"

Joe frowned. "It has elements of both."

"Maybe we should look at competitors." Sam hoped the pool of potential suspects would be smaller than cruise line employees and Hollingbrook's relatives.

They returned to the security office. Nico turned. "No luck finding our steward. He disappeared after he went toward the crew quarters."

"How did he do that?" Sam asked.

Chip glanced over his shoulder, a scowl marring his face. "If he's one of the crew, he knows the ship inside and out, including passageways that don't have security cameras."

And that pretty much shot holes in the argument for a civilian killer. How would a guest on the ship disappear that easily? "Where was he last seen?"

"Near the engine room," Caleb said. "There's a passageway on the aft side. No cameras in there."

"Go check it out," Nico told Sam and Joe.

"We'll drop off Sam's mike bag first, then go to the passageway." Joe glanced at Caleb. "Do we need temporary ID to access that area?"

"I have some here." Chip reached into an unsecured drawer and pulled out two generic red badges like the ones the security personnel wore but without a photo on the surface.

Nico scowled. "Do the badges in that drawer gain the wearer access to restricted areas?"

A hard swallow. "Yes, sir."

"Why are they in an unsecured drawer?"

"Someone is always in here."

"You're telling me you haven't visited the head since your shift started?"

"Well, sure. Caleb was here, though. He covered for me. No one could get in here and take a badge without one of us knowing about it." Chip shot a desperate look at his fellow employee. "Isn't that right?"

Caleb's face, however, told a different story. "A passenger dropped by and asked for help finding the fitness center." His skin flushed.

Sam guessed the passenger was a beautiful young female.

"How long were you out of the office to help this passenger?" Nico demanded.

"Five minutes, maybe ten."

"When you returned, was Chip in the office?"

A head shake in answer.

Joe eyed Chip. "Long visit to the head, buddy. You sick?"

"It was break time. I went for coffee and a snack."

"In other words, your office was unmanned for at least five minutes, maybe more."

"I locked the door behind me," Caleb protested. "No one could break in to steal a badge."

Nico looked at Sam. "You have your equipment on you?"

"Yes, sir."

"Want to demonstrate?"

She smiled. "Love to." Sam left the security office and waited in the hall for Joe to lock the door from the inside. She grabbed her lock picks from her pocket, slid the slender tips into the lock, and went to work. In seconds, the tumblers turned and Sam opened the door.

Both security men stared at her with gaping mouths.

"Of the five members of my team, Sam is the slowest at picking locks," Nico said. "She broke in the office in under thirty seconds. I'll ask you again. Why are you keeping badges in an unsecured drawer?"

Caleb handed two temporary badges to Joe and Sam. "We won't be anymore, sir."

Nico looked at Sam and Joe. "Report what you find. I'll be here going through the security feed, looking for stills to send Zane. Grab a meal after you return the badges. Mercy is still doing her demonstration. The team will meet in your suite when the demo is over."

"Yes, sir." Joe escorted Sam from the security office. "Their level of training makes me want to carry around every weapon in my arsenal," he muttered.

"Same here." Just the idea of having to depend on Winestock's personnel to protect her in the event of a takeover or attack made Sam's skin crawl.

They dropped off Sam's mike bag before continuing to the engine room and following the probable path the killer had taken. Joe opened the door to the passageway and stepped inside first. "Staircase."

Sam groaned. This guy could be anywhere on the ship by now. "This will be a wild goose chase."

"Probably. We still have to follow the trail until it disappears."

The operatives stepped onto the landing. No one was in the stairwell, not that Sam had expected the killer to be waiting for someone to find him and take him into custody. Some kind of clue would be nice.

"Maybe we'll get lucky."

"The way things have been going, I doubt that."

They took the stairs to the eighth deck. Sam swept her flashlight over each step, trailing behind her partner. At the landing, Joe held up his fist.

"What is it?" Sam peered around his broad back. Her gaze fell on an empty syringe in the corner of the stairwell.

CHAPTER SIXTEEN

Joe crouched beside the syringe. "This might be the murder weapon." Unless a diabetic had dropped the syringe from a pocket. He frowned. Possible, he supposed. People could take the stairwells to another deck, but this one was out of flow of traffic and harder to find. Added to that, the vanishing steward had entered this stairwell soon after he killed Bianca. Joe didn't believe in coincidence. In law enforcement and black ops work, everything happened for a reason, usually a bad one. Although he might be wrong, he believed the contents of this syringe killed the nanny.

With luck, the techs would find prints on the plastic. He longed to scoop up the evidence and process it himself, but held himself back. Fortress was supposed to work with Winestock and his security team, not take over the investigation no matter how tempted Joe was to do that.

Instead, he sent Nico a text reporting their discovery and requesting someone to secure this crime scene as well. Winestock would need another dozen people if the trail of clues continued.

His phone signaled an incoming text from Shadow's leader. Joe scanned it and turned to Sam. "He wants us to stay in place until Trace or Ben arrives."

"What do we do in the meantime?"

"See if we can find another clue to help us identify our perp."

He took out his flashlight and Sam joined him in searching the landing as well as the next flight of stairs. By the time they finished their examination, Ben entered the stairwell.

"What do we have?"

Joe indicated the syringe. "Winestock's people are stretched thin enough that he asked us to help track down the steward and detain him for questioning."

"That must have been a stab to his pride. Hated to hear about the nanny." He snapped several pictures with his phone and glanced at Joe. "Is the needle connected to her death?"

"Probably although there's a chance someone is using syringes for a legitimate medical reason and dropped it by accident."

"But you don't believe that."

"I think it's unlikely."

"Anything else I need to do before I bag and tag the syringe?"

"Sam and I went over the landing and another flight of stairs with no results. The ship's security personnel don't have enough people to process so many scenes. Not much choice but to take the syringe to the security office. Tell Caleb and Chip to lock it up the until the ship's doctor has time to test the contents. They need to check the syringe for fingerprints."

"Use gloves when you handle the syringe, Ben."

The EOD man stared at her. "I know how to preserve fingerprints."

She scowled at him. "I haven't shot anybody today. Keep it up and I'll make an exception."

"Ouch. You have a mean streak, lady."

Sam handed him a pair of gloves and a plastic bag she'd stashed in her pocket before they left the suite. "We don't know what's in the syringe. Be careful with the needle, too."

"Will do. Where are you two heading?"

"We'll continue climbing to the top deck," Joe said. "We might find something else to point us in the right direction. After that, we'll take our badges back to the security office and eat. Shadow is meeting in our suite when Mercy's demonstration is finished."

"You have an hour, then." Ben dropped the capped syringe into the plastic bag and slid it carefully into his jacket pocket. "Mercy is halfway through her program. She just finished her seminar and is now in the demonstration portion. As soon as I deliver this, I'll return to the dining room to keep an eye on things in there along with Trace and Curt." He turned to leave. "I thought about going on a cruise sometime with my future wife. This whole experience has shot holes in that plan." With that, he left the stairwell.

Joe understood that feeling. Knowing how unprepared the security team was to handle real trouble made him cringe at the thought of ceding control of his safety to them.

He wrapped his hand around Sam's. "Let's check the rest of the stairwell. I'm starving."

"You're always hungry."

"You should be, Sparky."

"I'm getting there," she said, her tone defensive.

Not as fast as he wanted. He'd never admit as much to the tough-as-nails woman at his side but he worried about the speed of her recovery. Reminding himself she almost died didn't help. In his mind, Sam was invincible. Seeing her having to fight her way back to full health scared him.

Instead of replying verbally and giving away his own inner turmoil, Joe squeezed her hand and motioned for her to scan the ground with the beam of her flashlight. They made their way to the top deck without stumbling across more clues left behind by the killer or encountering ship personnel.

After returning the security badges and reporting their lack of further progress, Nico joined them and the three operatives left the security office with Chip and Caleb's promise to continue searching for the mysterious steward ringing in their ears.

"I sent several head shots of the killer to Zane. I doubt even his magic program will be able to make anything out of the photos. Can't do much with shots of the back of the head or a chin."

"The steward never faced the camera?"

Nico shook his head. "He planned this out in excruciating detail."

"Why kill the nanny?" Sam asked. "What purpose did that serve?"

"Everything that's been happening points back to the client." Nico ignored two women who blatantly eyed him with flirtatious smiles curving their mouths and open invitations in their eyes. "Bianca was a convenient target, easy pickings."

Joe thought about Nico's reasoning and shook his head. "I don't think so."

"You have a different idea?"

"Bianca is connected to Charlaine, one of Hollingbrook's top executives. This man went to too much trouble and planning for a convenient target. This was a deliberate act."

"You think the nanny was the target?" Nico sounded skeptical. "She doesn't have a record or live a risky lifestyle. From the information I received from Zane a short time ago, Bianca lived a quiet life and adored children, especially babies. She loved her job as Kayla's nanny."

"Charlaine was the target."

"The steward killed the wrong woman?" Sam's eyes widened. "You're saying he was late or delayed for some reason and had to settle for Bianca?"

"He went to Charlaine's door, not Bianca's," Joe pointed out. "I've been thinking about the steward's encounter with Bianca. If you watch the footage again, you'll see there's a slight stiffening of the steward's shoulders when he saw who opened the door. He was surprised to see Bianca instead of Charlaine."

"Why didn't he wait for another opportunity? We would never take out the wrong target when we didn't have the opportunity to take the correct one."

"We're disciplined and well trained. This man isn't. He couldn't let Bianca live because she saw his face and could identify him. Think about it. This ship isn't large enough to hide for almost a month. Bianca was bound to see him again. If something happened to Charlaine and security checked the camera feed, the nanny might remember the steward and make the connection. She was too dangerous to leave alive."

Nico's hand fisted. "We need a face and name so we can ask him questions instead of speculating. I want this man located."

They returned to the dining room where the passengers were quietly talking and finishing their desserts and coffee while Mercy drew on a canvas with Curt standing off to the side of the platform, his gaze scanning the audience for potential threats. Nico led the way to the captain's table where the three operatives took their seats. The captain's steward leaned down and offered to bring them new meals and desserts.

"Thanks," Joe said, his stomach growling.

"What's going on?" Dax demanded. "First Charlaine leaves, then Lance, and they don't come back."

"You three left, then Captain Greer," Colt added. "You know what's going on." Suspicion gleamed in his eyes.

Nico studied the two executives. "We're not at liberty to discuss what we know."

The younger of the two men scowled. "We work for Hollingbrook Cruise Lines. Everything that happens on this ship is our business." When he realized he'd raised his voice and was drawing attention to himself, Colt leaned closer to Nico and lowered his voice. "What do you know? We'll find out anyway."

"Talk to Captain Greer. He's been in contact with Mr. Hollingbrook."

Colt's eyes narrowed. "I knew it. You're here for more than a vacation. Did Hollingbrook send you to check up on us? Has there been a threat against us or the ship?"

"Do you think I make a habit of bringing my wife on an operation?" Fury filled Nico's eyes. "Mercy is my heartbeat. I would never risk her life."

Swallowing hard, the man held up his hands in mock surrender. "No offense intended, man. I just think you know a lot more than you're saying."

Dax turned to stare at his co-worker. "Back off, Colt. If we need to know what's going on, Greer will tell us. Do you think Mike would leave us on this ship is there was a problem?"

"He's not here, is he? Mike can't know what's happening or isn't."

"Calm down. Drama won't help matters."

"Sorry. I'm just anxious to get off this ship. You know I hate being on the water." Colt glanced at Nico. "I apologize."

Shadow's leader inclined his head in acknowledgment.

Nicely done. Joe lifted Sam's hand from the table and kissed the back of it. He couldn't help but admire his teammate's ability to fit into the role he'd assumed. Nico had told the truth and turned the antagonism back on Colt. Shadow's leader had serious undercover skills. He'd have been a good asset as a cop. Joe didn't plan to tell the other man of his assessment since the knowledge would cause Nico's lip to curl.

In short order, the operatives tucked into their meals. By the time Mercy completed her demonstration and answered questions from the audience, they had finished their meals and the Hollingbrook executives had excused themselves to return to their cabins. From Colt's tight jaw and stiff body as he left the dining room and the heated discussion with Dax in the hallway, the younger executive planned to hunt down Captain Greer and demand answers.

As the audience gave Mercy a round of enthusiastic applause, Nico stood and hugged his wife. "You did a great job, sweetheart."

She smiled. "Did I keep them entertained long enough for you to do what you needed to?"

Nico brushed a kiss over her mouth. "We'll talk later. Do you need anything to eat or drink before we visit with Joe and Sam?"

"I would love iced tea and a piece of chocolate cake." She turned to the steward. "Would it be possible to have both to go?"

"Of course, Mrs. Rivera. Give me a couple minutes and I'll have that ready for you to take to your cabin."

"Thanks, Gregory. I appreciate it."

"My pleasure, ma'am." The steward's cheeks flushed as he hurried away to prepare the items Mercy had requested.

"Gregory?" Sam grinned. "You made friends fast."

She shrugged. "He's a nice man and went out of his way to make sure I had what I needed. Gregory's mother loves art."

Joe eyed the beautiful, detailed drawing of the lighthouse in the midst of a stormy sea still sitting on the easel on the platform. "What will you do with the lighthouse?"

Gregory returned at that moment. "Here you are, Mrs. Rivera." He handed her a large to-go glass of tea, plastic utensils, and a carry-out container with a see-through lid. Inside lay a large piece of chocolate cake with thick frosting.

"Call me Mercy."

"Yes, ma'am. May I get you anything else?" When Mercy shook her head, he turned to Nico, Joe, and Sam. "I'll be happy to bring something for you to take to the cabin as well."

Nico clapped him on the shoulder as Curt joined them, his gaze still scanning the audience who were now exiting the dining room. "We're fine, Gregory, but thanks for the offer. I also appreciate you making sure my wife had everything she needed while I was out."

The steward moved closer and dropped his voice. "I overheard Captain Greer talking about the incident with Chief Winestock and that you were helping with the investigation. How is the baby?"

"The doctor is keeping close tabs on her."

"This is terrible. We've never had something like this happen on board. What can I do to help catch this monster?"

"Listen to people as you work."

He looked disappointed. "Is that all? I hear people talk all the time."

"You're an employee," Mercy said. "I'm sorry to say most people will pay as much attention to you as they do a piece of furniture. They'll talk more freely because they don't notice your presence. You might hear something to point Nico in the right direction."

"Don't confront anyone in a bid to get answers." Joe laid a hand on Gregory's shoulder and squeezed. "That's a good way to thrust yourself into the path of the wrong person."

Gregory frowned. "You sound like a cop."

He grinned. "MP, remember?"

"Ah. Military police."

"That's right."

"I promise to listen while I'm out and about on the ship. If I hear anything, who do I report to?"

"Come to me, then talk to Winestock." Nico slid his arm around Mercy's shoulders. "Ready to go?"

"In a minute. Gregory, do you think your mother would like the picture I drew tonight?"

The steward's face brightened. "Yes, ma'am. Although she loves your art, she's not able to buy an original work."

Mercy glanced at Curt who passed her the canvas. After signing her name in the bottom right corner, she presented the canvas to Gregory. "Give this to your mother. I hope she enjoys it."

"I don't know how I can ever thank you for this, Mrs. Rivera."

"We'll see you tomorrow, Gregory."

"Have a good night, ma'am."

Trace signaled that he and Ben would join Shadow in a few minutes.

In the corridor outside the dining room, Nico pressed a kiss to Mercy's temple. "I think you have another conquest."

"Better keep an eye on her, Nico." Curt grinned. "She's capturing hearts all over the ship."

"The only heart I want is my husband's." Mercy leaned into Nico's side.

Watching the interaction created a longing in Joe's heart for the same type of freedom in his relationship with Sam.

When the group reached the stairwell, an alarm began to sound throughout the ship.

CHAPTER SEVENTEEN

Joe frowned as passengers hustled past the operatives, faces filled with fear. What was going on? He glanced at Nico who had his phone pressed to his ear.

"It's Nico. What's going on?" He listened a moment. "Can you tell where it is?" After a pause, he said, "I'll meet you there." He slid the phone into his pocket.

"What's going on?" Mercy asked.

"A fire in the kitchen. Go with Joe and Sam while I check this out. Curt, you're with me." Nico looked at Joe.

He nodded, acknowledging the silent order to protect Nico's wife with his own life. He understood his team leader's reluctance to leave Mercy's safety in the hands of another person. Joe felt the same handing off Sam's protection to anyone else.

Mercy brushed her lips over her husband's. "Be careful."

"Always, love." Nico and Curt hurried into the stairwell.

"Where do we go?" Mercy asked Joe.

"Our muster station." He clasped Sam's hand, gripped Mercy's arm, and urged the women into the stairwell.

"I don't like Nico and Curt going toward a fire instead of away from it."

"They'll take care of themselves. It's my job to take care of you."

"If this is a simple kitchen fire, why is Nico looking into it?"

How much did he tell her?

"Don't hedge the truth." Mercy speared him with a fierce glare. "No secrets, Joe."

He dropped his voice, not wanting to alarm passengers. "Based on the other problems, this incident might be a deliberate act to distract us from something bigger and more dangerous."

"It could also be a simple kitchen fire," Sam added. "Nico and Curt will know if this is an accident or not."

Within minutes, they arrived at their designated open-air muster station. They joined other excited or nervous passengers Joe recognized from the corridor where their suite was located.

One passenger was surrounded by a group of others, the elderly woman having difficulty breathing. A cruise employee pushed his way through the crowd, concern clear on his face.

Sam slid her hand from Joe's and followed. Retaining his hold on Mercy, Joe trailed Sam, determined not to let her out of his sight. Sam asked if she could be of assistance.

"Are you a doctor?" the employee asked.

"A medic."

"Fantastic." He turned to the distressed passenger. "Mrs. Cardwell, this woman is a medic. Is it all right if she helps you?"

The woman nodded.

Sam knelt in front of the woman sitting on a deck chair. "I'm Samantha. My friends call me Sam."

"You're too pretty to be called by a man's name."

Sam smiled. "You just made my day, Mrs. Cardwell. Tell me what's going on. Are you having chest pains?" She checked the woman's vitals as she asked a series of questions to diagnose the problem. The longer Sam spoke quietly with Mrs. Cardwell, the more her breathing calmed.

Joe scanned the area and nearby passengers, alert for potential threats to the ship and Sam and Mercy. If the fire was a distraction, Sam and Mercy would be targets out here in the open.

Within minutes, Sam patted the woman's hand and stood. "Feeling better now?"

Mrs. Cardwell smiled. "Thank you, my dear. I feel so silly."

"Stress can cause different types of reactions in our bodies."

"Including you?"

"Yes, ma'am. I'll let you in on a secret. I'm not a fan of being on a ship this far from shore."

"How are you remaining so calm?"

Sam's eyes met Joe's before she turned back to answer the question. "Joe keeps me grounded. He's been a huge help."

Joe cupped the side of Sam's neck with his left hand, ensuring Mrs. Cardwell saw the wedding band. This was the first time he had heard of Sam's reluctance to be on board a ship. Was she trying to help the woman feel better or did her words reveal her true feelings?

Mrs. Cardwell's eyes twinkled. "If my husband was still alive and as handsome as yours, I'd be glad to have him help me stay in the moment, too."

Joe chuckled, surprised at the light flirtation. The lady was a charmer.

"Martha!" Another older woman shoved through the crowd and stopped by Mrs. Cardwell's side. The two women shared a family resemblance. Joe figured they were sisters or cousins. "Are you all right? What happened?"

"Just a little trouble catching my breath, Anne. I'm fine now."

"Are you sure? Maybe you should see the ship's doctor."

"I don't think that's necessary, Sis." Mrs. Cardwell turned to Sam. "What do you think?"

"Having a doctor check you wouldn't hurt, especially if you begin having chest pains."

"Are you a nurse?" Anne asked.

"Medic."

At that moment, an announcement came over the loudspeaker informing those aboard that the ship's personnel had doused a minor kitchen fire and passengers could resume normal activities.

"Thank goodness." Anne turned to Mrs. Cardwell. "Come on. I think I've had enough excitement for one night."

"I agree."

Joe helped Martha Cardwell stand. "Take care of yourself, ma'am."

She patted his forearm. "Don't worry. I intend to do just that. Come on, Anne. We'll ask the cabin steward to bring us ice cream. After a scare like this, we deserve it."

"Sounds perfect." Anne glanced at Mercy. "I enjoyed your demonstration at dinner. Made me wish I could do more than draw terrible stick figures. You are very talented."

"Thank you, ma'am."

"It's Anne Claiborne. Call me Anne." She turned to Sam and Joe. "Thank you for helping Martha. We'll see you tomorrow." The two women left to return to their cabin, walking arm-in-arm.

When Mercy turned to follow them to the staircase, Joe laid a hand on her shoulder. "Wait."

"Why?"

"Too many people in a confined space. A stairwell is the perfect place for an intentional accident. Wait until the crowd thins."

Mercy's expression showed her unhappiness but she nodded in agreement.

A few minutes later, a text from Nico appeared on his phone screen. He scanned the message. "Nico and Curt will meet us at the suite in five minutes."

Still concerned about the women's safety, Joe motioned for Sam and Mercy to go down the stairs ahead of him. Sam nudged Mercy to walk near the wall while she took the outside position to better protect the artist.

When they entered the suite. Mercy glanced around. "Wow. This is nice. Nico and I would have enjoyed a suite like this."

Maybe. If Shadow's leader trusted the security officers aboard this ship. That was unlikely from what Joe had seen thus far.

A sharp knock sounded on the door.

Joe checked the peephole and opened the door for his teammates to enter the suite. He didn't have to ask if the fire was an accident. Their body language told the tale. "Anybody see anything?"

Curt snorted.

That's what Joe had been afraid of.

Mercy wrapped her arms around Nico. "What happened?"

He hugged her close. "One of the ovens caught fire."

Sam's eyebrows rose. "That sounds like a normal occurrence in my world."

"You don't toss clothes inside an oven in use."

"The steward's uniform?" Joe guessed.

Nico nodded.

Joe dragged a hand down his face, frustrated. The fake steward had covered his tracks. "Maybe a security camera recorded his movements."

"Security office is my next stop."

"I'll go with you," Mercy said. "Maybe I can tempt you into a moonlight walk on the deck afterward."

Nico's face softened. "Sounds like a great plan."

Another knock on the door heralded Trace and Ben's arrival. Joe waved them to the living room. "We have a lot to cover before Nico goes to the security office to check a possible lead."

Joe sat on the couch and gently tugged Sam down beside him. Before Nico gave Ben and Trace a rundown of events, Joe threaded his fingers through Sam's. When she stared at him in surprise, he winked at her. The medic needed to be comfortable with him holding and kissing her. He wouldn't stop unless she kicked him to the curb after this mission was completed. He intended to make sure he was lodged so deep in her heart she wouldn't want to push him away.

When his attention shifted to Nico, Joe noticed his teammates and Mercy staring at him and Sam. "What's wrong?"

"Nothing." Trace stretched his legs out in front of him. "We're glad you're smart enough to make a move on the lady."

"They have to act like they're married," Mercy pointed out.

"Outside the suite." Ben's lips curved slightly. "Trace is right. Joe finally got his act together."

Nico held up his hand. "Back on point."

"What's been happening?" Trace asked.

Between Nico, Curt, and Joe, they updated the other men.

Ben's brows knitted. "Why risk a larger fire aboard? Would have been simpler to weigh the clothes down with a heavy object and toss them overboard."

Nico shook his head. "More chances of someone seeing him throw the clothes overboard than tossing clothes in an oven. Passengers wander around the ship at all hours of the day and night. In an empty kitchen, the job takes two or three seconds."

Trace frowned. "He'd need precision timing or serious luck."

"He knows the ship routine," Sam pointed out. "If he has access to a steward's uniform, what prevents him from scoring a waiter's uniform?"

Mercy nodded. "Sam's right. Who questions the presence of a waiter in the kitchen?"

She had a good argument, Joe conceded. "Swipe the uniform and you're another invisible cog in the Pacific Star's machine."

Nico looked thoughtful. "No one would notice him until it was too late."

CHAPTER EIGHTEEN

Sam opened the suite's balcony door and walked to the railing, enjoying the cool breeze and the moonlight dancing on the surface of the Pacific Ocean. She should go to bed. Right. As if she wanted to face more nightmares. Every time she closed her eyes, Sam saw the bullet arrowing toward her chest in slow motion and no matter which direction she turned to evade it, the projectile slammed into her body anyway.

She didn't need Marcus Lang's counsel to know what she was feeling was normal. As a medic, Sam counseled her teammates on the body and mind's mechanisms to process trauma. Knowing she was normal didn't alleviate the frustration. Sam didn't want to be the weak link on her team and that's how PTSD made her feel. Weak.

Although Sam didn't hear movement, she knew Joe had joined her on the balcony. She wasn't surprised when his body heat warmed her back and his hands bracketed hers on the railing seconds later.

"Can't sleep?" he asked, voice soft. Joe had left the suite to find ice, bottled water, and soft drinks, encouraging her to go to bed.

She considered blowing off his question. Couldn't. In the past two days, her relationship with Joe had moved to a different level, one in which she felt compelled to tell him the truth. Conscious they still played a role outside the suite and voices carried at night on the water, she murmured, "Don't want to."

Somewhere close by, laughter from a couple on another balcony drifted on the breeze to Sam and Joe.

He kissed the side of her neck, eliciting a shiver from her. "You have to sleep sometime."

She didn't need the reminder. Her sleeping issue hampered her recovery. Yeah, she could have taken a mild sleep aid. Her lips curved. Guess the refusal made her as stubborn as her macho teammates.

Joe wrapped his arms around her waist and drew Sam back against his chest. As he spoke, his lips brushed her ear. "Have you tried sleeping outside?"

She turned her head toward him. "We live in a large city. Sleeping on the patio isn't safe."

He squeezed her waist. "You built a tree house in your backyard, Sparky. Why not sleep there?"

"What good would that do?"

"You were shot in a small, enclosed space. Maybe you need to know subconsciously that you have room to maneuver and defend yourself."

Sam stared, stunned at the simple solution to a problem she hadn't been able to diagnose for herself. Could it be that easy? Oh, she knew the nightmares wouldn't totally disappear with this one small change. If she could lessen the frequency and manage to sleep a few consecutive hours, though, her body would recover faster.

Already her mind jumped to several possibilities to beef up security in the tree house. She could design multiple escape routes including one leading her higher up the tree instead of down to the ground. The thick branch she was thinking of would give her access to her neighbor's yard where could she escape if one of Shadow's enemies attacked.

Joe turned Sam to face him, his arms circling her waist again. "We should try it tonight. The temperature is comfortable and rain isn't in the forecast."

She frowned. "You just said I have trouble sleeping because I feel trapped. This balcony isn't large and I would have no room to maneuver without being in danger of falling off the ship." Not a cheerful thought. Sam could hold her own in a pool but she wasn't an Olympic swimmer and had no desire to battle creatures of the deep.

"You won't be alone. I'll be here to watch your back." He rested his forehead against hers. "Will you try? If it doesn't work, we'll go inside and come up with another plan."

"What about you? You need sleep, too." Sam didn't want Joe to ignore taking care of himself to watch over her, never mind that she would have watched over him in a heartbeat if he needed her.

"I'll sleep out here, too. We'll leave the door to the suite open. We'll hear if anyone breaks in." He brushed his mouth over hers. "You game?"

What did she have to lose? She might gain a few more hours of sleep. At worst, she'd stay awake in the company of a handsome operative under a romantic moon. "I'd like that. Thanks."

Joe tightened his grip. "I would do anything for you. You know that, right?"

"I feel the same about you."

He was silent a moment. "Did you think about our conversation before dinner?"

She nodded. How could she not? Despite tracking a mysterious murdering steward, Joe dominated her thoughts.

Who was she kidding? Joe had dominated her thoughts since the first moment she'd seen him five years ago.

"Do you have questions?"

"One."

"What?"

"Did you mean what you said?"

Joe eased her closer. "Every word."

"We've worked together for five years and you pushed me away before now. What changed?"

"I thought I would lose you three months ago, Sam. I didn't want to waste another minute without you. Our job isn't the safest in the world. I didn't want to die with regrets. Not pursuing a relationship with you would have been the biggest regret of my life." He lowered his head and spoke against her ear, his warm breath causing a surge of goosebumps over her body. "Give me a chance, sweetheart. Give us a chance to explore this bond growing between us."

She longed to take the plunge with no thought for the possible fallout. She couldn't. "What if this new relationship doesn't work? You're my best friend, my partner. I don't want to lose you or our team."

"That won't happen. We'll figure it out. Take a leap of faith, Sam. Don't walk away from me because you're afraid. I am, too. I'm more afraid of missing out on a relationship with the most incredible woman I've ever known."

Sam looked into his eyes and saw the sincerity and restraint Joe exercised to keep himself from pressuring her to give in. She thought about their conversations through text, phone calls, and face-to-face encounters the past few months and knew her heart had already decided the matter. She drew in a deep breath and took that leap. "Yes."

Joe froze. "Yes?" he whispered. "You'll let this relationship between us develop naturally?"

Sam slid her hands up his chest and wrapped her arms around his neck. "Yes. Kiss me, Joe."

He flashed her a grin, his eyes lit with joy. In the next moment, his mouth captured hers, his kiss hot, ravenous, and so good. When he finally lifted his head, Joe nuzzled the side of her neck. "I swear you won't regret this. We'll take it one day at a time. Just don't hold back or hide. Talk to me. Promise?"

"I promise."

He held her tight against him for a few minutes until their breathing steadied. Easing back, Joe framed her face between his rough palms. "We need to sleep. I'll grab a couple blankets and pillows. We'll camp out here and enjoy the night breeze."

"I'll help." She followed him into the suite and found two blankets while Joe went after the pillows. Back on the balcony, Sam eyed the narrow couch and glanced around the small area. "How will we do this?"

"Easy." He dropped a pillow on one end of the couch and motioned for her to lay down. Joe covered her with the blanket, then stretched out on the floor beside the couch with his own pillow and blanket.

He turned on his side and positioned her hand on his shoulder. "Wake me if this doesn't work."

In answer, she squeezed his shoulder and began to relax the muscle groups in her body, starting at her feet and moving up. As she went through the process, her body let her know which muscles were tight and which were still healing from the extensive damage done by a would-be killer's bullet.

Although she didn't expect to sleep, Sam grew heavy lidded. Maybe Joe was right. Perhaps the root of her problem had been feeling trapped. Maybe she felt safe having Joe with her, knowing he had her back and always would.

She woke with a gasp twice during the night, remembering the pain and terror she experienced in that bathroom. Both times, Joe held her until the shakes disappeared, then kissed her and tucked the blanket around her again before returning to his pallet. The good news? The nightmares didn't wake her every hour or two as had been the recent pattern. Hopefully, the nightmares would ease off before the weather turned cold in Nashville. Maybe she should resume the intense sessions with Marcus when Shadow was between missions because Sam hated to be cold.

Joe sat up as the sun lightened the sky to a pearl gray. "Good morning."

"Hi."

"How do you feel?"

"Better," she admitted. "You were right."

He smiled. "We should write down today's date in case I need to refer to a time when I was actually right."

Sam's laughter was soft in deference to the early hour. "I'll make a note of it."

"Coffee?"

"Sounds fantastic." When she started to get up, Joe laid a hand on her shoulder to hold her in place.

"Enjoy the sunrise. I'll bring the coffee when it's ready." He gave her a quick kiss and went into the suite.

Sam swung her feet to the balcony floor and watched the world come to life. When Joe rejoined her, he brought two mugs of coffee and sat beside Sam. They sipped their drinks in companionable silence as the Pacific Star continued to power toward the next port, the sun continuing to rise on the horizon.

When her mug was empty, Joe set it aside along with his own. He gathered Sam into his arms and kissed her with gentle thoroughness. Minutes later, he raised his head. "That's a perfect start to the day." He stood and held out his hand. "Go shower. Nico will be here in thirty minutes. Zane has information for us."

"Did Nico give us a hint?"

"No, ma'am." He urged her inside the suite and closed the balcony door. "We'll find out soon enough. Want more coffee?"

She shook her head.

"I found ice, water, and soft drinks last night. Any of those sound interesting?"

Always taking care of her. The knowledge wrapped itself around her heart, nudging her closer to falling off the ledge into love. "Water."

Joe retrieved a bottle of water from the small refrigerator and handed it to Sam. "Take your time. I'll gather the blankets and pillows, then check email while you're getting ready."

Sam hurried into the bathroom. Minutes later, she was dressed in a short-sleeve shirt and jeans along with her boots. No, they weren't typical vacation clothes. However, with the murder and fire aboard ship yesterday, Sam needed the protection of more durable material and shoes. Her typical work gear would draw too much attention.

She opened the door to see Joe on the balcony, leaning against the railing. The sun's rays illuminated the beard shadowing his jaw, a beard that had reddened Sam's face when Joe kissed her. Totally worth the razzing from their teammates.

Joe made her heart turn over in her chest. She'd been crazy about him for years and still had a hard time believing he felt the same about her.

He glanced over his shoulder and smiled at her. "You look beautiful, Sparky." His fingers trailed lightly over her cheek as he passed her on the way to the bedroom. "I'll be out in a few minutes."

He grabbed the blankets and pillows from the couch and took them to the bedroom. By the time Joe returned to the living room, Nico had arrived.

"What's going on, Nico?" Sam joined Joe on the couch. The news must be bad. Nico's body language betrayed his tension.

"Zane got a hit on the man taking pictures at the San Diego terminal."

"Who is he?" Joe asked.

"Name's Reuben Flores. Ring a bell?"

Sam and Joe exchanged glances and shook their heads. "Should it?" Sam asked.

"He's second in command of the Maldonado trafficking ring."

A river of ice ran through Sam's veins as her past roared into the present with a vengeance.

CHAPTER NINETEEN

Joe reached for Sam's hand, unsurprised to find her skin as cold as ice. Every member of Shadow had a history with human traffickers, including him. While they didn't share details, the team knew the basics. He shoved his own painful memories into a deep, dark corner of his mind and slammed shut an imaginary door. Later. Sam was his priority now.

Sam never talked about her past except in the barest of details. The only reason Joe recognized the name was Sam's reaction to anesthesia. She'd talked in the recovery room three months ago. Most of her jumbled words didn't make sense. Maldonado's name was clear. Together with the information he knew and his observation of Sam, Joe had a pretty good idea what she survived.

"Breathe," he murmured. "Stay with me."

Nico frowned and appeared ready to launch into an interrogation.

Joe cut him off with a subtle hand signal, asking Nico to wait. He wrapped his arm around Sam, tugged her against his side, and held her while shudders wracked her body, helpless to do more than allow a woman he cared deeply about to process the news and work through the physical reaction. Knowing what she'd suffered made him want to punch those responsible for hurting her.

When the tremors stopped, she tipped her head back to look Joe in the eyes. "Thanks."

He pressed a brief, gentle kiss to her lips, then gave Nico a slight nod.

Shadow's leader sat in a chair near Sam. "Talk to me," he said, his voice low and soft. "What do you know about the Maldonado organization?"

Sam's hand tightened on Joe's. "Enough."

"Start at the beginning. Don't leave anything out no matter how uncomfortable you feel."

"You know I lost my parents in a plane crash when I was ten years old."

He nodded. "You went into the system because your parents were only children of only children and had no one to care for you."

"I was placed in foster care. My case worker hoped I'd be adopted quickly by a family." Her lips curved. "A great plan except I wasn't a baby and the families who took care of me wanted younger children or babies. Most of the families were nice." She stopped abruptly, her grip on Joe's hand painful.

"What happened, Sam?" Joe asked, keeping his voice calm, the opposite of the storm raging inside him. Invisible bands squeezed his heart and made drawing breath difficult.

"The last foster home was in a rundown neighborhood. Not a slum or anything. I guess I would classify it as old and tired. The couple who took me in were blue-collar workers who couldn't have children of their own. They were nice people but clueless about their neighbors."

Nico rested his forearms on his thighs. "What do you mean?"

"The Deans worked long hours in an automotive plant and left me to take care of myself in the mornings before school and in the afternoons."

Joe frowned. Child Protective Services couldn't have known about that plan. Leaving a child alone that long was a recipe for disaster.

"The people next door seemed normal. They waved and chatted whenever I saw them. Sergio Chavez and his wife, Rosita, made it a point to cultivate a friendship with the Deans and me in particular. In hindsight, I should have known something was up. Why would grown adults befriend a kid? Anyway, they continued the same pattern for a few weeks. One afternoon, Rosita came to the door and said she had something to show me, something she thought I would like."

Joe closed his eyes for a few seconds, dreading her next words. Not his Sam. He didn't know if he could sit here and listen. Jaw clenched, Joe forced himself to remain exactly where he was, his muscles relaxed. He'd have to deal because he refused to walk away from her no matter how much hearing what she'd endured gutted him.

"She and Sergio had been talking about getting a dog. I thought they wanted to show me their new dog. I went with her. As soon as their front door closed, Sergio clamped his hand around my mouth and dragged me into a windowless room on the second floor."

Joe seethed in silence. If Sergio Chavez and his wife were still alive, he intended to pay them a visit. No one hurt his woman.

"While he held me still, Rosita gave me a shot. Later, I heard the police tell my case worker I'd been given a sedative. The medicine was strong and knocked me out fast. When I woke, I was alone in that room with a collar around my neck. The collar had a chain which was attached to a grommet in the floor. I couldn't stand up or move more than two feet in any direction."

Nico scowled. "How long was it before someone found you?"

"Two days."

"Who discovered Chavez had taken you?" Joe had to force the words past his lips.

"My foster father. Rosita misjudged the sedative dosage and didn't give me enough to knock me out. I pretended to be more drugged than I actually was. When she took me to use the bathroom, I saw Roy Dean through the window. He was on his cell phone in the driveway. I broke away from Rosita, grabbed a decorative bowl from the bathroom counter and hurled it through the window. Once the glass shattered, I started screaming. Roy kicked in the front door and beat Sergio until he was unconscious. By the time the police arrived, he'd knocked out Rosita with one punch and took me out of the house to safety."

"Why did Chavez keep you so long?" Nico's voice was soft. "That's not standard procedure."

She gave a slight nod. "I know. The transport was delayed since another supplier had a special request to fill for the pick-up. Some sick creep in another state had placed an order for two girls with specific characteristics. Lucky me, I fulfilled the requirements for one of his requests. I have no idea if the other girl was rescued or not."

Joe's free hand fisted. He didn't want to ask the next question but knew from Nico's pointed glance his team leader was leaving it to Joe, assuming Sam would be more uncomfortable to have Nico prodding her for information.

Pointless to delay asking the question. The answer wouldn't change whether he asked now or later but he would know better how to anticipate her reactions if Shadow pursued the Maldonado organization. He cupped her cheek and turned Sam's face toward his. "Did Chavez rape you?"

Sam's cheeks flooded with color, her gaze breaking away from his. "No," she whispered.

Joe waited a beat. "But he molested you, didn't he?"

Her lips parted on a soft gasp. "How did you know?"

That explained why she didn't want any man but him to touch her. He felt like he'd won the ultimate prize because he'd gained her trust to that extent, a trust he would never break. "You let me see the real Samantha Coleman."

"How was Chavez tied to the Maldonado organization?" Nico asked.

"Sergio worked for them. He got a cut of the profit for every girl he kidnapped and forced into the trafficking ring. Because I was to fulfill a special request, Chavez was to receive a big bonus."

Their team leader studied her face a moment. "We have to pursue the lead Zane unearthed. Be honest with me, Sam. Are you able to continue with this mission?" He held up a hand before she could answer. "There's no shame in remaining on board the ship with Mercy and Curt if we're ordered to track down and dismantle this group. Of all people, you know what we'll face. Mercy would be glad to have you on her protection detail."

Sam shook her head. "I won't leave Shadow without a medic. You need me."

"We want you with us," Nico corrected. "You're a valuable member of our team. We trust you with our lives. You know that. If you need to bow out of this mission, Fortress will send a substitute medic. No one will hold it against you."

"No," she said flatly. "I'm not a vulnerable fourteen-year-old girl anymore. I can take care of myself and I trust Joe and the rest of Shadow to have my back."

Joe fought down the instinct to insist she remain aboard the Pacific Star. He didn't want her exposed to this organization again. Didn't matter that his logic was flawed. Eighty percent of their missions dealt with human traffickers. This was the first time, though, that Sam had been confronted directly by the group responsible for her childhood terror.

Sam was a well-trained operative and Army veteran. She wasn't helpless. That knowledge did little to ease the knot in his gut at the thought of his Sam facing the past head on while she wasn't quite full strength.

Nico was silent a moment longer, gaze assessing her, then nodded. "All right. If you want to set up a session with Marcus Lang, I'll find a way to make it happen. Do whatever is necessary to help yourself handle the emotions and memories, Sam."

Sam's grip on Joe's hand eased. "Thanks. I need to do this. It's time I face down the monster in the shadows."

"I understand. Mercy is waiting to go to breakfast with us. How much you tell Mercy about your past, if anything, is up to you, Sam. Don't feel compelled to bare your soul to the team. If you say nothing, they'll attribute your strong emotions to your shooting." Nico glanced at Joe. "Come to my cabin when you're ready."

"Yes, sir." Grateful for the chance to wall up his emotions before facing the team, he didn't argue. Joe also wanted to be sure Sam was all right. He walked Nico to the door. In the corridor, his friend said, "Take the time she needs." With that, he walked to his cabin.

"What did he say to you?" Sam stood at the balcony door, staring at the watery vista.

"Not to rush you." He crossed the room to her side, longing to hold her and offer what little comfort he could seventeen years too late. Joe feared the past was too close for her to be comfortable with him touching her. "Sam."

Without a word, she turned away from the balcony and wrapped her arms around him with a deep sigh.

Relief roared through him as he embraced Sam, glad to have her in his arms again. "Are you okay?"

"I am now." She tightened her hold. "Now you know my secret, do you regret asking me to date you?"

Joe kissed the top of her head. "Never. I thought you were amazing when I first met you."

"And now?"

"I'm astounded at your courage and grateful you're giving me a chance to win your heart."

Sam tilted her head back to stare at him, eyes wide. "What did you say?"

He pressed a finger against her lips. "Shh. No pressure. We have a job to do. Just know that I'm falling in love with you." Was probably already there if the strength of his feelings were anything to go by.

Joe eased her away from him. "Are you ready to face the others now?"

"I guess." She sounded stunned.

They walked to Nico's cabin, knocked on the door, and the couples headed for the dining room. They sat at a table out of the main traffic flow. Because of the early hour, the dining room was mostly empty.

Halfway through their meal, Gregory, the captain's steward stopped at their table. While Gregory talked to Mercy, Nico checked his phone screen and straightened.

He handed the phone to Joe who scanned the photo of the fake steward. His whistle was soft. Man, Zane's computer skills were impressive. His program had taken glimpses of this man and extrapolated his probable appearance.

As Gregory turned to leave, he glanced down and paused, frowning. "Why do you have a picture of Fitz?"

CHAPTER TWENTY

"You know this man?" Joe turned the phone for Gregory to see the photo better. Were they about to catch a break? Finding this man and stopping him from doing more damage to the ship or the people on board was at the top of Shadow's priority list.

"Sure. That's Fitz Thomas. He's a passenger." Gregory frowned. "Why is he wearing a steward's uniform?"

"That's what we want to know." Nico slid his phone away. "Do you know where to find him?"

"I've seen him on Deck 8 and at the pool. Sometimes in here but not often. He doesn't socialize with other passengers much. He's not comfortable around a lot of people. Beats me why he's on a cruise. We're wall-to-wall people most of the time. Why are you interested in Fitz?"

"He was in the area when the baby was drugged. He might have seen something."

"Fitz is a good guy. I'm sure he'll help if he knows anything."

Not likely if Joe's suspicions were correct.

"If I see him, should I tell him you want to talk to him?"

Nico shook his head. "We'll find him. We don't want to alert the wrong person of our interest."

Gregory stared at him a moment before horror filled his eyes. "You think he's responsible for hurting the baby? I can't imagine Fitz doing something like that."

Joe exchanged a glance with Sam and saw skepticism in her eyes. People could look normal to the outside world and yet be the worst of humanity inside until the evil slipped the leash and became apparent to the public. "Can you think of a reason to explain why he's in a steward's uniform when he's a passenger?"

A head shake.

"Do you know his cabin number?"

"No, but security can provide you the information." He glanced around the now busy dining room. "I'm sorry. I have to go back to work."

Mercy smiled at him. "Thanks for your help, Gregory."

"Sure. How did you like the cake?"

"Nico and I enjoyed it. We appreciate you boxing the treat for us."

"Glad to do it. I'll see you later."

Nico glanced at his companions. "When you finish, we'll go to the security office. We have a killer to catch."

Fifteen minutes later, Winestock's eyebrows rose when he saw the Fortress operatives and Mercy. "Have anything for me?"

"Maybe." Nico showed the security chief the picture of Thomas. "Does this man look familiar?"

A frown. "Should he?"

"The captain's steward identified him as Fitz Thomas. We need to find him."

"Why?"

"Security cameras captured this image of Thomas at the time the baby was drugged and Bianca was killed."

Winestock's expression darkened as he studied the photo again. "This is our fake steward?"

"He's dressed as one. We need to talk to him."

The chief swung around to his computer and typed in the man's name. He shook his head. "No passenger or employee is listed by that name."

Joe scowled. They were close to finding the killer. The man knew security would check. Maybe he didn't socialize to stay off their radar.

"Thousands of passengers are aboard the Pacific Star on this cruise. How will you find him?"

"He can't stay holed up in his cabin for a month," Joe pointed out. Especially if he intended to cause more mischief. He had a feeling Thomas hadn't finished his terror campaign.

Winestock dragged a hand down his face. "Yeah, you're probably right. The walls would close in on me if I was stuck in a cabin that long. Nico, send me the picture. I'll upload it to our computer system and search for this guy. He had to go through security to board. We require a photo ID. If he paused at the checkpoint long enough, I'll connect his face with a name."

"I doubt he used his legal name. He already lied to Gregory. I'd be surprised if he presented accurate identification. Start with passengers on Deck 8. Gregory mentioned seeing him there." Nico sent the picture to the chief's email address. "Let me know if you find him. In the meantime, we're going hunting."

"If you track him down, I want to talk to him."

Nico inclined his head without agreeing to Winestock's demand and escorted Mercy from the office.

In the corridor, Joe faced Nico. "Split up?"

"Mercy and I will take Deck 8. You and Sam head up to the pool. Maybe we'll get lucky and this guy will crawl out of his hole soon."

"What if he doesn't?" Mercy asked.

"Joe's right. Thomas can't stay hidden the rest of the cruise, love. We'll find him."

"I hope we locate him before he strikes again," Sam said.

"Thomas likes the pool," Joe added. "It's a perfect place to be out of the cabin and anonymous in the large crowd. Who pays attention to another man lounging around the pool?" That's why Nico assigned him and Sam to the pool. Less chance of Mercy running into Thomas on Deck 8.

Nico nodded. "If you run Thomas to ground, take him to the security office. Check in every hour."

"What about Ben, Trace and Curt?" Sam asked.

"Curt will stake out the main dining room. Ben and Trace will roam the ship. You and Joe watch your backs. I don't know what Thomas's agenda is, but he has one and will kill again to achieve his goal." With that, Nico and Mercy walked to the elevator.

Joe entwined his fingers with Sam's and headed toward the pool deck. "I think we have a while before Thomas shows his face at the pool."

"Why?"

"Not enough people to hide easily. This early in the morning, he'd stand out."

"You might be right. We'll stand out dressed as we are but I won't lounge around the pool in a swimsuit when I might have to tackle this man to prevent him from hurting innocent people. If circumstances were different, this would be the perfect time to swim."

"Not a fan of dodging beach balls and kids in the pool?"

"I don't mind that when I'm enjoying some sun and water. Swimming laps is more difficult with kids nearby." She smiled. "They don't mind crossing into the lap lane to retrieve a pool toy. I've swallowed more than my fair share of pool water when a kid startled me."

He slid her a sideways glance. "Have you thought about having children one day?"

Sam swung around to face him, eyes filled with wariness. "Do you want children?"

"Yes. My brothers and sisters have families and we have a ton of fun during the holidays when I'm not on a mission. I want a family of my own one day." He urged her into motion again. "Do you want a family?"

Sam not wanting kids wasn't a deal breaker. Joe was already in too deep to walk away now. However, he couldn't help but long to see Sam holding their child in her arms. She would be an amazing mother. Talk about a fierce protector of her child. Sam would literally fight to the death to protect her family. That she had the skills to defend those she loved was a huge turn on for him.

"I love kids, but I'm not ready to walk away from Fortress yet. Having a family would be next to impossible with me gone for weeks at a time with Shadow. I don't want to do that to my children. I know military moms do it all the time and I admire their courage and ability to nurture those kids while still serving and protecting our country. I don't have it in me to do the same, not after the childhood I had. I need to be with my children every night."

"But if you were ready to have a family?"

"I'd love to have a baby." Her voice sounded wistful.

The tension in Joe's body dissipated. "When the time comes, I think Maddox will find another role for you, one where you're stationed in Nashville so you can be the type of mother you want. He's always scrambling to staff the infirmary at Fortress headquarters. Maybe he would consider assigning you there."

A slow smile curved Sam's lips. "That's a great idea. I'll keep that in mind."

"There's no hurry. You're young and have several years before you have to give it serious thought."

She slid him a look. "I'm twenty-seven."

He snorted. "I have seven years on you." Made him feel old.

Her eyes widened. "That old? You'll be needing a cane to walk and hair dye to cover the gray soon."

Joe growled. "Hey, watch it." When Sam's laughter rang out in the stairwell, he gathered the medic against his side. He loved to hear her laugh.

On the pool deck, Joe pointed to the empty table under a large umbrella near the bar. "We'll be out of the sun and able to see anyone who comes and goes."

No sooner had he seated Sam and dropped into a chair himself when a steward appeared at their table.

"Good morning. What may I get for you?"

Joe requested iced coffee for both of them in deference to the heat already rising.

"What about breakfast? We have delicious muffins this morning. If you prefer something else, I'll arrange a delivery from the kitchen."

He was about to send the steward on his way when Sam asked, "What kind of muffins?"

"Blueberry, apple spice, or banana."

"Oh, man. They all sound fantastic. Both of us will have one of each."

When the steward hurried off, Joe stared at Sam. "We finished breakfast twenty minutes ago. Are you hungry again?"

She shook her head. "We have to look as though we're doing something besides watching people around the pool. No one will question us being here for a cozy breakfast. The weather's beautiful and newlyweds will want to spend as much time alone as possible."

For a couple hours. Then what? Joe could eat every hour. On missions, you never knew when you'd have the chance to eat again. Sam didn't enjoy eating all day.

The steward returned carrying a tray with their drinks, a basket of muffins, and two plates. "Here you are. May I bring you anything else?"

Sam laid her left hand on Joe's. The sun glinted off her wedding band. "Not right now. Thank you."

"If you need refills, let me know. My name is Jay."

"I'm Sam and this is my husband, Joe. Thanks for the coffee and muffins."

"My pleasure, ma'am." With a nod at Joe, the steward returned to his station at the bar.

Joe slowly ate an apple spice muffin and sipped his coffee, enjoying the breeze and his companion. He nodded at her half-eaten blueberry muffin. "How is it?"

"The best I've ever tasted." She smiled. "Wish I had more room in my stomach."

"We'll be here a while. You'll have time to finish the muffins."

"If I keep eating this much food, I'll need to jog every day while we're on board."

Joe snorted. "You lost several pounds while you recuperated and haven't regained them." A fact he hoped to change over the length of the cruise.

She rolled her eyes. "If you think I plan to regain that weight, I'll disappoint you. I like this weight on my frame."

Joe held his peace though he longed to protest. Sam needed more weight to take down an opponent with greater height and weight.

"Sam!"

Joe looked over at the two approaching women and stood. "Good morning, Mrs. Cardwell, Mrs. Claiborne."

Mrs. Cardwell smiled. "Please, call us Martha and Anne. May we join you this morning?"

"Of course." He seated both ladies, much to their surprise and pleasure. "How do you feel, Martha?"

"Fit as a fiddle and embarrassed about the hubbub I caused yesterday."

"We're glad we had a chance to meet both of you," Sam said, a twinkle in her eyes.

"Oh, you're too kind, my dear." Anne patted her hand. "I can't imagine you want to spend your honeymoon with two old ladies."

Joe smiled. "I see three beautiful women at this table."

Martha fanned her face. "I understand why you married this one, Sam. He's a keeper."

"He is special," Sam agreed. "That's why I plan to keep him around the rest of my life."

Joe's head whipped her direction. Was she serious or just playing the role Maddox and Nico cooked up for them? Man, he'd give anything to hear her say those words when they were alone and mean them.

"Smart woman." Anne nodded at her. "You have brains as well as beauty."

Sam laughed as Joe continued to stare at her, wondering and generally driving himself crazy. He turned his attention to the sisters and asked where they were from and about their families. Might as well enjoy the time with the sisters and let them provide camouflage in case their suspect showed his face at the pool.

Two hours later, the conversation was still going strong. Joe kept tabs on the passengers who came and went.

He went on alert the moment a familiar dark-haired man stepped out on the pool deck with a white towel draped across his arm. He wore dark blue swim trunks and mirrored sunglasses, his head swiveling as he took in his surroundings and whether people noticed him.

Joe tapped Sam's foot with his own. When she glanced at him, he inclined his head slightly toward Thomas.

Sam turned back to the women, listening to Martha talk about the value of reading a book a movie is based on before watching the film. When she paused, Sam said, "Martha, Anne, the heat is climbing fast out here. I'd love for you to meet our friend, Nico. He's married to Mercy. Would you eat lunch with us in the main dining room in thirty minutes?"

Anne looked at Martha. "She's right. Your cheeks are red, Sis. Come on. We'll enjoy the air conditioning, splash cold water on our faces, and cool down before lunch."

Joe stood and helped the women to their feet. "Thanks for sharing breakfast with us. We enjoyed visiting with you."

Martha patted his arm. "I haven't had that much fun for a long time except with my sister. Thank you for indulging a couple of old women."

"What old women?" He pressed her hand with his own. "I just see friends."

"Come on, Martha," Anne said. "We'll see you and Sam in a few minutes, Joe."

"If we're late, find Mercy. She'll be expecting you to have lunch with her."

Martha's eyes twinkled. "Oh, my. Honeymooners and young love. I remember those days." With those words, the two sisters left the pool deck.

Once the ladies were safely inside the ship, Joe returned to his seat.

Sam blew out a breath, her cheeks flushed. "I wanted them out of danger. I hope you don't mind."

"I enjoy their company, Sparky." He held out his hand to her. "You ready?"

"How should we do this? A lot of people are out here, including a bunch of kids. All of them are potential hostages."

"I know. We don't have a choice. Leaving him loose until he's in a safer location is not an option." He cupped her cheek and brushed his lips over her own. "I'll text the others and have them ready to assist. After Ben and Trace are in place, we'll run the same scenario we used in Columbia."

"Might not be as effective. He's in swimming trunks, not a tux."

"The ruse will work. Thomas won't want to stay by the pool with a drink all over him, especially when we draw attention to ourselves and him." Joe slid his phone from his pocket and sent a text to his teammates. Nico's response came a moment later. "Nico and Curt will meet us at the security office. Ben and Trace will be here in five."

"Who's going to be the klutz?"

"I have size 13 feet. I'd say I have the perfect excuse for tripping over the leg of a lounge chair."

"But he'll be less likely to spook if I do it. You're a big man and a threat from sheer size alone. I doubt Thomas will see me as anything more than your arm candy."

"He's a fool if he misses your sharp intelligence and confidence. We'll play it your way, though."

In low voices, they ran through different scenarios to anticipate his reaction, counter his moves, and contain the danger. Like Sam, Joe was concerned about the number of innocents around the pool, especially the children. If he was desperate enough, Thomas could hurt one of the kids.

At the five-minute mark, Trace and Ben arrived and stationed themselves at different vantage points.

"Go time, Sam." Joe raised her hand to his and kissed the back of it. "We'll ask the bartender for a glass of lemonade and make sure Thomas wants to leave the pool area to shower off the sticky mess."

After they obtained the lemonade, Joe and Sam started toward Thomas.

CHAPTER TWENTY-ONE

Sam drew in a steadying breath as she and Joe approached the suspected killer. Although the idea of touching this man made her skin crawl, Sam knew she'd made the right choice when Thomas's head turned their direction. She'd bet her next paycheck he was focused solely on Joe. There were advantages to being female. Men tended to underestimate her to their regret. She sipped the lemonade and gave a moan of appreciation.

Joe glanced down at her. "Is it good, baby?"

Amusement ripped through her. Baby? Sparky trumped that endearment any day. She smiled and decided to pay him back in kind. "Oh, sugar, it's wonderful. Here. Try it." Sam stopped beside Thomas's lounge chair, handed the glass to Joe, and watched him sip the concoction as she kept the other man in her peripheral vision. Thomas had stiffened, his hand clenching the towel at his side. Their suspect was antsy. Good thing they waited for Ben and Trace to arrive before moving on Thomas.

Her partner's eyebrows rose. "We'll ask Jay for the recipe. This is great. I would enjoy having a pitcher of this in our refrigerator at home."

She took back the glass and turned to continue toward the interior of the ship. Sam's foot caught on the lounger. She stumbled and fell across Thomas's legs, spilling part of her cold drink on the man's chest, stomach, and swim trunks. "I'm so sorry. I'm such a klutz. Are you all right?"

"Get off me," the man snapped, anger and disgust vying for dominance in his voice.

Instead of complying, Sam settled more of her weight on his legs while she fumbled with the glass and in the process spilled more of the lemonade.

Thomas cursed and reached for her.

Joe inserted himself between them. "Did you hurt yourself, babe?"

"I'm fine. I need a hand up, though. I'm stuck." She controlled the legs attempting to kick free of her. Rats. Wrestling with Thomas hurt more than the last time she and Joe used this scenario. Sam would be glad when she healed completely. Patience, she reminded herself. The healing rate inside the body was much slower than the outside. She was getting there. That had to be enough for now.

Trace approached in his borrowed security uniform. "Everything okay here?" he asked, gaze locked on Thomas's hands.

"We're fine," Thomas groused. He stilled his jerky movements to shake free of Sam. "The lady dumped her drink on me. No harm done."

"We're sorry about that," Joe said. He grabbed a towel. "Here. Let me wipe off the mess. Can we buy you a drink to make up for dousing you in lemonade?"

"That's not necessary." The man tried to push away Joe's hands. "I'll take care of wiping up the mess myself."

Between Sam, Joe, and Trace, Thomas didn't have a chance to slip away and hide.

"No, I insist. It's the least I can do." Ignoring his renewed cursing, Joe leaned down and wiped lemonade from Thomas's chest. When he finished, Joe tossed the towel aside and leaned closer to the suspect. In a low, clear voice, he said, "Get up and come with us right now."

Thomas froze, his body tense. "What?"

"You heard the man," Trace murmured. "If you run, we'll take you down and haul you off to the brig."

"I don't understand. What do you want with me?" The tightening of his facial muscles highlighted the lie.

Joe gripped one of his arms, Trace the other. Sam scrambled off Thomas, her attention focused on keeping the kids away from a potential altercation.

"We have questions and you have the answers." Joe hauled the man up with Trace's help. The two operatives marched Thomas off the deck with him repeating that he didn't know anything. Ben met them at the door to the interior of the ship. He went ahead of them and prevented other passengers from walking too close.

Rather than chance Thomas breaking loose in the stairwell, Joe and Trace led him to the elevator. An uneventful elevator ride later, the operatives walked him to the security office with Thomas protesting the entire way. The closer they came to the office, the more the man struggled to escape. Thomas definitely knew the layout of the ship and where the security office was located.

Thomas didn't declare his innocence, just repeated over and over that he didn't know anything and they were wasting their time with him.

Ben opened the door to the security office and Joe and Trace escorted Thomas inside the room. Sam shut the door behind them.

Winestock glowered at the man before glancing at Joe. "This our guy?"

"We'll find out. Do you have another room available?" One where they could interrogate their suspect in privacy. Wouldn't do to have a passenger walk in on them.

The security chief inclined his head toward the door on the left side of the main office.

Nico signaled Ben and Trace to resume their shift duties. Once they left the security office, Nico led the way to the other room. Although Thomas struggled in earnest, Joe easily countered every move and propelled him to the interior room.

Winestock walked to the room with the bank of security screens and had a low-voiced conversation with one of the men at the desk. When the employee turned, Sam recognized Chip. The younger man lifted his chin when he saw Sam, admiration in his gaze.

By the time she walked inside the interrogation room, Joe had seated Thomas at the table and zip-tied his hands to the chair.

"What's going on?" Thomas asked. "I don't know what you want with me." His demeanor had changed from puzzled to outright sullen.

Nico took the piece of paper in his hand with Thomas's picture and laid it on the table in front of the man. "You're a passenger on the Pacific Star. Why were you wearing the uniform of a steward?"

Thomas swallowed hard and shook his head. "That's not me. You have the wrong man."

Not him? Sam stared at the man. Sure looked like him. If it wasn't, why was he perspiring?

"It's you." Nico folded his arms across his chest. "Why are you pretending to be a cruise line employee?"

"You're part of the security team?"

"Answer the question," Joe snapped from his position behind the man's back. Thomas jumped at Joe's cold, angry tone. "Why are you pretending to be a steward?"

"I'm telling you that isn't me."

"You're such a lair, dude. I don't like liars."

Winestock shook his head. "This is a waste of time. I say we call law enforcement as soon as we dock at the next port. I want this clown off the ship. Better for him to rot in a local jail than run the risk of him hurting anyone else."

"You don't have anything on me."

Nico shook his head. "Wrong, Thomas, or whatever your real name is. You're on camera where an incident occurred. Same time, same place."

"That's it?" he scoffed. "I don't know about a crime. You have no right to hold me. I'll sue you for every penny you're worth."

"Good luck with that. Where's your steward uniform?"

Thomas sneered. "Charging me with theft? I'll get a slap on the wrist. You can't prove anything else."

Sam leaned against the wall, satisfaction swelling in her gut. Their suspect was rattled.

A sharp rap sounded on the door. Chip poked his head in the room. "Got it, Chief."

Winestock scanned the paper Chip handed him before giving it to Nico.

He snorted and stared at Thomas. "You couldn't be more original with the name on your fake passport?"

Thomas paled. "How did you know?"

"Tom Smith is a common name. Ranks up there with John Smith." Nico glanced at Winestock. "You want deniability?"

The chief's eyebrows rose. "Do I need it?"

A shrug. "Wouldn't hurt."

"What do you mean?" Thomas demanded. His gaze darted from Winestock to Nico and back again.

Winestock shook his head. "I'll stay."

"Suit yourself." Nico turned a chair backwards and straddled the seat. "Let's talk, Thomas."

The other man swore at Nico, hatred in his eyes, body tense.

Shadow's leader flicked a glance at Joe who gripped Thomas's shoulder near the neck, the hold unbreakable. "You don't want to do this. My friend is skilled in interrogation techniques." Nico's voice remained mild. "He enjoys inflicting pain. You sure you want to test him?"

"You're lying." The acrid scent of fear poured off Thomas. "I'm an American citizen. I have rights."

Another glance at Joe. "Give him a demonstration."

Sam's partner clamped a hand over the prisoner's mouth and changed the hold on his neck. Thomas's eyes widened in shock. He uttered a muffled scream, fighting to free himself. He failed.

Nico looked at Sam. "Get your bag."

"Yes, sir." She left the security office and returned to the honeymoon suite. Within minutes, she reentered the interrogation room to find tears streaming down Thomas's cheeks, skin pale and breath ragged.

"Let's try again." Nico signaled Joe to ease up. "What's your real name?"

Still shuddering in the aftermath of the pain, the prisoner said shakily, "Thomas."

When Joe laid a hand on his shoulder again, the man flinched away. "No, please. That's my real name. Thomas."

"Last name?"

His head sagged. "Ferguson. I'm Thomas Ferguson."

"What's your agenda, Thomas Ferguson?"

He shook his head and remained mute.

Joe grabbed Ferguson's hair and leaned close to speak in his ear. "Why did you hurt the baby? What did you have against an innocent infant?"

The prisoner shook his head. "No, I didn't do that. I swear. I like kids."

Joe glanced at Nico, received a nod of approval, and pulled out his Ka-Bar. He tugged Ferguson's head back at an uncomfortable angle and brandished his knife in front of the man's face. "Do you know how much damage I can do with this?"

Winestock stirred as if he planned to intervene. Out of Ferguson's eyesight, Sam motioned for the security chief to remain quiet. Face set in hard lines, he subsided though remained watchful.

"Don't," Ferguson pleaded, his voice hoarse.

"This is a Ka-Bar. The blade is full tang, one solid piece of steel. State of the art workmanship. The blade is razor-sharp and I can gut you like a fish or slice open your throat and watch you bleed out. One word from my friend and you're dead."

"You can't."

"Want to bet your life on that?" Joe leaned closer, his voice a low growl. "You could have killed the baby. Do you want to know what I do to people who hurt innocent children?"

Ferguson shook his head.

"Give us the right answers and you won't find out. Lie to us again and you'll wish you had never been born. The world will be better off without another terrorist who enjoys hurting the innocent."

"I'm not a terrorist."

Joe yanked Ferguson's head back further and placed the edge of the blade against the skin of his throat. Red beads of blood welled along the shallow cut.

"Wait! I'll talk. I swear."

"Why did you target the baby?"

He swallowed hard. Another shallow cut appeared. Blood slid over his skin. "I wanted the mother."

"The baby was a means to an end?" Nico asked.

"That's right."

"Why did you want the mother?"

"She's beautiful. I just wanted her."

Sam frowned. Charlaine was attractive, but his words didn't ring true. Charlaine's beauty wasn't why he targeted her.

Nico flicked her a look. She unzipped her mike bag and searched for the drug Nico had requested with a hand signal. She prepared the hypodermic and grabbed a packet with alcohol wipes.

When she straightened, Winestock's gaze locked on her with the intensity of a heat-seeking missile. She hoped he remained silent. If Thomas didn't believe the Fortress operatives would follow through on the threat, he'd remain silent.

"You're a rapist?" Joe raised his voice, his tone harsh.

Good thing Ferguson couldn't see Joe. Her partner played his role well. Only his eyes revealed the truth that he wasn't as angry as he sounded.

"What? No!"

"You expect us to believe you drugged the baby to capture the mother's attention? You got it."

"Where's the steward uniform?" Nico asked. "What did you do with it?"

Ferguson clammed up again.

"Let me kill him," Joe said to Nico. "We can't allow him to target other innocent women and children. No one will notice if we dump his body overboard after midnight and let the sharks have him."

"You're crazy." Ferguson renewed his efforts to free himself from the chair.

A huff of laughter. "You just now figured that out? You're not too bright, Thomas."

More fruitless struggles and Ferguson slid his glance toward Nico. "Don't let him kill me," he pleaded. "I'll tell you what you want to know."

"We gave you the opportunity to cooperate." He shrugged. "You didn't."

"Ask me anything. What do you want to know?"

"Where is the steward uniform?"

"I got rid of it." His voice rose to a shrill pitch as Joe shifted the angle of the knife and tightened his grip on Thomas's head as though preparing to cut his throat.

"How?"

"I threw the clothes into an oven."

"Why? What were you hiding?"

"I didn't want security to find the clothes if they managed to track me down."

"You stole a waiter's uniform before going to the kitchen?"

He scowled. "How do you know that? I was careful. Security wasn't lucky enough to catch me. I'm too good. But then you aren't cruise line security, are you?"

Nico tilted his head. "We aren't?"

"Not even close. The cruise line's security people are men and women who couldn't cut it in the military or police academies and now swagger around with a badge that doesn't mean anything."

No one spoke while Nico assessed their prisoner. "You're familiar with Holllingbrook ships. You used to work for them, Thomas."

CHAPTER TWENTY-TWO

Joe mentally reviewed their conversation with Thomas and realized Nico was correct. Thomas wouldn't have known about security and the cameras without inside knowledge. Joe believed another person was working with him, maybe one of the security staff. But that didn't explain the fact Thomas moved around the ship like he was intimately familiar with the layout. He must have worked on another cruise ship of the same design.

"I didn't say I was an employee." Thomas jerked in Joe's hold and ended up with another nick on his skin.

Joe rolled his eyes. Idiot. If this clown didn't stop flailing in the chair, he'd cut his own throat. Joe shifted the angle of the Ka-Bar.

"What did you do to the baby, Ferguson?" Nico folded his arms across the top of the chair back. "Before you lie to us, remember how much my friend hates those who prey on the weak. He also has a low tolerance for liars."

Thomas drew in a shaky breath. "I gave him the medicine in the diaper bag. I figured it was safe for him if the mother brought the medicine."

"Her," came the mild correction. The look in their team leader's eyes was anything but mild. "You didn't bother to read the dosing directions, did you? She had to be treated for an overdose. You're lucky the ship's doctor helped her. She could have died."

"I didn't mean to hurt her. Honest. I just wanted her to sleep so I could find the mother."

Nico shook his head. "You're still going with that story?" He glanced at Sam and inclined his head slightly toward the prisoner.

She stepped into Thomas's visual range and made a production out of readying the hypodermic needle for use.

"No. Wait."

Joe tightened his grip. "The truth, Ferguson. Last chance or we end your life now and dump you overboard in the dead of night."

"I don't know what you want from me."

"The truth. Why did you want the baby's mother?"

"Payback," he yelled.

"What did she do? Turn you down for a date? Cut you off in traffic? Spit on your shoes?"

Ferguson cursed. "I never saw her before in my life."

Joe frowned. What sense did that make? "I'm supposed to believe?"

Nico signaled Joe to hold off. "If you never met her, why choose this woman for payback? Payback for what, Ferguson?"

"She was an easy target." A cold smile curved his mouth despite the awkward angle Joe held his head. "Hollingbrook's a cheat and a liar. He deserves to die."

Nico's eyes narrowed. "A cheat and a liar. Care to explain that?"

The ugly grin on Thomas's face said the answer to that question was a resounding no.

A shrug. "Doesn't matter. By the time we finish tearing your life apart, you won't have any secrets left."

The smile faded from the prisoner's mouth. "You can't."

"When you realized the mother was away from the cabin, why did you take the nanny? You could have left the dinner and returned later for the mother. You chose to kill Bianca White. Why?"

"She would have recognized me and I still had a mission to complete."

Sam turned toward Thomas, needle glinting from the glare of the overhead light. "What did you inject her with?"

"Potassium chloride."

Joe's stomach twisted. Simple but effective. The nanny hadn't stood a chance once Thomas grabbed her. Joe tightened his grip. "What's your agenda?"

"Bring down Hollingbrook."

"You plant the bombs, too?"

A smug expression covered his face. "Had you scrambling, didn't it?"

Nico glanced at Winestock. "You have questions for him?"

"You covered them. What now?"

"I'm still in favor of dropping him in the ocean," Joe said. The world would be a better place without this man. Unless Thomas tried to kill him, though, Joe wouldn't follow through on the threat. He had a lot of plans for his future. None included spending time behind bars for homicide. He had long-term plans to romance Samantha Coleman.

Nico lifted one shoulder in a shrug. "We don't need sharks. Your woman is skilled at her job."

With those words, Sam set the hypodermic on the table in plain sight and ripped open the package with the alcohol wipe.

Thomas's eyes widened. "What are you doing?" he demanded. "I answered your questions."

Joe chuckled. "Did you think we would let you go? You admitted to killing a woman and poisoning a baby, Thomas. We can't let a menace wander around the ship."

"If I cooperated, you promised I'd live." His struggles renewed and intensified. "You promised."

A mean smile curved Nico's mouth. "Actually, I didn't. You deserve no mercy."

"I'll do anything. Ask me something else. I'll talk."

Shadow's leader stalked around the table to Thomas's side. "Are you working with anyone else?"

The man's gaze shifted down and to the left.

Joe shook his head, disgusted with the weasel.

Nico gripped Thomas's arm and held it still for Sam to administer the shot. Joe clamped his hand over Thomas's mouth. The man screamed as Sam inserted the needle in his vein and depressed the plunger. A moment later, the screams and struggles stopped and he went limp.

Winestock blew out a breath. "Tell me you didn't kill the little worm."

Sam capped the needle. "I sedated him. He won't be any trouble for at least 24 hours."

"Thank God. I wasn't looking forward to explaining to Mr. Hollingbrook that a passenger disappeared in the middle of the ocean. What do you plan to do with him? We can't keep him drugged for the next month."

"Our friends at the FBI will have plenty of questions for him. I'll contact Fortress and arrange for the feds to take Ferguson off our hands. We still have a job to do."

Joe stepped back from the prisoner. "We need to find his accomplice to stop the attacks against Hollingbrook and the cruise line."

"That's only one of the tasks," Nico said.

Winestock frowned. "You have another mission?"

"Someone is targeting female passengers from your cruise line, this route in particular."

The security chief stiffened. "That doesn't have anything to do with us. I'm not responsible for passenger safety when they're off the ship."

Joe folded his arms across his chest. "You have a human trafficking ring targeting passengers, buddy."

"Those women wandered off into areas that aren't recommended for tourists."

Joe pulled out his cell phone and brought up the picture of the man he'd noticed on the dock in San Diego. He turned his phone toward the security chief. "Recognize this man?"

Winestock glanced at the screen. "Nope. Should I?"

"He's a scout for the Maldonado human trafficking ring. He took pictures of women boarding the ship in San Diego."

"Maybe he was seeing a friend off."

"He took pictures of several groups of women and left without acknowledging anyone on board the ship." Nico frowned. "Don't lie to yourself, Winestock. He's trolling for merchandise for the Maldonado group."

"You knew and did nothing about it." Sam glared at him over her shoulder before turning to store the used needle in her bag. "Why didn't you warn the women to stay in groups and stick to the safe areas at the ports? You left them to fend for themselves in a hostile environment with no idea they were being hunted."

"I'm not responsible for passengers once they leave the ship," he insisted.

"Keep telling yourself that and you'll be looking for another job," Nico said. "Part of our mission is to evaluate you and your security team. Your department is understaffed with people not trained to handle what's happening on the Pacific Star. Hollingbrook is to blame for the number of people in your department. The blame for inadequate employee training sits squarely on your shoulders."

Winestock grimaced. "I need this job. I have a kid going to college next year. What will you tell the owner?"

"The security teams on Hollingbrook cruise ships need better training. Fortress has a training facility in Otter Creek, Tennessee. Personal Security International. We train bodyguards and security teams to handle crime and terrorist threats. We'll teach you what you need to know if you're willing to learn."

The chief whistled. "You don't pull any punches, Nico."

"What's the point? If I don't tell you the truth, you and your team could end up dead along with hundreds of passengers. Now, is there a place we can dump the prisoner until we dock at the next port?"

"We use a cabin across the hall for detention. One of my people has to stay with Ferguson at all times until the feds take him." His lips curved. "We'll be more shorthanded than before. Will your men supplement my workforce?"

Nico inclined his head. "We still have to find Ferguson's partner. Working security gives Ben and Trace a chance to roam the ship without arousing suspicion. They're excellent at blending in. The rest of us will be more visible." He turned to Joe. "Cut Ferguson loose and we'll take him to the detention cabin. We need to make an appearance before people question our disappearance."

"Rumors must be circulating as it is." Sam hoisted her mike bag over her shoulder. "Although we hustled Thomas off the pool deck, many swimmers and sunbathers saw me dump a drink on him and the guys escort him off the deck. He wasn't shy about voicing his displeasure."

Nico chuckled. "You used the Columbian maneuver. Nice. Bet Ferguson never saw the real Sam. He won't be the last man to make that mistake."

Sam shrugged and opened the door as Nico and Joe each draped one of Ferguson's arms over their shoulders and maneuvered the unconscious man across the hall to the other cabin.

Chip followed them into the room and closed the door. "What's the story with this one?"

"Thomas Ferguson killed the nanny, poisoned the baby, started the fire, and planted the bombs."

The security employee scowled. "Did he say why?"

"Revenge against Hollingbrook."

"We'll find out the motive behind the attacks," Joe said as he and Nico laid the man on the bed and zip-tied his wrists to the iron rail of the headboard. Ferguson wasn't going anywhere unless someone freed him. "Don't let anyone inside this cabin except the Fortress team, your buddy Caleb, or Winestock."

Chip blinked. "Why?"

"You have another traitor on board. We need to find that person before someone else is injured or dies."

CHAPTER TWENTY-THREE

"I want to check on Kayla and Ferguson," Sam told Joe as they walked from the dining room.

Joe gave her a sidelong glance. "I understand why you want to check on the baby. Why Ferguson?"

"He's sedated and helpless." A state that would terrify any operative.

"I told Chip to keep everybody out of the cabin except those we trust."

Sam headed toward the stairs. "You saw how angry he was with Ferguson. Do you think we can trust him to stand up to his shipmates if they want justice by their own hands?"

"You're right. Kayla first, then we'll check Ferguson."

Minutes later, they walked into the infirmary and heard Kayla Bennett crying. Charlaine looked frazzled as her daughter voiced her displeasure at having her diaper changed.

"Need help?" Sam asked.

"Please. Would you hold her while I fix her bottle? She's hungry."

"I'd love to hold your sweet angel."

Relief flooded the other woman's face. "Thank you, Sam. Lance said he'd be here by now. I don't know what's keeping him."

"Work?" Joe suggested as Charlaine transferred the baby from the bed to Sam's extended arms.

"Maybe. Marketing is ignored until we need a campaign. I keep telling Mike if we know information sooner, we'll create better marketing campaigns." Charlaine shook a bottle filled with warm water and baby formula and returned to Sam and Kayla. "Do you want to feed her?"

"If you want a short break, I'd love to feed her."

"I've been by my daughter's side since we brought her to the infirmary." Her cheeks pinked. "I'd love to change clothes and brush my hair. I promise I won't be more than fifteen minutes."

"We'll be fine. Take a few minutes for yourself." After Charlaine left, Sam settled into a nearby chair, repositioned Kayla, and gave her the bottle. The baby latched on and began to drink.

Tenderness wrapped delicate tendrils around Sam's heart. Kayla made Sam long for a baby of her own. One day, she promised herself. It wasn't time yet.

She glanced at Joe and found his gaze locked on her, an odd expression on his face. Her eyebrow rose in silent inquiry.

He knelt beside the chair. "She's beautiful." His attention shifted to Sam. "So are you. Watching you with Kayla in your arms makes me want a family all the more." Joe leaned over and brushed his mouth over hers. "You're a natural at this, Sparky. Maybe you will hold our baby in your arms one day."

Sam's breath caught as shock rocketed through her system. Before she could gather her wits and formulate a response, muffled shouts could be heard in the corridor, growing louder by the second.

Between one heartbeat and the next, Joe placed himself between Sam and Kayla and the potential threat, weapon in his hand.

The door to the infirmary burst open and Trace entered the cabin with a furious Lance Farraday in tow, the executive's face marred by blood from a split lip and a reddened eye. He'd been on the losing end of a scuffle and from the thunderous expression on Trace's face, the scuffle had been with him.

Their teammate was ticked off. He shut the door with more force than necessary as Joe relaxed his stance and moved aside for Sam to see better.

Lance's gaze dropped to the baby in her arms. His eyes widened. "That's my daughter. Where is Charlaine?"

"Changing clothes. She'll be back in a few minutes."

"Is Kayla all right?"

"She's perfect. You're a lucky man, Lance."

He smiled in agreement and winced, hand to his mouth. "Ow."

"Need some ice on your lip and eye."

Lance glared. "No kidding, sweet cheeks." He yanked his arm from Trace's grip.

Joe slid his weapon into his holster. "Watch your mouth, Farraday."

A snort. "What will you do if I don't?"

A slow smile formed on Joe's mouth. "Turn my wife loose on you. She'll take you down, hard. Sam is dynamite in a small package. How were you injured?"

"Your Neanderthal friend punched me."

Trace wouldn't have inflicted injuries unless he had no choice. "What did you do, Lance?"

"Nothing I don't have a right to do. That creep hurt my daughter." By the end of his statement, Lance's voice rose to a shout.

Kayla whimpered.

"Calm down," Sam said, voice soft. "You're scaring Kayla."

Guilt filled Lance's eyes. "Sorry."

"How did you know about Ferguson?" Joe asked.

"I'm upper management for Hollingbrook Cruise Lines. I have access to every part of the ship, including security. I wanted to know if my daughter and Charlaine were still in danger. I have an obligation to protect them. I can't do that if I don't know what's going on. No one will stop me from protecting my family." He cast a pointed glance at Trace. "Not even you, tough guy. I'll be talking to Winestock. Expect your walking papers by day's end. You chose to screw with the wrong man."

Trace stared at Lance. "You can try to have me fired. You'll be disappointed with the results."

"Need ice for your hand?" Sam asked him. The knuckles on his right hand were red.

"I'm fine for now." He turned back to Farraday. "Stay away from the security corridor. You said you wanted to protect your woman and daughter. The best way is to stay with them. Ferguson will answer for his actions. Don't make yourself a target of law enforcement officials. Ferguson won't cause more trouble. Focus on your family, Farraday. Let security handle the rest." Trace nodded at Joe and Sam and left.

The doctor walked out of the treatment room where he'd been tending a patient. His eyebrows rose. "Wow. What does the other guy look like?"

Joe grinned. "Red knuckles. Mr. Farraday needs ice packs, Dr. Martin."

"Got those." He gestured toward the back room. "I'll check your lip to see if you need stitches first. Ice will help but expect a shiner by the end of the day."

Lance shuffled toward the doctor, leading Sam to believe Trace had slammed a fist into the man's gut, too.

Joe sighed. "I need to have another talk with Chip."

"Winestock, too. If you want to go to the security office, I'll be fine here."

"I'm not leaving you and Kayla alone. Too much risk."

"The doctor and Lance are in the next room."

"They're not me."

No question about that. "All right. After Charlaine returns, we'll go together." When Joe's gaze shifted and softened as he watched Kayla drink, she said, "Do you want to hold her?"

Joe's eyes lit up. He cradled the baby in one arm and held the bottle to her lips with his free hand. "She's so tiny."

"She'll grow fast. In a few months, Kayla will be crawling. Didn't you say you have nieces and nephews?"

"Seven nieces and two nephews. Since my family is scattered throughout the US, I don't have the opportunity to be with the kids much except during holidays. I'm not with them long enough to see the growth stages."

When Kayla finished her bottle, Joe shifted the baby to his shoulder, and patted her back like an expert. Before long, she let out a loud belch.

Joe chuckled. "Good job, little lady."

Sam's heart turned over in her chest. She would never forget the sight of the tough operative cuddling a small baby in his arms.

And that's when she knew the truth. During the past five years, Sam had fallen in love with Joe. She might have been teetering before the shooting three months ago, but this cinched her fate. And the knowledge scared her. He had the ability to savage her. If Joe changed his mind, he would shatter her heart.

"Sam?" Joe's eyes were filled with concern. "You okay?"

"I'm fine."

"You don't look like you're fine. What's going on?"

Although she longed to share the knowledge, this wasn't the time or place. They could be interrupted at any moment.

As though to reinforce that point, the door to the corridor opened. Sam spun around, weapon in hand, and placed her body between Joe and the baby and the door.

Charlaine walked inside and pulled up short at the sight of the weapon. "Is something wrong? Is Kayla safe?"

"She's fine," Joe assured her. He turned for Charlaine to see her sleeping daughter in his arms. "Kayla finished her bottle and decided we weren't entertaining enough to keep her awake."

The mother relaxed. "Good. Have you seen Lance?"

"He's with the doctor." Sam motioned toward the treatment room where a steady stream of swearing could be heard.

"Is he sick?"

"He got into a scuffle with one of the security guards."

Charlaine's mouth gaped. "Why?"

"Here." Joe walked to her. "Take Kayla and ask him. Sam and I have an appointment. Thanks for letting us hold her for a few minutes, Charlaine. She's a beautiful baby."

She lifted her sleeping daughter from Joe's arms. "Thank you for giving me a break." Once Kayla's breathing settled into an easy rhythm, Charlaine hurried into the treatment room.

As Sam and Joe walked into the corridor, they heard the woman gasp. "Lance! What happened?"

"Why don't they get married?" Sam grasped the railing in the stairwell. "They're crazy about each other."

"No fraternization rule, remember?"

"Short-sighted on Hollingbrook's part. Charlaine and Lance have work experience. Neither one should have a difficult time finding a job." She gave him a sidelong glance. "We have skills useful in other fields. If Maddox instituted the same ban in our company, we have other options."

"Would you be willing to find another job?"

Sam turned to face him. "If the choice was finding another job or losing you, I'd find another job."

Her foot landed on the next stair when Joe stopped her, wrapped an arm around her waist, and drew her against his chest. "I would never ask you to make the sacrifice. I would use my contacts and experience to hire on with a local police force. If it came down to you or me having to make a change, I would hunt for a new job."

Tears stung Sam's eyes. She loved this amazing man so much. Not the time or place, she reminded herself. Soon, though. Unable to say what was in her heart, she pressed her mouth to his for a series of gentle kisses, hoping to tell him the truth of her heart with her touch.

Joe groaned, pulled her close, and deepened the kiss. Minutes or hours later, he lifted his head to grab a breath. "We have to stop. My control is razor thin."

She cupped his jaw. "Same here. You go straight to my head, Joe."

A slight smile curved his kiss-swollen mouth. "Close, but not where I want to be."

"Where do you want to be?"

Joe's lips touched hers. "Your heart." He drew back and turned toward the stairs again.

Sam touched his hand, making him pause. "Your name is engraved on my heart and always will be."

Hope flared in his eyes. "Tell me you're saying what I think you are."

"We should talk about this later."

"Sam, please." Joe wrapped his arms around her waist and held her in place. "Say it."

She wound her arms around his neck and whispered against his lips, "I love you, Joe Gray."

He shuddered, his eyes closing for a second before opening again to stare deep into hers. "I love you, too. I was afraid you would decide I wasn't worth the trouble to keep."

"I'm never letting you go."

"Ditto, my love." He planted a hard kiss on her mouth before setting her to his side and getting them moving again. "Let's check in with the security team before I lose focus more than I already have."

When they neared the security office, Joe laid a hand on Sam's arm and nodded toward the open door of the detention cabin.

The operatives drew their weapons. Joe signaled he'd go in first. Sam wanted to argue that she was just as capable but this wasn't a matter of capability. Joe was a better shot. If a gunman waited inside, Joe had a better chance of taking down the threat than she did. Playing to their strengths was the beauty of their partnership. She nodded and signaled for Joe to proceed.

Sig raised, Joe peeked around the cabin's door frame. "Sam." He holstered his weapon and rushed inside the room, Sam on his heels.

She glanced at Thomas Ferguson. A bullet in the forehead had ended his life the second the projectile burrowed into his brain.

CHAPTER TWENTY-FOUR

After darting to the security office, Joe returned with Winestock and Caleb on his heels. "How is Chip?" he asked Sam as he entered the cabin. The security employee sat on the floor, his back against a wall.

"The killer hit him on the head. Chip needs to go to the infirmary."

"Creep clobbered me good," Chip complained.

"Did you see his face?" Winestock asked.

"No, sir. He wore a mask, the kind people who have allergies or a cold wear. I'm sorry, Chief. I messed up. Joe told me not to let anybody in. The killer knocked on the door and said he brought food for me."

Joe frowned. "Did you call for a meal delivery?"

A nod. "I was starving. I thought this was legitimate."

"You're sure the attacker was a man?"

Another nod. "About six two, brown hair, and brown eyes."

"Did he say anything?" Winestock asked.

"Aside from claiming to be a steward, no."

"You're lucky to be alive, Chip." The chief turned weary eyes to Joe. "The killer used a suppressor. I was across the hall and didn't hear a thing." He glanced at Caleb. "Take him to the infirmary and have Dr. Martin check him."

Caleb hurried forward and knelt beside his friend. "Come on, buddy. Maybe Lucy will check on you."

Despite his pallor, Chip's lips curved. "Hope so. I'd love to take her to dinner when the headache eases."

"Women love to nurture a wounded soldier." The two security men left the cabin, Chip leaning heavily on his friend.

"I'll call in my crime scene team." Winestock stared at Ferguson's body. "They haven't seen this much action in the five years they've worked for me. We need to contact the feds and make sure the meet us in Puerto Vallarta. Two bodies in two days. I'll let them hash things out with the locals."

Nico walked in with Trace. Shadow's leader stared down at Ferguson's lifeless body. "What happened to the guard in this room?"

"Knocked out," Sam said. "Caleb took Chip to the infirmary."

"Leads?" Trace asked.

Joe blew out a breath. "Not much. Killer was six two, brown hair and eyes with a dust mask over his face. Haven't had a chance to check the security feed yet."

"I'll set it up." Winestock dragged a hand down his face. "I have to contact my crime team anyway. Nico, you and Trace secure the scene until I return." He led Joe and Sam to the security office. Winestock cued the footage and showed Joe had to work the system. "I need to contact my crime team."

"Go ahead." Joe dropped into the chair the chief had vacated. "This system is similar to one we sell at Fortress." One of the low-end models.

"I'll be in the outer office for a minute, then across the hall. Lock up when you're finished. If you find anything useful, I want to know about it."

Joe saluted.

After Winestock left, Sam sat in a chair beside Joe. "We won't get much from the security footage, will we?"

"Doubt it. We still have to check. The killer could have made a mistake." He started the footage from the time Ferguson entered the detention cabin. Several passengers passed the cabin, a few workers. He and Sam watched as Farraday used a key card to unlock the cabin door and walked inside. Two minutes later, Trace arrived. In less than two minutes, their teammate escorted a protesting Farraday from the room with facial injuries.

After watching several minutes of empty corridor, a figure appeared in camera range. He wore a dark shirt and pants and the mask Chip mentioned. He pulled a weapon from his pocket, screwed on a suppressor, and knocked on the door. As soon as it opened, the man slammed the butt of his weapon on Chip's head. The security man dropped to the ground. The killer shoved him inside and shut the door. One minute later, strolled away, the weapon a bulge at his lower back under the shirt.

"How could security miss this?" Sam looked at Joe. "It's all here on the footage."

Joe motioned to the bank of cameras. "Easy. The guard could have been keeping an eye on another screen or he might have had to leave the office to help out. Winestock's workforce is short-handed and Chip was keeping an eye on a sleeping Ferguson. Of all places on this ship, Caleb probably thought the detention cabin was the safest area."

"Can you follow the killer's progress?"

"Maybe." He keyed in the time immediately after the murder as he surfed through the other screen footage. The process took longer than it would have taken Chip or Caleb but he managed to track the killer until he disappeared in the bowels of the ship in areas not covered by cameras.

Joe blew out a breath, frustrated with their lack of progress. "That's it. Like Ferguson, he knew the layout of the ship and took advantage of it to disappear. He probably had a shirt stashed somewhere. He'd blend in with other passengers or the crew if he managed to steal a crew member's shirt."

"Send a copy of the footage to Zane and Nico. We'll leave the original cued for Winestock. Maybe he'll recognize the killer."

"At least we know he's Caucasian." A few taps of the keyboard later, Joe shoved his chair away from the table. He and Sam returned to the detention cabin where Nico observed the crime team at work. "Where's Winestock?"

"On another deck. He should return soon. Find anything?"

"Ran the security footage. Farraday accessed this cabin with a key card. Chip had his hands full keeping Farraday from going after Ferguson and calling for reinforcements. Trace showed up two minutes later. When Trace escorted him from the cabin, Farraday had the injuries we saw when he arrived at the infirmary. Within forty minutes, the killer pistol-whipped Chip with a suppressed weapon. He killed Ferguson and left a minute later."

"You track him?"

"Tried. He knew the ship as well as Ferguson and disappeared. No identification. Dude was wearing a mask, black pants, black shirt. I sent the footage to your email and Fortress. Maybe Zane will work more magic."

Nico scowled. "Maybe."

Winestock returned. "Tell me the security cameras helped."

Sam shook her head. "Joe has the footage ready in the screen room. Maybe you'll recognize the killer."

"It's not likely," Joe warned. "We have a lot of nothing to work with. Did you send Trace to the detention cabin when Farraday barged in?"

The chief nodded. "Caleb and I were on the wrong side of the ship. Trace was the closest person to help Chip. Figured he could handle one irate passenger."

"You haven't heard the last word from Farraday. He says he's going to talk to you about firing Trace."

Winestock snorted. "I'm not surprised. He and the other executives throw their weight around each time they're on board Hollingbrook ships. I appreciate that they have a job to do. I wish they respected our jobs enough not to interfere in our operations."

"Need me to stay longer?" Nico asked.

A head shake. "Caleb is on his way back. Between the two of us, we'll manage. If I need help, I'll call." His expression grew grim. "I hope that won't be necessary or I can guarantee I won't be working for Hollingbrook after this cruise is completed."

The crime team members looked at each other, then stared at their boss, shock on their faces.

Winestock motioned for them to return to work, then faced the Fortress operatives. "Thanks for your assistance. I'll let you know what we find. I expect you to do the same."

"What makes you think we'll find anything else?" Sam asked.

"You have information at your disposal. Got a feeling a lot of it is not from the normal sources. I want to know what you learn."

Nico gave a short nod. "We'll be in touch after we do some research." In the corridor, he glanced at Joe and Sam. "I'm going to check on Mercy. I'll meet you at the suite. We have a lot of work to do and not much time to do it."

"You think our man will try to slip off the boat when we dock?"

"Depends on how worried he is about another interview with the feds. I'm more concerned with the time line. The problems haven't been this pervasive on this route over the past few months. Something triggered the escalation."

"He's not finished," Sam said.

"I'm afraid he won't stop until Mike Hollingbrook is dead and his cruise line destroyed." Nico turned away. "I'll see you soon."

Joe walked with Sam in the opposite direction. "We'll call Z and bring him up to speed on everything that's been happening."

Together, they entered the stairwell and headed toward their deck. Halfway to their destination, a crowd of people entered the stairwell, many grumbling about an elevator malfunction.

He nudged Sam closer to the wall and angled himself to protect her from an accidental bump. The last thing he wanted was for the woman he loved to fall down the stairs.

Joe waited for the crowd to pass before he resumed the journey toward their suite. The skin at the back of his neck tingled. As he started to turn, he caught a tall figure in black in his peripheral vision. Before he could react, a hard hand landed on his back and shoved.

CHAPTER TWENTY-FIVE

One minute Joe sheltered Sam from the crowd in the stairwell. The next he pushed her away from him as he fell. "Joe!" People scrambled out of the way as he tumbled. Joe landed hard on the next landing, his back and head slamming against the wall. He slumped to the floor and remained motionless.

Horror stricken, Sam pushed through the crowd gathering around him. "Joe." She dropped to her knees. For a second, she remained frozen. Her medic training kicked in and she assessed him for injuries with one hand. With the other, she grabbed her phone and called Nico, grateful Fortress provided cell phones that worked anywhere.

When her team leader answered, she said, "South stairwell. Now. Joe's hurt." After shoving the phone back into her pocket, she resumed checking the man she loved for broken bones. By the time Nico and Ben arrived on the run, she'd ruled out broken limbs.

"How bad?" Nico asked.

"No broken bones so far. I need to check his ribs. Ben, see if the infirmary has a litter, a backboard, and a C-collar to stabilize Joe's neck until we take x-rays."

At that moment, Joe groaned and his eyelids fluttered.

"Joe?" Sam laid a restraining hand on his chest. "Don't move. You had a bad fall."

"Don't need a litter or horse collar. Just give me a minute to catch my breath."

"Tough," Nico said. "You're going to the infirmary to be checked anyway. Ben, go." As the EOD man hurried off, Shadow's leader thanked the passengers who lingered for their concern and urged them to clear the stairwell for the medical personnel who would respond to the accident. Once the bystanders were gone, he knelt by Joe's side. "You're the most sure footed of us all, buddy. What happened?"

Joe cut his eyes toward Sam. "Did you see the man in black?"

She blinked. "No." What man?

"I didn't fall by accident, Nico. Someone pushed me from behind. As I fell, I twisted in mid-air and saw a man dressed in black run up the stairs while everyone else in the crowd moved down the stairwell. Lost sight of him when my head hit the wall or floor."

"Wall," Sam confirmed. She'd never forget the sight of his body flying through the air and landing against the wall. She'd see that in her nightmares.

She dragged her attention back to assessing Joe's injuries. She checked his head for injuries, careful to keep his head and neck aligned with his body. Joe hissed when she reached the area near his left ear.

Sam glanced at Nico. "He has a large knot and a gash. You need stitches, Joe."

He scowled. "Great. You're doing them. Don't trust the ship's doctor."

Understandable. They didn't know who was involved in the conspiracy. She held up two fingers. "How many fingers do you see?"

"Too many. Two or five. Hard to tell with the blurry vision."

Concussion. She prayed that was the only injury aside from bruising and the gash.

"I know what will cure me," he murmured.

"Four weeks of vacation?"

"As long as I was with you, that would be a bonus. I'm sure a kiss would solve my problem."

Nico snorted. "He's not hurt that bad if he can still flirt with you, Sam."

She pretended to consider the cure. "A kiss, huh? Too bad I didn't know about this miracle cure before now. Would have saved myself much stress and worry on missions."

"Not the rest of the guys. Only cures what ails me." Joe winked at her.

Despite her worry, his words brought a smile. "You're something else."

"Kiss?" he prompted.

Sam glanced at Nico.

He held up his hands. "Don't look at me, lady. My kisses belong to Mercy."

"Turn around."

Nico rolled his eyes and turned his back to them. "Hurry up, will you? This is embarrassing."

Sam leaned down. "Don't move," she whispered against his mouth. Tilting her head, she pressed a series of gentle kisses to his lips.

"I want a real one when the doc clears me," he grumbled.

"As many as you want," Sam agreed.

"I'll hold you to that promise, Sparky."

Ben returned a minute later with a litter and backboard in hand and the doctor on his heels.

"No broken limbs," Sam reported. "He has a large bump on his head and a gash that needs stitches. He insists I do them."

Martin's eyebrows soared. "All right."

Between her and the doctor, they slipped the C-collar around Joe's neck. Nico and Ben slid Joe onto the backboard and fastened the board to the litter.

"This is ridiculous." Joe scowled. "I'm fine."

"Then you will walk out of the infirmary under your own steam in a couple hours." The doctor patted his arm before leading the way to the medical facility.

After taking Joe to the examination room for the doctor to take x-rays, Nico turned to Ben. "Go back on patrol. Keep your eyes open for a man dressed in all black."

"He's probably changed clothes by now," the EOD man murmured.

"He might not realize Joe saw him."

"Not enough to ID him," Joe said. "I saw his back and the black clothes as he ran the other direction."

While Sam cleaned the area around the cut at the side of Joe's head and injected the medicine to numb the affected area, Dr. Martin used the time to prep Joe for the x-rays. By the time the scalp was numb, the doctor had finished taking the x-rays and disappeared into the other room to examine the images.

Sam laid her hand on Joe's arm. "Ready?"

"Do it. I want to be ready to go as soon as Martin says I'm clear."

"What do you need me to do, Sam?" Nico asked.

"I need better light to work. Find a lamp or a flashlight."

He returned with an adjustable lamp. "This work?"

"Perfect." She washed her hands and tugged on the rubber gloves she had laid out beside the stitch kit Martin provided.

Sam sat on a stool and got to work. Five stitches later, she sat back and tugged off her gloves. "I made the stitches as small as I possible. Don't shave your head anytime soon."

"Thanks."

By the time Sam cleared the last of the trash from her work, Martin returned, a smile on his face. "Good news, Joe. I don't see signs of cracks or broken bones. Your spine and neck are fine."

"Told you."

"Better to be sure. I can give you pain pills. You'll be sore and bruised tomorrow. Of course, your wife might have meds to help with that."

"She does. I still don't want anything."

Sam couldn't blame him. With a second killer still on the loose, none of them could afford to be down. "I'll give him mild pain meds if he needs them."

Martin nodded. "Good enough. You know what to look for, Sam. If your husband has complications, let me know." He grinned. "I still do house calls."

Joe held out his hand. "Thanks, Doc."

After a shake, the doctor said, "Let's get you out of here. I might have a run on people who need meds for nausea or a hangover."

Nico and Sam helped Joe to sit up. His face went white and he swayed on the exam table.

Nico steadied him with a hand to Joe's shoulder. "Easy."

Joe blew out a breath. "Oh, man."

"It's the concussion." Sam positioned herself to keep him from hitting the floor in case he went down. "You need to sleep for a while. How bad is the headache?"

"Bad enough."

From Joe, that was an admission of a monster-size headache. She looked at Nico. "Help me get him to the suite. He needs to be off rotation for a few hours."

"I'm okay," Joe protested.

"You will be. Right now, you're taking a breather." Nico draped Joe's arm over his shoulder and assisted him from the table. "The sooner you take a nap, the quicker I'll have you back where I need you."

"Yeah, yeah." Joe stumbled along beside Nico in the corridor. "You just want more time to whisper sweet nothings in Mercy's ear."

"I'm a smart man."

Sam led the men to the elevator. When the car arrived, the interior was empty. Good. If the killer thought Joe was seriously injured, the Fortress team might be able to capitalize on the mistaken notion.

Her jaw clenched. If the killer came after Joe while he was down, she wouldn't hesitate to kill him.

Inside the suite, she directed Nico to help Joe into the bedroom. "Are you nauseated?" she asked Joe.

"Oh, yeah. I'm pretty sure I'll embarrass myself by puking my guts out before the night is over."

"Nico, find a soft drink, preferably one with ginger in it."

"I'll be back." Once Sam handed Nico her key card, their team leader left the suite.

Sam dimmed the lights and blocked the sunlight coming in from the window. "Better?"

He sighed. "Much. Thanks."

She went to her mike bag and found a packet of the mild pain meds the members of Shadow preferred to use. The medicine knocked the edge off the pain yet allowed them to function. She located a chemically-activated ice pack and grabbed a wash cloth from the bathroom.

Sam laid the pain meds on the nightstand and shook the ice pack. She wrapped the pack in the cloth and laid it against his head.

"You owe me a kiss, Sparky," he murmured.

"I will happily pay what I owe when you aren't sick to your stomach."

A pause. "How long will I be laid up?"

"Not sure. Depends on the severity of your concussion. I'll have to wake you frequently through the night to check. I doubt you'll be running at top speed for a couple days."

His expression grew grim. "I need to be mobile. This killer won't stop. He has an agenda."

"He must know we're friends with Nico and Mercy. She's vulnerable."

Joe lifted her hand to his lips and kissed the back of it. "That's why Curt is on board. He's extra protection for Mercy."

Sam hoped the extra precaution would be enough.

Nico returned with the soft drink and a container of crackers. "Courtesy of the kitchen staff."

She smiled. "This is great." Sam encouraged Joe to sip part of the liquid before handing him a couple capsules. "Your preferred pain killer. Do you think you can keep down a few crackers?"

He flinched. "Not likely."

"All right. Let's see if the soft drink does the trick."

"Anything else I can do, Sam?" Nico asked.

"I've got this. Check on Mercy. We're concerned the killer might go after her next."

"So am I. I'll check on you later. Joe, you and Sam are off duty until tomorrow morning. One team member will be in the other room at all times. We'll split the shifts so no one is on duty too long."

"I can handle the watch." Sam could protect Joe as well as the rest of her teammates.

Nico's gaze locked on hers. "We always have the back of an injured teammate and the medic tending to him. Knock that chip off your shoulder. No one is calling into question your bodyguard skills. This is about protecting both of you while Joe heals and your focus is on him."

Sam's cheeks burned, part shame and part temper, both aimed at herself. Setting up watch shifts was standard procedure. Her teammates had followed the same procedure when she was laid up. "I'm sorry. I know it's for the best."

After another moment, Nico nodded. "Curt will take the first watch. If you need me, contact me."

"Thanks."

Nico laid his hand on Joe's shoulder and squeezed. "Rest as much as you can. I need you on your feet."

"Copy that."

He handed Sam her key card and left. Ten minutes later, Curt arrived, checked on Joe, and set up his laptop in the living room.

Joe squeezed Sam's hand. "Promise to rest between checks on me."

"Promise." As long as he was rested comfortably and wasn't in danger.

He frowned. "Why do I feel like there are qualifiers in that one word?"

"Because there are. Focus on you instead of me."

"Never going to happen. I love you. You are at the center of everything that matters to me. You will always be first."

Arguing with Joe was pointless. She brushed his lips with hers. "I love you. Sleep now. I'll check on you in a while. If you need me, call out. I'll be in the living room."

"Resting, right?"

She gave a short nod. Resting with a weapon at hand to protect the man who meant everything to her.

CHAPTER TWENTY-SIX

Throughout the long night, Joe slept fitfully in part because he knew Sam was awake. Bone-deep bruises on his aching body didn't help, either. He wanted nothing more than to let Sam dope him up with heavier pain meds but he wouldn't take a chance with her safety. Yeah, his teammates were taking turns watching over them both. Didn't matter. Samantha Coleman was his to protect and he intended to do that even if it meant toughing out the pain for a few hours.

Near dawn, Sam returned to his bedside with another soft drink and more pain meds. "How do you feel?"

"Headache's manageable and I don't feel like barfing." A blessing. He'd been aggravated and humiliated to have the woman he loved tend to him while he puked in the middle of the night.

She smiled. "Progress. Are you hungry?"

"A little," he admitted. "Aside from that kiss you promised me, I want out of this cabin."

Sam cupped his jaw. "You want the kiss now or after you shower?"

His heart leapt. Good thing he'd taken the time to brush his teeth after the last episode of illness. "Do you need to ask? Now."

With a soft laugh, she leaned down and kissed him. The kiss started out as a gentle brush of her lips against his and progressed to the deep, hot kiss he longed for.

Joe groaned, lifted his hands, and threaded his fingers through her hair. Man, this woman was everything to him. He couldn't wait to put his ring on her finger and marry the beautiful medic. But after what Sam had experienced in her past, he refused to rush the romance. She needed him to court her. Didn't matter that he'd known and worked with her for years. They hadn't been together as a couple for those years. She deserved the best he could give her.

Joe had seen her watching Nico and Mercy with longing in her eyes when she thought no one was looking. Sam needed time to trust him with everything. Her life, her heart, her body. The last, he knew, would be the hardest step.

He tilted his head and deepened the kiss, urging Sam to sit on the edge of the bed. When he finally eased her back, Joe smiled. "Definitely worth a few bruises."

"And five stitches."

"A mere scratch."

"Let me check your injury before you shower." No signs of infection. Excellent. Sam applied a waterproof bandage over the stitches. "The bandage will keep the stitches dry for a few minutes. I didn't want to shave your head. I like your hair long enough to run my fingers through."

Warmth filled him. When she said things like that, he fell deeper in love with her. "I won't take long." Minutes later, he left the bedroom and walked into the living room dressed in cargo pants and a black t-shirt. Sam and Nico sat on the couch.

"Shower's yours," Joe said as he walked to Sam. He captured her chin in the palm of his hand and dropped a quick kiss on her mouth. She looked surprised. He winked at her, hoping she would soon expect him to be openly affectionate in front of their teammates.

"I'll be back in a few minutes." She squeezed his wrist and stepped around him to go into the bedroom. She closed the door behind her.

Nico's gaze skimmed over Joe, evaluating. "You look better. You operational?"

Joe was tempted to say he was ready for anything. Not a smart move, though. Nico depended on them to tell the truth about their physical readiness and Joe wasn't at peak efficiency. "Light duty today. Maybe full rotation tomorrow."

A nod. "We're docking in Puerto Vallarta in a few hours. We'll be tied up with the feds when we arrive."

Joe grimaced. "Figured. Any chance they'll do the interviews in the suite? I don't want to sit in the open." Someone on board the ship was hunting. Joe didn't intend to make himself or Sam an easy target.

"I'll see what I can do. They want answers. They'll cooperate to get them. Mercy and Curt are waiting for us in the dining room if you're up to it."

"As soon as Sam is ready, we'll go. Anything suspicious happening around Mercy?"

"Not so far. One of us is always with her." Nico studied him a moment. "How serious are things between you and Sam?"

"I'm in love with her and want to marry her as soon as she'll let me."

His friend's lips curved. "Does she know?"

"She knows I love her. She doesn't know I want to marry her. Don't tell her. I'll have to ease her into the idea."

"When will you tell her?"

"I don't know yet. I want to romance her. She takes care of Shadow. It's my turn to take care of her. She needs me to date her and give her time to trust me with every part of her. I refuse to screw this up by rushing her down the church aisle so I can slide a wedding band on her finger and declare her off limits to other men. I love Sam enough to wait until she's ready. She deserves the time to adjust and this allows me time to treat her like a princess."

A slow nod. "I'm glad you're wise enough to see that. You have my support. One thing, though. If you hurt Sam, I'll rip you up one side and down the other." Though his tone was conversational, Nico's gaze bored into Joe's. His team leader meant every word.

"I hear you." Wouldn't be necessary for Nico to follow through. Joe would sooner slit his own throat than hurt Sam.

When Sam returned to the living room, the three operatives made their way to the dining room. Because of the early hour, the place was almost empty.

Gregory, the captain's steward, hailed them with a cheerful greeting. "Captain Greer will be here soon. He'd like to join your table."

Nico's eyebrows rose. "How did he know we'd be here this early?"

Gregory's cheeks flushed. "He requested that I notify him when you arrived. I contacted him when Mrs. Rivera said she was expecting you. I hope that's all right. I'm not a spy."

"I planned to track Greer down after breakfast. This saves me time."

The steward relaxed. "Good. Have a seat. I'll pour coffee for your group while you visit the breakfast bar. If you want something different for breakfast, let me know. I'll have the kitchen staff prepare whatever you want."

"Thanks, Gregory." Nico glanced at Joe and inclined his head toward the food, then bent to kiss his wife.

"Come on." Joe pressed his hand to Sam's lower back. "Let's see what they're serving." After filling his plate, he escorted Sam to the table and sat next to Curt.

"You okay?" his friend murmured.

"Better. Sore, stiff, low-level headache."

"You scared your woman."

"I know." He hated causing Sam to worry. "I'll make it up to her."

Sam glanced at Joe and Curt. "Mercy says the boss called Nico before he came to the suite for his watch shift this morning."

"Sounds like we need to meet before the ship docks in Puerto Vallarta."

Nico returned from the food bar in time to hear Joe's comment. "We'll talk after breakfast. I'm letting our teammates sleep as long as possible. They're on duty in a couple hours."

Captain Greer entered the dining room and approached their table with long, ground-eating strides. "May I join you?"

"Please." Nico motioned to the seat on his left.

After Gregory took the captain's order and left to fill a plate, Greer looked at Joe, his gaze assessing. "Heard what happened yesterday. How are you?"

"I'm fine."

A nod. "What can you tell me, Nico?"

"Not much. We'll check security footage this morning. If we're lucky, the man screwed up in his haste to leave the stairwell."

"He wasn't wearing a mask." Joe picked up a biscuit. "Gives us better than even odds one of the security cameras caught part of his face."

"Word's starting to circulate among the crew that odd things are happening on board." Greer nodded his thanks at Gregory as the steward set his filled plate and coffee mug on the table in front of him.

"What about the passengers?"

"A few inquiries. Most are intent on enjoying their vacation."

"Better than the alternative."

"You're right. Wouldn't take much to start a panic. Do you know who is behind this?"

"If we did, he'd be in custody."

Nico set down his coffee mug. "We have a few leads we're pursuing but nothing is confirmed. When we have concrete information, we'll pass it along."

Greer sighed. "Guess I can't ask for more than that." As soon as he finished breakfast, the captain excused himself to return to the bridge.

Five minutes later, Trace and Ben arrived and loaded their plates. They sat at the next table over. "Meeting in the suite in fifteen," Nico said to them although his gaze was fixed on his wife.

"Copy that," Ben murmured.

As Joe ate, he kept an eye on the passengers trickling into the dining room. He doubted the man who shoved him down the stair still wore all black. However, he might recognize the man's body movements and the way he held himself. Joe would love to capture the killer before he had a chance to do more damage to the ship or hurt anyone else.

Nico caught Sam and Joe's eye and lifted his chin slightly. By unspoken consent, the operatives at their table and Mercy rose to leave. Trace and Ben would follow soon.

Once all the operatives were seated around the suite's living room, Nico said, "Maddox called."

CHAPTER TWENTY-SEVEN

Joe dragged a hand down his face and flinched. Man, he needed to do light training today to loosen his muscles. "Let me guess. We have another problem."

"Give the man a prize," Ben muttered as he settled deeper into the chair he occupied. "What's the bad news, Nico?"

"Three things. Mike Hollingbrook received more threats against him and the cruise line."

Curt frowned. "Specific threats?"

A nod. "The email said he'd beg for mercy before the sender granted him an escape in death and his ships would go down in flames."

Joe's blood ran cold. "More bombs?" The Pacific Star was a huge ship. The chances of them finding explosive devices in places other than the obvious was slim to none. "Bomb-sniffing dogs searched the ship before we left San Diego."

"Maddox wants us to check anyway. It's possible Ferguson and his partner found a way to conceal the explosives from the dogs."

Ben scowled. "Does Maddox know how many places could hold a bomb on this tub?"

"We have to finish the search by the time we dock in Puerto Vallarta. The second piece of information Maddox shared came from Zane's research. I asked Z to look into Tom Ferguson's background. He discovered something very interesting about our dead man. Tom is the only child of Kirk Ferguson."

Joe frowned. "Wait. Isn't that the man who owns Ferguson Cruises?"

"Owned. Kirk is dead. The cruise line was on the verge of bankruptcy a year ago. One of his main competitors was Hollingbrook Cruise Lines. When he knew the company was going under and he couldn't save it, Kirk approached Hollingbrook and sold him the company. Tom fought against the decision to sell out, insisting he and his father could turn the company around. Kirk disagreed and sold it anyway, then overdosed on sleeping pills and scotch."

"So, this is about revenge," Sam said. "Tom said Hollingbrook was a liar and cheat who deserved to die but Tom's dead. The danger should be over."

"Tom's partner doesn't agree. He's determined to carry out this vendetta to the end."

"What's the point?" Trace scowled. "Tom would have been Kirk's heir if anything was left to inherit. What's the partner's motive?"

"That's the question we need to answer. If we answer that question, we'll know the culprit's identity."

"Have Z send us the information he unearthed about Tom's background."

"It's already in your email."

"What's the third piece of bad news?" Mercy asked.

Nico glanced at Sam before refocusing on the rest of the team.

Joe tensed at Nico's unspoken warning. The news would probably upset Sam. Joe draped his arm across her shoulders, ignoring the renewed pain in his back. She was not facing this alone.

"Zane has been scouring the Internet for references to the Maldonado trafficking group. Activity in the Maldonado strongholds is heightened and there are rumors Maldonado has his eye on a big prize, one that will net him big bucks in a special auction."

"Sick creep," Ben muttered.

"Zane's working as fast as he can to find out more information and Maddox is tapping his sources in Mexico. So far, nothing."

"The Maldonado might not have anything to do with Hollingbrook." Sam pressed closer to Joe's side. "We shouldn't discount other big targets."

Nico inclined his head. "We won't. However, since Maldonado's second in command is snapping pictures of female passengers on the Pacific Star, I suspect we'll face Maldonado and his organization soon."

Sam shuddered.

Joe tucked her closer and pressed a kiss to her temple. "We'll handle whatever comes together, baby. I give you my word that they won't touch you again."

Trace's eyebrows knitted, concern filling his eyes. "Sam?"

Joe shook his head. "Don't ask."

Sam nestled her hand in his. "No, it's okay."

"No one will force you to discuss your past," Nico reminded her.

Curt's expression hardened. "No way," he growled out. "Not Sam."

Ben leaped to his feet and stalked to the balcony doors, his back to the room, face a mask of rage.

"Tell me the man who touched her is dead." Trace's voice was flat.

"He is," Joe confirmed. "He worked for the human trafficking groups that's stalking Pacific Star passengers."

Ben swung around and glared daggers at him. "And you're allowing her to work this op? What's wrong with you, Gray?"

His cheeks burned and for a moment, Joe saw red. "The choice is Sam's." Didn't matter that Joe longed to bundle her onto the next plane and send her away from danger. As much as he wanted to protect her from life, he couldn't do it. If he safeguarded the woman he loved to that extent, he'd lose her.

"If she was mine, I wouldn't give her an option." Ben's voice rose. He strode to stand in front of Sam and loomed over hers. "Go home, Samantha. You shouldn't be here."

Unable to contain himself any longer, Joe stood and shifted to stand in front of Sam, forcing Ben to back up. "Knock it off, Ben."

"Stop." Sam's soft voice was as effective as a shout. Silence reined in the suite as everyone's gaze shifted to her. "I decide what ops to work. I'm not a terrified fourteen-year-old anymore. I'm as well trained as you are."

"More," Nico said.

"You're more vulnerable because you're a woman and on the small side." Ben's hands clenched into rock-hard fists. "You're gorgeous, Sam. Why would you chance this group deciding you're worth the risk to snatch you for their stable?"

"I'll be more trouble than I'm worth."

"No doubts about that," Curt said. "It's not a good enough deterrent and you know it."

"Enough," Nico said. "Sam made her position clear. We accept it and move on. You're worried Sam's at risk? Watch her back. None of us would be here if Sam had opted out of missions where we were injured. She wants a part in taking down Maldonado's organization. At fourteen, she didn't have the knowledge and training. Now she does. Sam has the right to confront her worst nightmare. Instead of fighting to send her home, fight to keep her safe while she does her job."

That was the end of the argument. Joe kept his gaze on Ben. His teammate struggled to reign in his temper. Jaw clenched tight, Ben returned to the balcony door to stare at the ocean. Something was there, Joe thought. Something ugly in his past was eating Ben alive and human trafficking missions made the pitched battle inside his friend harder to handle. Someday soon, Ben would have to deal with the tragedy.

"First priority is searching the ship," Nico said. "We need security badges from Winestock. We start at the bottom of the ship and work our way to the top. Passenger cabins are off limits unless we have probable cause to search them."

"Would Tom's partner set off another bomb before he left the ship?" Mercy asked.

"His best option is to trigger the bomb once he's safely on land."

Joe noted the worry in his team leader's eyes as he spoke to his wife. Nico could lose Mercy if the killer set off another bomb before the artist left the ship.

He understood the temptation Nico faced to spirit the woman he loved away from danger. Even though Joe had called out Ben, he longed to protect the woman he wanted to marry. If something happened to her, Joe didn't know if he'd survive. He had no desire to return to the loneliness and isolation he'd wrapped around him like a blanket after the horrible operation in New York City that had changed his life. Memories of that locked windowless room filled with children and teen girls filled his worst nightmares.

"We split up to cover the ship faster. Joe and Sam will work together so she can keep an eye on him. Ben, Curt, Trace work separately. Mercy will be with me."

"Still too much ground to cover," Ben snapped with a glance over his shoulder. "We don't have enough hours or people to search this miniature town."

"I've already touched base with Winestock. He's calling in all of his crew to search."

"Do they know not to touch whatever they find?"

Nico stared at the EOD man without saying a word.

Ben flushed and held up his hands in mock surrender.

"Let's go." Holding hands with Mercy, Nico led the way to the security office where Winestock's people gathered for instructions.

Winestock motioned for the Fortress team leader to join him. "This is Nico. He's head of the unit from Fortress Security. He and his team are here to assist us. Two of his team members defused the bombs found earlier. Nico has instructions for you. Follow them to the letter. He and his team know what they're doing." He stepped back and ceded the leadership role to Nico.

Shadow's team leader made eye contact with every member of Winestock's staff. "It's possible another bomb may be on board." He waited for the shocked gasps and whispers to die down before continuing. "You walk these corridors every day so you know how large the Pacific Star is. We need every available person to help search. Between my team and the security employees, we have twenty people to search a ship the size of a small city. Winestock divided you into two groups. Group one, search the even numbered decks. Group two, take the odd numbered decks. Both groups start on the top decks. Search for things that don't belong."

An employee with a sour expression on his face called out, "What about your team? You plan to help out or just order the rest of us around?"

"Sallinger," Winestock snapped. "One more word and you'll be written up."

Nico held up his hand to stop the security chief from reaming his worker further. "We'll start in the engine room and work our way up to meet the security teams. If you find anything suspicious, contact Winestock. Under no circumstances are you to touch a device to disarm or move it. The bombs we dismantled were tricky to disarm. Wouldn't have taken much to set them off. Be thorough but fast. We have to complete the search before we dock in Puerto Vallarta."

"Who is doing this?" another employee asked.

"That's what we're trying to find out. We have some leads but they have to wait until we make sure this creep can't blow a hole in the ship."

"Is it true we've had two murders since we left San Diego?" asked a third person.

Nico gave a short nod. "A nanny who had the misfortune of being in the wrong place at the wrong time and the man who murdered the nanny."

"Can't say I'm crying over the loss of a murderer," someone muttered.

"The second murderer hurt your co-worker, Chip. This man wouldn't hesitate to kill someone else. He's a stone-cold killer with an agenda that could include sinking this ship with all of us on board. Don't alarm the passengers. Come up with a good cover story fast and get going. Winestock has your group assignments."

Once the employees left the security office, Winestock leaned against his desk, arms folded across his chest. "Was it wise to tell all that information? Might start a panic."

"Would you rather work in the dark?" Joe asked.

The chief grimaced. "Not if I can help it although I did it often enough in the Navy."

"They needed to know this wasn't a drill," Nico said.

"Yeah, I get it. I want to help search but someone has to be in the office while the teams search the ship."

"Search the security office and detention cell plus the other rooms on this corridor. We'll cover the other half of the deck."

Winestock nodded. "I can do that. Any word from Fortress on the security footage?"

"Not yet. Besides the potential bomb, we have another problem to handle."

"The human trafficking group?"

Nico nodded. "They're ready to make a tactical strike, one where they'll reap a big profit."

Winestock cursed. "Guess that takes precedence over security footage."

"We need security badges so we don't alarm passengers more than necessary and the ship's personnel won't stop us from accessing restricted areas." Two minutes later with badges in hand, Nico led his team into the corridor. He assigned areas to search. "Move fast. Time is running out."

CHAPTER TWENTY-EIGHT

Worry gnawed at Sam's gut as she worked side by side in the engine room with Joe. The moment they stepped inside the room, color had drained from his face. She felt sure the heat or strong odors caused that reaction. "What do you need?" she asked as they moved to search the next part of their grid.

"A long vacation with you on a beach or in the mountains. Anywhere I can feel a breeze on my face as long as it isn't on a ship."

She smiled. "I like both ideas. Are you nauseated again or is your head hurting?"

"Both," he admitted. "I can't afford to be down, Sam."

"I'll be back in one minute."

Sam jogged to the breakroom she'd spotted down the corridor. She grabbed a soft drink and returned to the engine room. After handing him the drink, Sam gave Joe two mild pain killers. Once he'd swallowed the pills and guzzled part of the cold liquid, she placed an anti-nausea patch behind his ear. "You'll feel better in a few minutes."

He dropped a quick kiss to her mouth. "Thanks."

A simple touch that made her heart turn to mush. Although she longed to indulge in more long kisses with Joe, the situation was too dire to steal a few minutes for themselves. Sam turned back to the task at hand. The safety of thousands of passengers depended on their work. They continued the search but came up empty in their area. The rest of their team also found nothing.

"Next deck," Nico said.

Again, they split up and searched the deck in a grid pattern. Still nothing.

Four decks later, Sam froze when she saw a tube attached to a flashing digital timer. Chill bumps surged up her spine. "Joe." Her voice came out strangled. Even as she watched, the clock counted down the minutes until detonation. The bomb was set to go off when they docked in Puerto Vallarta.

Joe swiveled and looked in the direction she pointed. Grabbing a flashlight from the pocket of his cargo pants, Joe aimed the beam at the tube, timer, and wiring. His expression darkened. "Find Nico and Ben."

Sam hurried to the corridor and sprinted for the last place she'd seen Shadow's leader.

Nico spun on his heel when she entered the room he and Mercy were searching. He'd automatically moved in front of his wife, hand on his weapon. "Find something, Sam?"

She nodded. "Joe said we need Ben."

"I'll get him," Mercy said.

Nico followed Sam to the enclosed observation area. Her gut clenched when she saw Joe on his back underneath the table, examining the device.

Their team leader crouched. "What do we have?"

"Not sure. This isn't like the other bombs Ben and I handled in San Diego."

Ben ran into the room with Mercy on his heels. He set his equipment bag to the side, got on his back and slid under the table, flashlight in hand. The EOD man was silent a moment as he studied the tube, timer, and wiring. "Sam, find out if Martin has a sealed container to handle hazardous material."

"What does that mean?" Mercy asked. "Isn't this a bomb?"

"It definitely is. This device will spew a chemical instead of shrapnel."

Sam spun on her heel and sprinted for the stairs. What kind of chemical lurked in that tube? A nerve agent? Many children were on this vessel. The thought spurred Sam to run faster.

She hit the door of the infirmary at a dead run. "Dr. Martin!"

The physician came out of his treatment room, alarm on his face. "What's wrong? Is it Joe?"

"Do you have a sealed container to handle hazardous material?"

He frowned. "Yes. Why?"

"I need it right now."

Martin walked to the locked room where he kept his supplies. A moment later, he returned with a dusty square box that he handed to Sam. "What's going on?"

"I'll explain later." If she was able.

Sam ran back to Joe and Ben. She glanced around the room. "Where are Nico and Mercy?"

"They returned to the search." Joe took the box from her. "He wanted her away from here. Can't say that I blame him."

"We can't afford to assume this is the only chemical device planted on board the ship." Ben pointed at one end of the tube. "See this, Joe?"

"Yep."

"Turn the wire cutters away from that end. If the metal touches the tube here, the contact will trigger the device. We'll be taking a bath in this stuff. When we detach the tube from the table, keep it level. We don't know how volatile the chemical is. Might do nothing if we stand it upright since he had to bring this on board a ship. Let's not find out if we're wrong. Ready?"

"Go ahead."

Sam waited, heart in her throat, until Joe and Ben removed the device. Joe slid out from under the table, took the tube from Ben, and slowly moved the tube into the box and sealed the container.

Some of Sam's tension eased. One device down. Hopefully, no more devices were on board. Martin's box was small.

"Back to work." Ben took the hazardous materials box from Joe and headed for the door with smooth, easy strides. "This may only be the beginning."

After the Fortress team finished the search of that deck and the next, Nico received a call from Winestock. He glanced at Ben. "Security team two found another one." He told Joe and Ben the location. "You two and Sam head to Deck 8. The rest of us will search the next deck. I hope the searchers didn't miss another device."

Twenty minutes later, the second bomb was dismantled and secured in the box. Once Joe sealed the container, the security team and the operatives relaxed.

Ben turned to the security team's leader. "Good work."

The woman beamed. "Thank you, sir."

"Call me Ben."

"Come on, Sandy," one of her teammates called. "We have to search the rest of the deck."

"See you later, Ben." With a smile, Sandy rushed off with the rest of her team.

Joe laughed. "I think perky Sandy is sweet on you, my friend."

The EOD man rolled his eyes. "She looks like she's twelve and she works on a ship with a route down the west coast, a long way from Nashville. I'll pass."

"She might be worth the effort."

"Don't push your luck, Gray." His gaze tracked to where Sandy had left the room with her team. "What would a woman filled with sunshine want to do with a man living in the shadows?"

A woman filled with sunshine might be exactly what a man filled with darkness needed. A woman filled with sunshine must live in Nashville. Ben deserved more than an empty life.

The operatives returned to the rest of their teammates and resumed work. The search of the ship concluded without another device being found by the operatives or the security teams.

"Let's hope this is the last of the nasty tricks," Trace murmured. "What should we do with the box?"

"Return it to the infirmary," Sam said. "Martin keeps the box in a secured room with his medicine supply. The box should be safe until the feds take possession of it." She glanced at Joe. "The doctor will need another hazardous materials container. Think the feds will have one?"

"Doubt it." Amusement gleamed in his eyes. "I'll let Nico contact Maddox. The boss loves dealing with feds."

Sam grinned at Joe's wry wit. Brent Maddox hated working with the federal agencies. Operations involving federal agents usually went south at the most inopportune time.

"Let's break the good news to Nico." Joe wrapped an arm around Sam's waist and guided her to the elevator.

"No stairs?"

"Not this time."

She ran an assessing gaze over him once they were inside the elevator. Joe was still too pale and he looked exhausted. He needed downtime. Once they briefed Nico, Sam would convince him to rest until the Pacific Star docked.

They located Shadow's leader in the security office, conferring with Winestock who looked ill.

Sam's eyebrows rose. "Are you feeling all right, Chief Winestock?"

A head shake. "I may never be okay again. This man planned to set off chemical weapons inside the ship. We could have lost everyone on board and that would have been on me. I'm in charge of security. I may not wait for my pink slip. I might submit my resignation. I don't understand how the killer got the weapons on board the ship."

"I have some ideas on that," Nico said. "We'll talk after my team and I discover who is to blame."

Winestock's fist clenched. "I'll tell you one thing. Hollingbrook needs to send the security teams through PSI. We need more training and more personnel. If he doesn't get ahead of this, the next time a terrorist sabotages one of the cruise ships, the attack might succeed." His knuckles whitened. "If you and your team weren't here, this ship would have been doomed."

Nico clapped him on the shoulder and turned to Sam and Joe. "Find more devices?"

Joe shook his head, winced slightly. "We secured them in Martin's hazardous materials box. Ben took the box to the infirmary where the doctor locked it up until the feds take possession."

"The Pacific Star needs another hazardous materials box, Nico. Unless the feds travel with one routinely, Martin needs one before the ship leaves port."

"I'll find out from Zane if Fortress has assets in the area. If not, he'll make arrangements to have one delivered." Nico paused. "Are you okay, Joe?"

A faint smile curved Joe's mouth. "Do I look that bad?"

"You look as though a good gust of wind could blow you over." He leaned against Winestock's desk. "You're off duty until we dock."

"If something comes up, let me know."

Nico lifted his chin in acknowledgment. "Sam, I need him on his feet as fast as possible."

"I've done all I can. It will take time for him to heal."

Time they might not have.

CHAPTER TWENTY-NINE

Joe walked with Sam to the suite, nauseated and suffering with a pounding headache. Although the patch Sam placed behind his ear had helped, it wasn't enough to get rid of the feeling he was going to hurl any second.

The light pouring into the suite's windows made him want to dive into a deep, dark cave and hide until the misery had passed. Unfortunately, that wasn't an option at the moment.

As soon as the door was secured, Sam urged Joe toward the bedroom and closed the curtains again. "Rest. I'll be back in a minute."

Joe captured her wrist. "Where are you going?" With all the problems popping up on this floating death trap, he didn't want Sam out of his sight. Whoever targeted the cruise line was growing desperate and Sam was part of the team thwarting his efforts. The Fortress operatives and Mercy were prime targets for revenge.

"To get you another soft drink, water, and ice. I'll be back in two minutes."

"I'll go with you."

Sam placed her hand over his heart. "Give yourself a break. You heard Nico. We need you in top form, fast. I'm not going far and I'll leave the door open. You'll hear if I run into trouble."

Once again, Joe had to check his automatic denial of her request. Sam was a well-trained operative. She could handle a simple trip two hundred feet down the corridor. He brushed her lips with his and released her.

Joe followed her to the door and watched her progress. In less than two minutes, she reappeared, bottled water, soft drink, and a container of ice in her hands.

Sam frowned. "You're supposed to be resting," she said as she drew near.

He shrugged. "You're my first priority."

"And you're mine." She nudged him inside the suite and led the way to the bedroom. "While you sip the soft drink, I'll make a couple ice packs."

Joe sat on the side of the bed and broke the seal on the drink. All he wanted to do was stretch out and close his eyes for a few minutes. Maybe then the nagging headache would ease. He'd forgotten how much he hated concussions.

Sam returned with the ice packs. "Lie down and I'll arrange the ice packs for you. Did the patch help?"

"Not enough. The overhead lights and smells triggered the nausea and headache. Working with Ben to dismantle the chemical weapons made the symptoms worse." Joe unlaced his boots. He groaned as the back of his head sank into the pillow. Man, it felt good to lay flat.

A moment later, Sam slid an ice pack wrapped in a washcloth behind his neck and draped the other over his forehead.

"I feel like a wuss," he muttered. "I've had concussions before and they're no picnic. This one, though, seems worse than the others."

"You hit the wall hard. Martin also doesn't know you have a high tolerance for pain. The concussion may be more severe than the doctor thought." Sam's lips pressed against his in a lingering kiss before she pulled away and walked toward the door.

"Stay with me."

She smiled. "Can't. You're too great a temptation for me, Mr. Gray, and you need sleep."

He needed her more. "You need a nap as much as I do, probably more." He knew Sam. She watched over him all night with a cat nap here and there.

"I'll sleep on the couch. Call out if you need me."

"Promise you won't leave the suite without waking me."

"You have my word. Let go and sleep, Joe. No one will slip past me."

Although he longed to hold her in his arms as he drifted off, the beautiful medic was a temptation to him as well. Joe needed to be mobile and functional. His gut said this killer was just getting started and Sam and his teammates were in the line of fire.

When Sam left the bedroom, he willed himself to relax. Sam was safe inside their suite where he'd hear if something happened. The ice packs and soft drink eased his discomfort enough for Joe to fall asleep. Sometime later, he woke to the sound of Nico's voice. Was the ship ready to dock or had something else prompted Shadow's leader to come to the suite?

Joe removed the packs of melted ice and carefully sat up. The room didn't spin and he didn't feel like throwing up. A definite improvement. After tying on his boots, he stood, breathing a sigh of relief. So far, so good. If the headache and nausea remained at bay, he'd be better able to protect Sam, Mercy, and his teammates.

He walked into the living room where his team leader sat in a chair. Mercy was on the couch with Sam. "Anything new?"

Sam jumped up and came toward him. "How do you feel?"

"Better." Ignoring their interested audience, he wrapped his arms around her and eased Sam to his chest. She fit perfectly in his arms. "Did you rest?"

She nodded.

Joe tightened his grip, pressed a kiss to her mouth, then sat with her and Mercy on the couch. "Where are we, Nico?"

"Thirty minutes from port. The feds are waiting for us to dock."

"Do we know who they sent?"

"Same bunch we dealt with in San Diego minus the SDPD detective and the Coast Guard. The FBI sent another agent with Brock this time."

Joe grunted. "Hope this one is more competent than Brock."

"Not holding my breath. Communications from the Maldonado group are heating up. They mentioned the name Hollingbrook."

Joe blew out a breath. Not what he wanted to hear. "The company or the man?"

"Both."

"Think they're the ones responsible for killing Janine Hollingbrook?"

Nico frowned. "It's possible, but that's not their standard procedure. They prefer to grab and go. I would have expected them to grab Janine and take off with her if they had a vendetta against Hollingbrook. Make him pay through the nose for his daughter's safe return."

"They never would have returned her, though."

Mercy turned to stare at her husband. "Why not? They want money. If he paid up, why wouldn't they release her?"

"You're right about the money. Hollingbrook would have paid them but the human trafficking group would have sold Janine to the highest bidder for a quick, tidy extra profit."

His wife shivered. "That sounds so cold."

"It's an ugly business, love. They profit on human suffering." He turned his attention to Joe. "Something about this doesn't feel right."

"Explain."

"I can't see the Maldonado group going after Hollingbrook personally or his business empire. If they're targeting the cruise ship passengers, why put him out of business? It's the perfect place to choose their next victims."

Joe considered the alternatives. "If Ferguson was still alive, I'd look at him. He'd strike a deal with Maldonado to get the result he wanted. When Hollingbrook Cruise Lines was bankrupt, the route could be taken over by another cruise line."

Sam frowned. "But Ferguson's not alive. What other alternative do you see?"

"We need to look at the rest of Hollingbrook's competitors, dig deeper into the backgrounds of the Hollingbrook executives. Maybe one of them has a hidden past that's forcing them to work with Maldonado. The strongest scenario is one of the executives is behind all the incidents and formed a partnership with Maldonado to make extra money and take down the high and mighty Mike Hollingbrook."

"I can't disagree with your reasoning, but why focus on one of the executives?" Nico asked. "Wouldn't they have the most to lose if Hollingbrook's company goes down?"

"They know everything about the cruise business, the ships themselves, and have access to every part of the ship. Who would raise an eyebrow if an executive took a cruise to see how smoothly things ran? A coincidence if he or she were on a ship when a passenger disappeared during one of the port visits."

Nico dragged a hand down his face. "And it would have been easy to stash the bombs aboard ship. Who's going to question one of Hollingbrook's executives? I didn't think to ask Zane to check for overlaps between the foursome's travel schedule and the disappearances. I'll contact him before the feds invade the Pacific Star."

"I don't want the culprit to be Charlaine or Lance," Mercy said. "Kayla deserves to have two parents who love her and are available when she needs them. What about Janine's murder? Weren't the executives on board the Pacific Star at the time?"

Joe shrugged. "Hired gun. If an executive is guilty, it's possible he or she pointed the human trafficking group her direction. Janine fought back. Perhaps the shooter concluded she was too much trouble and killed her instead of holding her for ransom."

She stared at him a moment. "You know, it's a good thing I trust Nico and the rest of Shadow to keep me safe. Remarks like that make me realize how vulnerable I am."

"We're all vulnerable." Sam laid her hand over Mercy's. "Look at Joe's fall down the stairs. The killer tried to injure Joe so he couldn't function as part of our team."

"We still have a two-pronged investigation," Joe said. "The two prongs might be working together or Hollingbrook might have had the misfortune to make a personal enemy and catch the attention of a vicious human trafficking ring. What's our next move, Nico?"

"Deal with the feds. They're waiting for us in Puerto Vallarta. The passengers will be questioned again before they're allowed to disembark. I wish I had another team at my disposal. We need eyes on the executives. If they aren't involved, they're targets."

"Ask Winestock to keep the executives on board until we're free to serve as their bodyguards. There's been a credible threat. Let's capitalize on that and keep them contained until we've been questioned."

"Good plan. I'll talk to Winestock." Nico rose and held out his hand to his wife. "Joe, Sam, I'll meet you in the security office. The interrogation room is the best place to answer questions from the feds. Trace and Ben will join us there." With that, he escorted Mercy from the suite.

"Are you hungry?" Joe asked Sam. He was starving and needed to eat while he could. He wouldn't have an opportunity for several hours once the agents were on board.

Sam's stomach growled, her face flushing.

He chuckled. "I'll take that as a definite yes. We have enough time for a quick meal."

Forty-five minutes later, Joe escorted Sam to the security office. A low rumble of heated voices greeted them as they walked inside.

Caleb glanced up from his desk. He inclined his head to the interrogation room. "Go on in. They're waiting for you. Good luck."

From the furious look on Special Agent Travis Brock's face, they might need Caleb's good wishes.

CHAPTER THIRTY

"Agent Brock." Joe nodded at the blond-haired man glaring at him. He ignored the show of temper and seated Sam before dropping into the chair next to hers. "Can't say I'm happy to see you again."

Ben, Curt, and Trace grinned behind the FBI agent's back. They leaned against the wall beside Nico, waiting to see how the interview played out. How could Brock sit with his back to the four operatives? Joe's skin would be crawling if he didn't know and trust the men.

A snort. "I'll bet. You just couldn't help yourself, could you, Gray."

He remained silent, figuring the other man would fill him in. Brock didn't disappoint him.

"You and your friends had to be heroes and dismantle deadly weapons when you should have called professionals to handle an unknown substance."

"Is your memory faulty, Brock?" Nico snapped. "We couldn't wait until you showed up. The timers were set to go off as we docked the ship. The safety of thousands of people was at stake. You couldn't dismantle the devices and contain them in time. I trust Ben to handle a bomb more than I trust you and your team. You're just ticked off because we took care of it without your permission. I'll remind you again that I don't work for you. I'm not answerable to you and neither is my team."

"The FBI has the authority to deal with the situation and the fallout from it, not you. Local law enforcement won't work with you."

"Do I look like I care? My wife is on board this ship. I'm not risking her life to pander to your ego."

The second FBI agent, a man in his mid-thirties with dark hair and eyes and skin tone that spoke of his Hispanic heritage, straightened from his position against the wall. "Lock up your ego, Brock," he said, his voice mild. "We have a job to do and so does the Fortress team."

The first agent turned and narrowed his eyes at his partner. "You know these people?"

"I know the man who created Fortress. Used to serve in the same military unit. Brent Maddox doesn't hire inept operatives. He's tough, disciplined, and knows his own limitations. He expects his people to exhibit the same qualities." The second agent turned to Joe and held out his hand. "Rafe Torres. Brent was my commanding officer."

Respect for the agent rose several notches. Rafe Torres was a Navy SEAL. He gripped the agent's hand. "Joe Gray. This is Samantha Coleman."

"I wish we'd met under better circumstances." A quick smile flashed. "I have stories about your boss I'd love to share. Makes my day to embarrass him."

"Next time you're in Nashville, look us up. I'll throw steaks and potatoes on the grill while you spill Brent's secrets."

"I'll do that."

Brock scowled. "If you're finished setting up a date, can we get on with this? I'd like to find out if these mercenaries had anything to do with planting explosives on this ship."

Winestock dragged a hand over his bald head. "You're way off base, Brock. Don't waste time chasing that crazy theory. Nico and his teammates are not your culprits."

A sneer settled on Brock's face. "You think you're in a position to tell me how to do my job? Get a clue, Winestock. You're just a rent-a-cop without any authority. I'm the one with a real badge."

"Enough," Torres snapped.

Brock's face reddened. "Fine. I've got a few years on you in the Bureau, Torres, but if you think you can get answers better than an experienced agent, go for it. You take the lead on this one."

Excellent. Joe saw satisfaction gleam in Torres' eyes when the SEAL turned his direction. Suited Joe to have Brent's battle buddy questioning them instead of his less-than-stellar sidekick.

"I imagine Nico's unit has more tasks to complete." Torres returned his attention to Joe. "We'll start with you and move on to Samantha, then the rest of your teammates."

"More teammates?" His co-worker looked stunned. "What teammates are you talking about? I thought there were only three of them."

Winestock rolled his eyes.

Joe snorted as he rested his arm across Sam's shoulders. Agent Brock was an idiot.

Torres stared at Brock. "There are six Fortress operatives in this room. How could you miss the other three?"

The first agent glanced around the room. He flinched when his gaze landed on Ben. Joe didn't blame him. Ben's eyes were ice cold and locked on Brock. His teammate had the death glare down pat.

Brock turned back to Torres. "I thought they were Winestock's people." He waved a hand at the SEAL. "Go on. Show me how good you are."

A muscle ticked in his jaw. "We have a lot of ground to cover in a short amount of time. Joe, let's start with you. Tell me what happened after the Pacific Star left San Diego."

Joe recounted the events of the past few days, ending with his fall and the nerve-wracking minutes when he'd helped Ben dismantle a chemical weapon.

Torres remained quiet until he was finished, then took him through the events again, stopping him occasionally to ask clarifying questions. When he finished, he asked Joe another question. "Have you seen this type of chemical weapon before?"

"Seen them, yes. Handled them, no. I had basic training in EOD when I was in the Rangers. Everything else I've picked up from Fortress, Ben especially."

"What's your specialty on this team?"

"Spotter."

Torres' eyes gleamed with interest. "Huh. So was I. Let's go back to the stairwell incident. Were you injured?"

Sam spoke up. "Joe has a concussion and stitches from his impact with the wall along with significant bruising."

"What's your role in the unit, Samantha?"

"Medic."

"A nurse?" Brock scoffed. "Figures."

Sam wrapped her hand around Joe's fist, holding him in place and silently asking him to let her handle the obnoxious agent. "I'm a medic. I have more training than a nurse, Agent Brock. I've performed field surgery while under fire. Can you say the same?"

His face flamed and he lapsed into silence.

Torres's hands were flat on the table, his gaze locked on Joe.

Waiting for him to make a move on his partner? He'd love to do just that but didn't fancy spending time in prison for the momentary satisfaction of punching Brock's face for insulting Sam. Joe had too many plans involving a certain beautiful medic. He didn't intend to waste years of his life without his lady by his side. He used a hand signal to tell Torres he was in control.

The SEAL gave a chin lift in acknowledgment and turned his attention to Sam. "Tell me what happened since the ship left San Diego from your perspective."

Sam complied, adding the medical details of Bianca's death and Joe's injuries.

Brock opened his mouth to spout something at Sam. From the expression on his face, his comment wouldn't be complimentary.

Joe pointed at him. "Don't say it. I won't tolerate anyone insulting Sam. You already got one free pass. You won't get another one."

Torres looked at Joe, a silent warning in his eyes. "Did you recognize the man in the stairwell, Samantha?"

Sam shook her head. "I saw a glimpse of someone in black, then Joe pushed me toward the wall as he fell."

"I saw the back of him as he ran up the stairs while I tumbled down them. Dark hair, six two, Caucasian, wearing all black. From the way he moved, this was the same man who killed Ferguson."

"How do you know it's the same man?" Brock's eyes narrowed with suspicion. "I thought you said you didn't recognize him."

"Security footage caught Ferguson's killer. He was careful not to show his face to the camera." Joe glanced at Torres. "None of the cameras caught his face."

"He knew where the security cameras were located."

"Looks like it."

"Inside job?"

Joe nodded.

"Have any suspects?"

"No proof."

"Tell me anyway."

"Another competitor of Hollingbrook or someone connected to Hollingbrook Cruise Lines."

"Why do you suspect a competitor?"

"Ferguson was the heir to Ferguson Cruises and would have been a direct competitor except the business went under and Mike Hollingbrook bought his father out. Tom wanted to save the business. His father sold it anyway. Not long after that, Kirk Ferguson committed suicide."

Torres whistled. "Excellent motive for murder and sabotage. Cold, hard revenge."

"Another competitor could try to take down Hollingbrook and his company for market share."

Brock snorted. "If you have all the answers, why is Ferguson dead?"

"His partner believed he was a weak link. The partner killed him to keep him quiet."

"The partner created the plan and planted chemical weapons on board the Pacific Star in his bid to destroy the cruise line. Maybe he was carrying out Ferguson's agenda or had a separate one of his own and used Ferguson as the patsy." Torres shook his head, expression grim. "Anything else I should know?"

Joe glanced at Nico. Should he tell the SEAL about the Maldonado group? They weren't sure the two prongs of the Fortress investigation were connected and Joe didn't want to send the feds in the wrong direction.

Shadow's leader gave a slight nod.

He told Torres about Maldonado's heightened communication level with the name Hollingbrook in their messages and the scout who had been photographing women as they boarded the Pacific Star.

"Oh, come on," Brock scoffed. "A human trafficking group? You're trying to create drama to get your names in the paper. What breathing man doesn't appreciate a beautiful woman?"

Torres pinned Joe with another warning look before turning to his partner. "We need to interview the Hollingbrook executives. Find a quiet place and question them."

Brock heaved himself to his feet. "Fine with me. I could use the fresh air." The senior agent stalked from the room.

"How do you stand to work with him?" Trace muttered.

"No choice."

"Turn in your badge and join Fortress," Nico said. "Brent would love to have you work for him."

The corners of Torres's lips edged up. "He's already made the offer. I'm thinking about it."

Ben stirred. "Stop thinking and do it. The perks include more money and better teammates. You won't regret it."

The agent gave a slight nod and turned back to Joe and Sam. "You can go. Stay out of Brock's way."

He shrugged. "May not be possible." Joe glanced at Nico. "Orders?"

"Find out where the executives are being interviewed. Stick close to Charlaine and Lance when Brock finishes with them. The killer already targeted Charlaine and the baby once. I don't want to give him another shot at them. They won't escape a second time."

"Yes, sir." He stood and helped Sam to her feet.

"Check in every hour."

Joe saluted.

In the corridor, Sam said, "I guess Nico concluded Charlaine isn't part of the plot to destroy Hollingbrook."

"She was on the bottom of my suspect list. I can't see Charlaine putting her daughter in danger. That still leaves the other three executives and who knows how many competitors who would love to take over Hollingbrook's market share."

They located Brock in the main dining room. He occupied a table in the corner with Charlaine sitting across from him. The agent recoiled at the loud scream from Kayla. "Can't you do anything about that?" he demanded of the frazzled mother.

"I told you this was her nap time. She's tired and hungry. I need to take care of her."

"I haven't finished questioning you. Where's your babysitter?"

"She's dead, killed by a crazy man in a steward's uniform."

"There has to be someone else capable of holding her for a few minutes," Brock said, clearly exasperated with this turn of events. "I'm hunting for a killer, lady. That's more important than your baby."

She gestured toward the other three executives cradling cups of coffee several tables away as they awaited their turn answering Brock's questions. "Kayla comes first for me. If you're in such a hurry to ask your questions, start with one of the others while I get her settled."

Sam looked at Joe. "I can look after Kayla while Charlaine talks to Agent Brock."

He glanced back to the agent and the mother, still arguing over Kayla's escalating cries. "Might be a good idea, especially for Kayla. Brock will blow our cover. He won't be able to resist the temptation to get back at us over the confrontation earlier."

"Maybe the truth will make it easier for us to protect Charlaine and her daughter."

Perhaps. Sometimes the truth made things more difficult, especially when emotions were involved. Sam and Charlaine had begun to form a bond. When the executive realized Sam had been playing an assigned role, she might feel betrayed.

Joe pressed his hand to Sam's lower back. "We should go before Charlaine punches Brock."

As they walked toward the corner table, Brock glanced up and scowled. "What are you two doing here? If you interfere with my investigation, I'll slap the cuffs on you and haul you off this metal tub."

Sam focused her attention on Charlaine and the baby. "Do you need help with your daughter? I'll be glad to watch her while you talk to Agent Brock."

The mother's eyes widened. "You know each other?"

"We've met," Joe said.

"We're busy here, Gray." Brock's eyes glittered. "If you want to be a glory hound, go somewhere else. I don't have time for a couple of mercenaries."

Charlaine's jaw dropped. The other executives twisted in their seats to stare at Joe and Sam, their expressions an odd mixture of disbelief and anger.

Joe sighed and exchanged a glance with Sam. "Told you," he murmured.

"What's he talking about?" Charlaine looked from Joe to Sam. "I thought you were in the Army."

"We were in the Army," Joe confirmed. "We work for Fortress Security now."

"We can talk about why we're on board the Pacific Star later." Sam held out her arms. "Let me help you with Kayla."

"I don't know if I can trust you with her. You lied to me."

"Misled," Sam corrected. "I'll take her to the other side of the dining room. You can see me but her crying won't bother Agent Brock. The sooner you answer his questions, the faster you'll have Kayla in your arms."

Lacking another option, Charlaine placed her daughter in Sam's arms. "Don't leave this room with her."

A nod. "I'll stay in your sight."

After Joe and Sam moved across the room, Brock resumed questioning Charlaine. The worried mother volleyed her glances between Sam and the FBI agent.

"Do you want to hold her?" Sam asked fifteen minutes later.

"I'd love to but I don't think Charlaine would be comfortable with me holding her baby."

More long minutes passed. Sam fed Kayla, changed her diaper, and patted the baby's back until she fell asleep.

When Brock finished questioning Charlaine, she rose and hurried toward Sam and Joe without glancing at Lance. Kayla's father, however, couldn't take his eyes from his girlfriend and daughter.

"Thank you for taking care of her for me."

"I'm sorry about the deception, Charlaine." Sam carefully shifted Kayla from her arms to the mother's. "We had a job to do. Playing the role of vacationing tourists was our cover story."

"Are you two really married?"

"Not yet," Joe said.

Sam's head whipped his direction, her eyes wide.

"We are dating, though. I'm not letting her get away."

Some of the stiffness in Charlaine's stance eased. "You're so lucky," she whispered, her own gaze darting to Lance who was still watching her while Dax made his way to the table to talk to Brock.

"What do you plan to do the rest of the day?"

"I want to see some of Puerto Vallarta." She smiled down at her sleeping child. "I can't be gone long and I don't want to be too far from her baby supplies. Carting around baby stuff is almost like moving. When we go anywhere together, I carry three times more stuff for her than I do for myself."

"Mind if we tag along?" Joe asked.

"Why would you want to?"

He shifted closer and lowered his voice. "We're worried about your safety."

Charlaine stared at him. "I don't understand."

"The steward who killed your nanny was named Tom Ferguson. Is the name familiar to you?"

"I know a Tom Ferguson. His father owned a competing cruise line. I can't imagine it's the same one, though."

Sam laid her hand on Charlaine's shoulder. "It's the same man. He wanted to hurt Hollingbrook and his business. He planned to use you to accomplish his goal."

"That doesn't make sense. I can't believe Tom's on board the ship and I haven't seen him." She motioned toward her co-workers. "If the others had seen him, they would have mentioned it. Have you arrested him?"

"We're not cops. We can detain, not arrest. We did detain him, but his accomplice killed him."

Blood drained from the woman's face. "He's dead?" She cast a glance Lance's direction, fear evident on her face.

He got to his feet immediately and came to her. The other men stared after him, speculation in their gazes. "What is it? What's happened?" Lance laid a hand gently on Kayla. "Is the baby okay?"

"She's fine. It's Tom Ferguson. He's been on this cruise. Someone murdered him, Lance."

Lance stared at Joe and Sam. "I haven't heard anything about it. Are you sure he was murdered?"

"No question."

The other man wrapped his arm around Charlaine's shoulder and drew her close to his body. "I need to get Charlaine and Kayla off this ship. Can you help me do that?"

"Depends," Joe said. "Are you talking about getting them away from the ship for a day at Puerto Vallarta or sending them home?"

"Home."

Charlaine shook her head. "I can't go home. You know Mike insists his executives take at least one cruise a year. I had to beg off the others because I was either pregnant or recovering from Kayla's birth. I need this job, Lance."

"No job is worth your life. Kayla needs her mother." He glanced around to be sure the other executives weren't within earshot and murmured, "I need you, honey. Please, for our sake, let me make arrangements for you to go home."

She turned to Joe and Sam, appeal in her eyes. "What do you think I should do?"

"Go home. Better yet, go on vacation somewhere with Lance and your baby. If you can't take more time off, hire a bodyguard."

"Why?"

Joe grimaced. "Ferguson didn't target Bianca. He was after you, Charlaine. If you had still been in the cabin when Ferguson showed up, you would be the one on the way to the morgue, not Bianca."

Lance cursed, then cupped his girlfriend's cheek with his palm and turned her face to his. "Charlaine, please. Kayla and I need you safe. If you won't go home for my sake, go home for Kayla's."

She leaned her head against his shoulder. "All right. I'll go if you come with me. If I'm a target, you might be, too. I couldn't stand it if something happened to you."

He dropped a kiss on her lips. "Deal." Lance turned to Joe. "I need my family away from here as soon as possible. Do you have any suggestions?"

"Let me make a call. I'll see what Fortress can arrange for you." Joe went out to the corridor and called Zane.

"Yeah, Murphy."

"It's Joe. I need a favor."

"Name it."

"We need to get Lance Farraday and Charlaine and Kayla Bennett out of Puerto Vallarta as soon as possible. We think Charlaine and possibly the baby are still targets for the killer."

"Hold." Sounds of Zane's fingers flying over his laptop keyboard came over the cell connection. "Bravo is returning from a mission in South America. I've rerouted them. They'll be on the ground in three hours at Gustavo Diaz Ordaz International Airport. Have Farraday and the Bennetts there with their belongings. Bravo will make sure they arrive in the US safely. Are they going home or somewhere else?"

"Preferably somewhere else."

"Find out if they like the beach. If they do, I'll arrange for them to stay in a condo on the beach front. If not, I'll work out something else."

"Thanks, Z."

"Yep. How are you?"

"Better. Sam did a great job."

"Not surprising. She's a top-flight medic. More important, she cares a great deal about you."

"I'll send you Lance and Charlaine's preferences in a couple minutes. Also, send St. Claire a message to keep an eye on Lance and Charlaine. If we find out they're involved in what's happening, he'll have to turn them over to the feds."

"Copy that. I assigned the geeks to your deeper background search on the executives and the security footage from the stairwell incident. I should know more in less than an hour." With that, his friend ended the call.

Joe returned to the dining room as Brock finished questioning Dax and called for Colt to join him at the table. He stopped at Sam's side. "All set, Lance. You're leaving Puerto Vallarta in three hours on board a Fortress jet. One of our teams will escort you to the States. Would you prefer a vacation at the beach or somewhere else?"

Charlaine's face lit up. "Beach. I'd love to take Kayla there."

He smiled. "Excellent. We'll arrange for a condo on the beach for the three of you."

Lance held out his hand. "Thank you."

"What's going on?" Dax strode up to them, a scowl on his face, his gaze locked on the other two executives.

"I'm getting Kayla and Charlaine out of here. They're not safe."

"You two look pretty cozy." He lowered his voice. "You know how Mike feels about his employees seeing each other."

"Tough," Lance snapped. "There are other jobs. I'll find another one if he fires me. The one thing I won't do is give up Charlaine or my daughter."

"Please don't say anything to Mike, Dax," Charlaine begged.

"I'm not the one you need to worry about." The executive inclined his head to the younger executive watching them with glittering eyes.

CHAPTER THIRTY-ONE

Sam folded Kayla's clothes and placed them in her adorable pink suitcase. She marveled at the tiny clothes. Sam hoped to pack clothes like this for her own daughter one day. Her lips curved. Maybe a daughter with dark hair and eyes like Joe's.

What had Joe meant when he said they weren't married yet but he wasn't planning to let her go? Did he mean what she hoped? As soon as Shadow finished this mission, Sam intended to find out. Not knowing would drive her crazy.

"How long have you and Joe been together?"

"We've worked together for five years. We recently started dating."

"He's in love with you."

Sam swung around to face Charlaine, hope unfurling in her heart. "How do you know?"

"His feelings are obvious every time he looks at you or touches you. That man adores you."

Was Charlaine right? "The feeling is mutual."

"You haven't told him how you feel?"

"Not yet."

"What are you waiting for?" The young mother snapped closed her own suitcase. "Don't let circumstances stop you from doing what's best for you and Joe."

"Will you take your own advice?"

A sad smile curved Charlaine's mouth. "I want to. I'm afraid to give up my job."

"You and Lance have a few days together to decide what you want to do. There are other jobs." She smiled. "In the words of a wise friend, don't let circumstances stop you from doing what's best for you, Kayla, and Lance."

Soft laughter. "Serves me right for offering unwanted advice."

"Would you marry him if he asked?"

"He already has. Several times." Her gaze shifted to Kayla. "I'm thinking about saying yes the next time he asks."

Sam glanced at her. "Maybe you should ask him to marry you this time. The beach vacation could be turned into a nice honeymoon for three."

Charlaine's eyes lit. "I might do that. He'd be surprised."

"And thrilled, I bet."

They finished packing Charlaine's and Kayla's belongings as a knock sounded on the door.

Charlaine turned to answer the door, but Sam laid a hand on her arm. "Let me make sure it's safe." She eased her Sig from the holster at her back and held it down by her side. A peek through the peephole showed Joe waiting in the corridor.

Sam slid the weapon away and opened the door.

"Ready?" Joe asked as he stepped inside the cabin, followed by Trace and Ben.

"Just finished."

The three men gathered the baby gear and Charlaine's luggage while she grabbed the diaper bag and her carry-on luggage. As she and Charlaine had discussed, Sam cuddled

Kayla close. She smiled as the little one melted against her shoulder. Such a sweet baby. Being Kayla's bodyguard was no hardship.

The group met Lance and Curt at the other end of the corridor and left the ship together. They walked to the car rental area where a large SUV waited on them. Lance and Charlaine climbed into the backseat with their daughter while the operatives loaded the luggage in the cargo area. Once Kayla was strapped into the car seat Zane had requested, Joe climbed behind the wheel and Sam hopped into the shotgun seat. With a wave at his teammates, Joe drove toward the airport.

Sam and Joe watched their surroundings and the mirrors. She breathed a sigh of relief when they arrived at the airfield without incident. A few more minutes and the little family would be safely off the ground.

Near the Fortress jet, Joe turned off the engine. "Wait here for a moment." He exited the SUV and scanned for potential threats to their passengers.

"Is this necessary?" Lance asked. "Our trip to the airport was unplanned."

Sam glanced back at him. "We don't know who masterminded the events on board the Pacific Star or what kind of connections he has. The feds know about our plans and Agent Brock isn't capable of discretion."

Joe pressed his phone to his ear. In less than a minute, three men exited the jet and crossed the tarmac to the SUV. Joe greeted Trent St. Claire, Bravo's leader, along with Cade Ramsey and Matt Rainer, two of his teammates.

Joe opened the back door of the SUV and extended his hand to Charlaine. "Let's get you and your family on the jet." In short order, the five men were loaded down with luggage and baby supplies. As they trekked across the airfield, Sam carried the baby while Charlaine hoisted the diaper bag and her own carry-on luggage.

One of the men dropped a stuffed rabbit. Charlaine hurried ahead of Sam to scoop the toy from the ground. Sam continued toward the jet, murmuring to the stirring baby, hoping Kayla wouldn't rouse until the jet was in the air.

She approached an area of shadows, the one place where the lights around the airfield didn't reach. Uneasy, Sam searched the darkened area even as she gave it a wider berth. Movement caused her to tighten her grip on the baby and quicken her pace. Ahead of her, Charlaine, Lance, and most of the operatives were near the jet's stairs. Joe turned back to wait for her and Kayla.

The alarm in Joe's face and a whoosh of air were Sam's only warnings before a hard arm gripped her waist and yanked her against a massive chest. The cold steel of a gun barrel pressed to her head.

Joe dropped the luggage he carried and drew his weapon. Charlaine cried out in fear. The other operatives freed their hands and drew their weapons, expressions grim and determined.

Joe slowly moved toward Sam and her captor. "Let her go, Flores, and you might leave this airfield alive."

Ice flowed through Sam's veins. Oh, man. Reuben Flores, the second-in-command of the Maldonado human trafficking ring. Why was he at the airfield? Why face off with armed men alone?

More feet shuffling in the darkness told Sam that Flores brought friends to the party. Careful to pitch her voice so Joe heard her words but she wouldn't scare Kayla, Sam said, "Tell your friends to drop their weapons and back away if they want to live, Flores."

Joe signaled Trent and the other operatives. They shifted position.

Flores's tight grip made breathing difficult for Sam. If she passed out, Kayla would fall.

"Your bodyguards won't shoot with you and the brat at risk," he said in accented English.

Her bodyguards? Sam's eyes locked with Joe's. Fear for her and the baby as well as grim determination to free them filled his eyes as he moved closer.

"Stop right there," Flores ordered.

"What do you want?" Joe kept his weapon trained on the thug at Sam's back.

A triumphant laugh filled the night air. "I have what I came for. Put down your gun."

Joe shook his head, shifting to the right, angling for a better shot. "Not going to happen. Let them go."

Flores snorted. "And give you a free shot at me? You must think I'm stupid."

Joe signaled Bravo to take Charlaine and Lance to safety. Flores believed Sam was Kayla's mother. If he learned the truth from the panicked mother, the trafficker would order his friends to grab Charlaine. At least Sam had a chance to defend herself. Charlaine wouldn't.

Kayla started to squirm and whimper.

"Shh." Sam tried to soothe the baby back to sleep to no avail. Kayla gave a few fretful cries. "Let my friend take the baby," she urged Flores. "A crying baby will draw attention you don't want."

"Shut her up before I do it for you," he growled.

"It doesn't work that way. The crying will grow louder the longer we wait. Please, she's just a baby. She can't help crying."

Flores uttered vile curses in Spanish. "If your man does anything but take the baby, the first bullet goes into your head. The second goes into his."

Matt Rainer spoke softly to Kayla's parents and hurried them inside the jet.

Sam looked at Joe, willing him to understand. "Take our baby."

"Gun on the ground first," Flores ordered Joe. "Do anything but take the brat and I put a bullet in your woman's head. Then my friends will kill you and your buddies."

Joe placed his Sig on the ground near his feet. "Take me instead of my girlfriend. I'll be your hostage."

The thug laughed. "You're not my type. Your woman, however, is exactly the kind of woman I want in my bed. Take your brat before I shut her up myself. Jorge, if her boyfriend disobeys my instructions, kill the brat. Diego, keep your attention on the boyfriend. If he twitches the wrong way, fill him full of lead."

Another man separated himself from the other shadowy figures on the tarmac and lifted his weapon. A moment later, a red laser light centered on Kayla. The second man trained his weapon on Joe's heart.

Panic and nausea built inside Sam. Joe wasn't wearing a vest. If Diego's bullet hit Joe's heart, the man she loved with every beat of her heart would die.

Sam tried to twist her body to shield the baby from danger. Flores's hold tightened enough that Sam was in excruciating pain and held completely immobile. Frustrated, she caught Joe's eye and shook her head slightly. Whatever went down on the tarmac, she wouldn't be able to help.

Joe glided further to the right by a few inches before he closed the distance between himself and Sam. "Easy, Flores. Don't hurt my daughter or woman."

The thug barked out a laugh. "You're more interested in your brat than your woman. What kind of man are you?" Flores stuck his face near Sam's hair and drew in a deep breath. "Maybe you aren't man enough to know what to do with her."

Joe's expression hardened as fury filled his eyes.

Although Sam felt as though she would barf any second, if she lost it, so would Joe. If he lost control, he was dead. Sam couldn't live with that. She couldn't live without him. Not knowing how else to help him maintain control, Sam signaled that she was okay. A total lie. Joe's eyes narrowed. Good. At least he was still thinking clearly.

When he neared, more of Flores's friends aimed their laser sights at Joe. One light centered on his forehead, another at his gut, still another at his groin. The weapon aimed at his heart didn't waiver.

"Don't," she mouthed to him.

"Don't ask me to do this," he murmured.

"Please. I have to know you and the baby are safe." If she was to survive the ordeal to come, Sam needed some hope to hold in her heart. When Kayla's wails increased in volume, she handed Kayla to Joe.

He wrapped his muscle-bound arms around the baby, covering her head with one hand, anguish burning deep in his eyes. "Hold on for me, baby."

"Always."

Flores jerked Sam tighter against his chest and slowly backed away from Joe. His buddies closed ranks and followed their boss, all their weapons pointed at Joe and Kayla. A glance told her the other Fortress operatives couldn't take out all Flores's associates without at least one of the thugs' bullets hitting Joe or the baby.

Vehicles screeched to a stop somewhere behind Sam and Flores. Oh, man. The men had a quick escape worked out. Sam broke out into a cold sweat at the thought of being alone with men who were part of the Maldonado trafficking ring. She knew what lay in store if Joe and the other operatives didn't reach her fast enough.

Flores tossed Sam inside an SUV and climbed in after her. She scrambled to the opposite door and yanked on the handle, desperate to escape before the vehicle was in motion. The door refused to open.

An ugly laugh from Flores. "Did you think me careless enough to let you escape?"

The driver handed a filled syringe to his boss.

Sam's heart rate soared into the stratosphere. "No!"

Flores backhanded her. Sam's head whipped to the left and slammed into the frame of the SUV, stunning her. Her captor grabbed her arm, shoved the needle into her vein, and depressed the plunger.

Sam fought against the effects of the drug. Wasted effort. In less than a minute, the world around her grew hazy. She regretted her own cowardice in not telling Joe that she loved him. Now she might never have the chance.

She slumped against the door. As the darkness closed in, she felt Flores's hard hand fist in her hair.

CHAPTER THIRTY-TWO

Joe boarded the Fortress jet and handed a still-crying Kayla to her frantic mother. He turned to find a wall of operatives. "Move. I'm going after Sam."

Trent shook his head. "Nico's orders are to wait for the rest of Shadow."

"Forget it. Flores has his hands on the woman I'm going to marry. I'm not leaving her with him one minute more than necessary."

"Going without backup and zero intel is a death sentence. How do you think Sam will feel if you die?"

"You don't understand." His gut screamed at him to get off this jet and rescue the love of his life. He couldn't leave her in the hands of the same trafficking ring that targeted her as a teen. "Would you wait for your teammates if Grace was in the hands of human traffickers?"

"I hope my fellow operatives would be stubborn enough and wise enough to force me to wait and formulate a plan so all of us survive. You're not thinking straight, Joe. Sam is a trained operative. She can handle herself."

"This same group took Sam captive when she was fourteen. I can't leave her in their hands. I swore they wouldn't touch her again." And he'd failed. When he rescued her, would she trust him to keep her safe from this point forward? He wouldn't blame her if she rejected him and his heart. If Sam walked away, she'd take his heart with her.

"Why did she let herself be taken?" Lance demanded. "I'm grateful my daughter is safe, but Sam is trained. She could have fought back and escaped or given you and the others a chance to rescue her. Why would she allow them to take her?"

"To protect me and Kayla. Seven weapons were trained on us and I'm not wearing a vest. Sam let them take her so they wouldn't kill me or your daughter." Joe's voice sounded thick as he fought to contain the rage and guilt. He had to force the chaos of emotion behind a brick wall to deal with later. If he didn't, Sam would die. Even if she ultimately rejected him, Joe couldn't live in a world where she didn't exist. She owned his heart even if she didn't know the truth.

He should have told her. Knowing how he felt would have given her more reason to fight to survive until he arrived. Now he might not have the chance.

No. He wouldn't think that way or he'd be paralyzed. Joe would reach Sam in time. He would accept no other outcome. As soon as their team was out of danger, he would tell Sam he loved her and beg her to give him another chance to prove himself worthy of her love. "Nico has fifteen more minutes. If he doesn't arrive by that time, I'm leaving without Shadow."

"I can't let you do that, buddy." Trent folded his arms across his massive chest and positioned himself to block the exit.

St. Claire had him by at least fifty pounds and seven inches. Didn't matter. No one would prevent him from going after the woman he loved. "You won't stop me. If I have to, I'll take down every member of Bravo."

Trent was silent a moment, assessing Joe's determination. He sighed. "Fifteen minutes. Let's use the time to come up with a plan."

The team and Joe met around the conference table and hashed out several ideas. Which plan they chose depended on the set up when they located Sam.

Joe called Zane five minutes before his deadline.

"Heard about Sam. What do you need, Joe?" was his friend's greeting.

"Activate Sam's tracker and send me the satellite link to track her movements."

Zane's fingers tapped on the keyboard. A moment later, he said, "Done. She's still on the move."

"Copy that. Anything you can tell me about the background of Dax and Colt?"

"Dax has quite a few drunk and disorderlies on his record, most of them around the times of his divorces. From all indications, he's loyal to Mike Hollingbrook and the company."

"And Colt?"

"On the surface, his background is perfect."

Joe stilled. "Too perfect?" Who didn't have a dent or two on their record? He'd had plenty of scrapes and close calls with law enforcement before he joined the military and law enforcement.

"The geeks checked into his background, including school records. None of the schools listed had heard of Colt Riley. On the surface, he's a model citizen. Dig deeper and you find out Colt Riley doesn't exist."

His grip tightened around the cell phone. "Send me everything you and the geeks discovered."

"Copy. Sam is a tough cookie, Joe. She'll be okay."

Joe's throat tightened again. "Yeah." He ended the call, praying his friend was right. Sam had to be okay. The alternative was unthinkable.

"News?" Trent asked.

"Zane activated Sam's tracker. She's still moving. Riley's background is raising red flags. The schools he claimed to attend have never heard of him."

"You have a contact aboard the ship?"

"Chief of security. Ben has Winestock's number."

"Have Winestock detain Riley. We'll chat with him after we spring Sam and deliver a little Fortress retribution."

While Joe called Ben for the information he needed, Trent and the rest of Bravo suited up.

"Talk to me," Ben greeted him when he answered his cell phone.

"Colt Riley's background is raising red flags. I want Winestock to detain him on board the ship. I need his number."

Ben rattled off the information. "We're five minutes out. Don't move from that jet, Gray. We have two SUVs. Curt and Mercy will escort Charlaine, Kayla, and Lance stateside. We have your gear and Sam's. You can suit up on the way. Four minutes out." He ended the call.

Joe blew out a breath. He was ready to jump out of his skin. Joe called Winestock. "Find Colt Riley and detain him."

"Is he behind this mess?"

"Possibly. Won't know for sure until we interrogate him." This wouldn't be an interview. If Riley was guilty, he'd murdered two people and was responsible for Sam's abduction. The Hollingbrook executive would spill every secret he ever knew by the time Joe and his teammates were finished with him. If Riley was guilty, they would find out. If he was innocent, Joe would move forward in the investigation. He wouldn't stop until the person responsible was revealed and Maldonado's group destroyed.

"Hold on a minute." Winestock's voice was muffled as he contacted the security member who'd been assigned to watch the executive. A moment later, the chief said to Joe,

"He's gone. That's on me, Joe. I didn't tell my people to follow the remaining executives if they left the Pacific Star. I'm sorry."

"So am I. The Maldonado group abducted Sam. If Riley is working with the human traffickers, he may be meeting with them right now." Riley would know the other men had screwed up and taken the wrong woman. If they learned the truth, Sam was dead.

Feeling as though the walls of the cabin were closing in, Joe strode to the exit and down the stairs to wait for his team. He wasn't surprised to hear footsteps behind him. One of the members of Bravo was ensuring he didn't leave the team behind.

His hands fisted. "Hold on for me, Sparky," he murmured. "Just hold on. I'm coming for you."

Two minutes later, twin sets of headlights appeared on the access road. Two vehicles raced toward the tarmac and skidded to a stop beside Joe's SUV. Operatives poured from the vehicles and hurried to unload Mercy's luggage and Curt's gear.

Joe ignored the activity. Instead, he found his gear and suited up. He added weapons to the arsenal he already carried on his person plus a second Ka-Bar, more ammunition, and his vest. Last, he attached the webbing for his comm system.

By the time he finished with his preparations, his teammates and Bravo were at the SUVs and the jet was powering up.

Nico held out his hand. "Give me the keys. You're not driving." He shook his head when Joe opened his mouth to protest. "We're wasting time. Keys."

Anxious to be gone already, Joe tossed his team leader the keys and climbed into the shotgun seat of the SUV. Trent and Liam, Bravo's sniper, climbed into the backseat as the jet taxied down the runway.

Nico led the caravan from the tarmac. "You're navigating, Joe. Where is she?"

Joe grabbed his phone and clicked on the link Zane had sent. "Still in motion. Turn right at the next intersection."

In between Joe's instructions, Nico and Trent discussed options, finally narrowing down their choices to two.

Joe glared at Trent over his shoulder. "I don't like either option. Too dangerous for Sam."

"They're the best choices we have."

"If we wait for full dark to fall, Flores and his cronies could hurt her. Maybe kill her." A full frontal assault into an unknown situation the moment they arrived on site didn't give Sam much better odds of surviving. An invisible knife stabbed him in the heart at that thought. He dragged a ragged breath into his lungs. "There has to be another way to do this."

"If you have an idea, I'm open to suggestions."

Joe wracked his brain for a better choice and come up with zip. "I want to assess the situation before I sign off on either plan." Listen to him talk as though he had a leadership role in either team. He was a spotter, period. As long as Nico was functional, Joe had no say in the plan chosen. Except this plan affected his life and the woman he needed more than air.

Nico slid him a glance. "You need to think with your head, not your heart. Sam's life isn't the only one at stake. The lives of two teams are at risk if we go in daylight. Samantha Coleman is as tough as nails. If we can't come up with a way to slip inside the building without being seen, we'll have to depend on her to handle the situation until we can reach her."

"I'll agree only if her life is not at immediate risk. The minute I know otherwise, all bets are off. No one will stop me from going after her."

"We'll be one step behind you."

The next hour passed in relative silence as Joe followed the electronic trail from Sam's tracker. He watched the flashing marker on the screen, waiting for it to move again. It didn't.

Joe's stomach tightened into a knot. "Hurry, Nico. They stopped moving." The operatives were twenty minutes behind the Maldonado group. Terrible things could happen in twenty minutes.

The SUV surged ahead. "Where?" Nico asked.

"Los Lobos."

"Send Zane the coordinates. If we're very lucky, one of the satellites will be in position to get us more intel."

Joe called Zane.

"What do you need?" was the tech guru's greeting.

"Satellite image of the following coordinates." He gave Z the information.

A minute later, Zane said, "Got it. I also sent you a map of the area. Looks like you have plenty of cover if you want to try a daytime operation to free Sam."

"Any clue how many people are in the area?"

"She's in a warehouse district. Looks like most of the warehouses are abandoned. In fact, the only building with vehicles nearby is the one Sam was taken to. Tell me you aren't going in there alone, my friend."

"Shadow and Bravo are working this as a joint operation."

"Excellent. What about Curt?"

"On the jet with Mercy, Kayla, Charlaine, and Lance. By the way, Charlaine and Lance love the beach."

"Great. I've already arranged for them to have a condo for a week in Gulf Shores. I'll book them seats on a commercial flight leaving from Nashville International Airport this evening."

"Thanks for arranging everything, Z."

"Yep. The Murphy Travel Agency is happy to be of service."

Joe gave a huff of laughter despite the growing anguish in his heart and ended the call after promising to keep Zane updated. He clicked on the first link in his email, then shared it with the members of Bravo, Nico, Ben, and Trace.

Liam and Trace conferred and chose high ground on two nearby warehouses that looked like the snipers would have an excellent line of sight into the building where Sam had been taken.

The last few miles, Nico and Trent refined the strategy they had chosen.

"Z said we would have plenty of cover." Joe checked his weapons one more time as Nico slowed and hunted for a safe place to park, one that wouldn't alert a passerby to their presence in the area.

"As long as the Maldonado group doesn't have surveillance cameras to pick up our movement, we might be able to go after Sam sooner. No guarantees, though."

Joe gritted his teeth to hold back the scathing retort on the tip of his tongue.

Nico parked inside one of the abandoned warehouses three blocks from their target location. The other two SUVs were parked in nearby abandoned warehouses. Wouldn't be smart for them all to park in the same location in case the hiding place was discovered.

As soon as Nico turned off the engine, the operatives left the vehicle. The rest of the teams joined them. "Shadow will take the right flank, Bravo the left. Liam, Trace, report in when you're in position. The rest of us will hold until then. Go."

The two snipers checked that the area outside the warehouse was clear, then melted into the shadows. Joe's body practically vibrated with tension and the clawing need to go to Sam. He shifted to the entrance of the warehouse to keep watch.

Five minutes later, Trace's voice came through the comm system. "In position."

Before long, Liam reported in, confirming he was also in position.

"Copy," Trent murmured to his teammate. "We're moving."

Finally. Joe fell in behind Nico with Ben at his back.

Shadow's leader glanced over his shoulder at Joe, a silent warning in his eyes. "Assessment only unless I say otherwise. Clear?"

He clenched his jaw as he nodded. The teams were taking too long. Who knew what was happening to Sam? He had to get to her before it was too late.

Joe silently willed Nico to move faster even though he knew fast movement drew the eye. One block from Sam, Nico held up his fist, signaling Ben and Joe to stop.

The team leader hugged the shadows as he crept closer to the corner of another abandoned warehouse. He peered around the corner, then eased back against the wall. He signaled his teammates to do the same.

Joe frowned until he heard a vehicle approaching. With his back pressed to the wall, he watched as the silver luxury SUV slowly crept past their location. From this angle, he couldn't see well enough to know the identity of the driver. The sticker on the bumper declared it a rental. The vehicle passed out of sight and the team resumed their careful approach to Sam's location.

Two minutes later, Trace's voice came over the comm system. "We have a problem."

"Sit rep," Nico snapped.

"Colt Riley just climbed out of a silver SUV and is heading into the warehouse."

Adrenaline poured into Joe's veins. "Nico." His voice came out strangled. The seconds were literally ticking away on Sam's life. If the Fortress teams waited any longer, Sam would die.

Shadow's leader ignored Joe. "Bravo leader, is your team in position?"

"Roger," came the immediate response from Trent. "Bravo team is ready to roll."

"Security?"

"No surveillance cameras," Liam said.

"One guard at the front and back entrances," Trace added.

"On my mark, take out the guards."

Both snipers acknowledged Nico's order.

"Shadow will be in position in one minute." Nico signaled Ben and Joe to follow him. At their designated location, Nico's gaze locked with Joe's. "Your only job is to get to Sam. The rest of us will take care of the garbage. Watch your six and use that ice you're famous for on missions."

Joe drew in a deep breath, sharpened his focus, and nodded at Nico. He was ready.

CHAPTER THIRTY-THREE

Sam woke to the realization that she was sitting in a wooden chair, her wrists cinched to the slats behind her back. The drug Flores shot into her vein had left her weak, dizzy, and sluggish.

She was in deep trouble. If Joe and the rest of her team didn't arrive soon, she wouldn't live to share another sunrise with the man of her dreams.

Sam let her head continue to hang and slowly flexed her hands and wrists. Flores had used zip ties cinched tight enough to cut off circulation. Not enough play in the bindings to slip her hands free to defend herself if the drug wore off fast enough. Patience didn't seem to be high on Flores's priority list which dropped Sam's chances of survival even further.

A cold sweat beaded on her back at being helpless again. Sam fought to control her heart rate. Giving in to panic wouldn't help her rescue herself if her team couldn't find her in time. At least Flores and his cronies didn't know they'd grabbed the wrong woman. That was one of the only reasons she was still alive. The moment that changed, Sam would be fighting for her life with her feet and the chair she was tied to.

If Flores learned of his error, the mercenary-minded man might be inclined to take her for himself or sell her at an auction, ridding himself of the problem and still profiting from the mistake.

Her hands fisted. Flores was in for a surprise if he thought she would give up. The Army and Fortress had spent a fortune training her to handle every conceivable situation. She would fight. Hard. Sam wanted the life she dreamed of with Joe Gray and no two-bit Neanderthal was going to take that life from her.

She opened her eyes to slits and blinked at the sunlight streaming into the room. Concrete floor. Sam cut her gaze to the left, then right without moving her head. Scarred wooden walls. Echoing interior. Musty smell of disuse. A warehouse?

Still no sound in the room to indicate she had company in her prison. She needed more intel to formulate a plan. Sam raised her head and took in her surroundings. The room was large and barren of furniture aside from her chair. No bars on the window. If she freed herself from the zip ties, she could escape through the window and run for safety.

Maybe Flores hadn't confiscated her phone. The cargo pockets were deep. If he didn't search her while she was unconscious, he wouldn't know she had access to help.

Sam shifted her leg until the pocket where she'd hidden her phone nudged against the chair frame. Something hard pressed against her leg. Relief had her muscles relaxing a fraction. Thank God. She still had her phone.

What about her Sig? Had Flores and his goons found her weapon? Sam shifted her leg. The holster was empty. All right, then. No gun. She had a knife hidden in her boot. That was something, at least. Not her choice of weapon.

Knives were for close contact confrontations. Based on the way she felt, Sam would be better off not engaging in hand-to-hand combat. For now, anyway. Already her head felt clearer. If she had a few more minutes, Sam might be able to take on Flores and company.

Her lips curved. Good thing she had trackers embedded beneath her skin. Sam had no idea where Flores had taken her.

Was the drug in her system habit forming? No need to worry at this point. If he'd hooked her body on the drug, she'd detox her system after she was free. She thought about the plan of treating herself and reconsidered. Might be best to go to Dr. Sorenson's clinic in case something had happened while she'd been knocked out or Flores had used a dirty needle.

Sam fought down the nausea boiling in her stomach. No. She couldn't lose it. Everything hinged on her being able to think and act when the opportunity presented itself.

She froze as the sound of male voices filtered through the flimsy door. Flores's voice she recognized immediately. The second man's voice sounded familiar but she couldn't place it.

"Good work." The second male laughed. "I can't believe you grabbed her despite the two bodyguards with her. Guess that Fortress group is all hot air, boasting how good they are."

"I'm better," Flores said.

"Is the auction set up?"

"Not yet."

A pause. "Why not? I told you to take care of it immediately. That's what I'm paying you for."

"What do you care what happens to the woman as long as she never surfaces again? You paid me to take care of her. I plan to do that. After."

"After what?" The second man's voice rose.

"After I take what I want. She's very beautiful. With my personal training, she will bring a great price if I decide to sell her." A laugh escaped. "I might keep her for myself."

"We had a deal."

"You made demands. I never agreed to them. What's done is done. The woman is no longer your concern. She is my property now."

Fury burned in Sam's gut, blasting away the nausea. She was no man's property. As for training? Flores was in for a shock. Given the opportunity, she would kill him without an ounce of regret. That sick cretin would rue the day he'd laid his hands on her.

At least he hadn't killed Joe or Kayla. Sam knew in her heart Joe was coming for her. The skin under her right shoulder blade burned as another tracking tag was activated. The warmth reminded her that Shadow had her back. She had to survive until help arrived or she could free herself from this building and disappear into the shadows.

"If she ever sees the light of day again, I'll destroy you and throw you on the not-so-tender mercies of your boss. Maldonado and I have a profitable arrangement going. He won't be happy if something interferes with the supply of women."

A long pause. "A wise man wouldn't threaten me. My enemies don't live long."

Flores's voice had dropped and taken on a dangerous edge. Did the other man hear it? Suited Sam's purposes if there was dissension between the men. Better for Sam if they turned on each other instead of her.

"Take me to the woman," the second man demanded. "I want to tell her why she's going to suffer before I get out of this stinking town."

A loud growl. "Careful, my friend. Los Lobos is my hometown. It is dear to my heart. For the sake of your health, choose your words carefully."

"The woman. Now."

"This way."

The men's footsteps drew closer. Sam raised her head and stared at the door, mentally preparing herself for the confrontation to come.

Flores threw open the door and stepped inside first. A moment later, Colt Riley entered the room. His gaze swung to her. The triumphant expression on his face faded, replaced by shock, then fury.

He swung around to face Flores. "Is this some kind of joke or a ploy to milk more money from me? It won't work, Flores."

Maldonado's man frowned. "You told me to capture the woman with the baby and take her to a safe place."

Riley shook his head, his glittering gaze locked on Sam. "This is the wrong woman, you dolt. This is Charlaine's bodyguard. She's married to another bodyguard who is as solid as a brick wall and could easily take down both of us without breaking a sweat." Fear glimmered in the depths of his eyes. "Are you sure her husband didn't follow you here?"

A snort. "No one followed. My men made sure. We are safe for the moment." Left unspoken was the threat that they might not be secure for much longer.

Riley was afraid of Joe. Good. Given half a chance, Joe would kill this worm if she didn't get to the executive first. "Surprise, Riley or whatever your name is. Screwed up, didn't you?"

"Shut up." Riley covered the distance between them in six strides and backhanded her with his fist.

Her head whipped to the side. Pain exploded in Sam's cheekbone. She blinked back the sting of tears, unwilling to give Riley the satisfaction of knowing he'd hurt her.

She turned back to glare at him. "You're the one behind the trouble at Hollingbrook Cruise Line."

Riley smiled. "Very good, Sam. And not only the problems plaguing the cruise line."

"You killed Janine Hollingbrook."

"Not directly. My friend, Maldonado, took care of the job for me."

"How much did you pay his organization?"

A laugh. "Not a penny. We have an arrangement. When I take over Hollingbrook's cruise line, Maldonado's people will cruise for free and have a chance to peruse the merchandise."

Disgust filled Sam. This lowlife would run a floating human trafficking market. "It doesn't bother you that these women won't have a life if they're taken?"

He shrugged. "Won't be my problem. Maldonado's men won't take them directly from the ship. The women will disappear when they're visiting a port. All kinds of bad things happen when tourists stray from the safe areas of a city."

"Why kill Janine? What did she do to you?"

"Nothing except have Mike Hollingbrook as her father."

"You murdered an innocent woman to hurt Mike."

Fury darkened his eyes. "My father is dead because of him. He was a good man and Hollingbrook destroyed him. I'll take everything he cares about away from him, then kill him."

"Who is your father?"

"Kirk Ferguson. Tom was my brother."

Shock rolled through Sam. According to the research she and Joe had conducted earlier into Ferguson, Tom was his only offspring. "Tom was an only child."

A scowl marred his face. "My mother had a short affair with Kirk. I'm the result of their fling. My father loved his wife and didn't want her to know the affair. He supported my mother and me financially in return for us staying in the background and remaining silent. His name isn't on my birth certificate because Kirk's wife wasn't in good health. He feared the news might kill her. She desperately wanted a second child and her health prevented her from carrying another pregnancy to term. While she was recuperating from one of the miscarriages, Kirk met my mother."

"Who are you?"

He stared at her a moment. "I suppose it won't hurt to tell you. You won't be able to divulge the information to anyone who will listen. Flores knows to keep his mouth shut. If he decides to sell you, you'll be too broken to spill what you know and your buyer won't care. My name is Wade Andrews."

The name sounded familiar to her. She wracked her brain to remember where she'd heard or seen his name. Must have been during Shadow's research into the backgrounds of their suspects.

The memory piece fell into place. "You were lower-level management at Ferguson Cruises for a while." Didn't make sense for Ferguson to give his illegitimate son a job when he'd insisted no one know of their relationship. "Why did Ferguson hire you? If he wanted to maintain that distance between the two of you but give you a break, he should have helped you find a job in another company."

Andrews laughed. "He did. When it became apparent that I had inherited my old man's business savvy in the cruise industry, he made a few phone calls and got me a job with Hollingbrook. Didn't hurt that I'd crossed paths with him several times. Hollingbrook hired me on Kirk's recommendation and I worked hard enough to earn fast promotions."

Sam frowned. "Don't you see what Kirk did?"

His smile faded. "What do you mean? He helped his son find a job. Kirk was a great father."

A great father didn't ignore his own son and refuse to acknowledge the blood relationship to the world. "Kirk's wife died a few years ago. What kept him from acknowledging you then?" She shook her head. "You're lying to yourself, Andrews. Old Kirk helped you get a job with his competition so you wouldn't be a threat to Tom's position in the company. You were the one most like him. You had the ambition. But Tom was the acknowledged heir. Kirk protected his legitimate son over you."

Andrews backhanded Sam on the opposite cheek with his fist. Great. She'd have matching bruises on her cheeks. Sam blew hair away from her eyes and turned toward the angry executive again. "Feel better beating up on a defenseless woman?"

Flores chuckled, his eyes glowing with heat. "This one, she has spirit. I look forward to taming her."

"You're a fool, Flores." Andrews sneered. "You'll never train this woman. She'll die before she becomes your slave."

Andrews wasn't as stupid as he seemed. Sam knew her teammates were close. She just had to stall. "Why did you kill Tom?"

"Weak link. He would have talked. I don't intend to spend time behind bars." He folded his arms across his chest. "Now, where is Charlaine?"

Sam shrugged. Another blow from his fist rocked the chair. She sucked in a breath. When she was free, Sam would take this abusive jerk down.

"Try again, Sam." Andrews smirked. "I can keep this up all night."

"No," Flores said, voice sharp. "She is my property and I have plans for her this night."

"After I get answers to my questions," the executive insisted.

"Why do you want Charlaine?" Sam's face swelled where his blows had landed.

"Hollingbrook assigned guards for her and still she's vulnerable. If she's taken, no one will be safe. The downfall of the man himself and the company he built will be a sweet reward as I avenge my father's death at his hands."

Outside the warehouse, two rifles fired.

CHAPTER THIRTY-FOUR

The second Liam and Trace fired their sniper rifles, taking out the guards at the front and back doors, Joe sprinted for the window near the corner of the warehouse where Sam was being held, Ben and Nico at his back.

He peered through the window, thankful this side of the building was in the shadows cast by the warehouse next door. An enemy soldier would have to walk by the narrow alley and look right at them to see the operatives.

The room on the other side of the glass was empty. Excellent. "Room clear," he whispered into his comm system. Joe tried lifting the window. Locked.

When flashbangs exploded inside the building followed by shouts and screams, he smashed the glass with his gloved fist. Joe reached up and unlocked the window. Within seconds, all three operatives were inside the room, weapons up and ready in case one of the traffickers pinpointed the location of the noise and raced into the room.

No one came. Bravo team's distraction was giving Joe, Nico, and Ben the chance to find Sam.

Joe crossed the room and eased the door open a crack. No movement yet. That would change soon. They needed to move. This warehouse was at least 10,000 square feet and Sam's captors now knew they were under attack. He prayed they didn't panic, kill her, and run. That possibility was why Joe had been against this plan from the beginning. Riley showing up at the warehouse had forced his hand and those of his teammates. Time had run out to come up with another option.

He eased the door open further. Mission clock ticking in his head, Joe signaled Nico and Ben. The three operatives exited the room. Nico indicated he and Ben would take the rooms on the right side of the corridor while Joe searched the ones on the left. He cleared room after room, growing more frustrated with every minute that passed with no sign of Sam. Fear beat at him. Where was she? He closed the door to the last room, glanced at Nico, and shook his head. "Clear."

"Same. Second floor."

Joe led the way to the stairs and stepped into the stairwell. A second later, he saw movement on the landing, aimed, and fired. One of the Maldonado soldiers fell to the floor with a bullet in his heart, his sightless eyes staring into Joe's.

He rushed up the remaining stairs to the second-floor landing and eased the door open. Joe grimaced. "Three heading this way," he murmured.

Nico motioned for Ben to take position on the right wall. Joe took the left wall, bashing the dim light bulb with the butt of his Sig. Shadow's leader crouched on the stairs, nearly invisible in the darkness. "Ben and I will take care of these clowns. Find Sam. She's your only priority."

"Roger that."

The wooden door burst open and three men surged into the confined space. Nico dropped the first man with a shot to the forehead. Joe shoved the third man toward Ben and slipped into the corridor, Sig up and tracking. He turned off the lights. The operatives hadn't had time to cut the power with Riley showing up unexpectedly. Turning off the lights made him more difficult to spot.

A grim smile curved his lips. As long as Maldonado's people left the lights off. The moment the lights came on, Joe would be a prime target with limited places to dive for safety.

He moved swiftly to the first door on the right and renewed his search for Sam. Three rooms later, he heard booted feet running toward him. Not one of his teammates since they were trained to move in silence.

Joe pressed his back to the inside wall of the room he'd been searching, leaving the door ajar to see and hear what was going on. A male voice called out to Ruben as he ran down the corridor to the farthest room in the corner.

His hand tightened around the hand grip of his Sig. Was the thug calling out to Ruben Flores?

A door opened. "Jorge, what is it? What's going on?"

Joe's lips curled. He recognized that voice. Was Sam with the sleaze ball?

"We're under attack. There must be at least fifty men."

He frowned. How did nine operatives become a contingent of fifty men?

"Do you recognize any of them? Are they from a rival group?"

"No, sir. I've never seen them before. They're everywhere, Ruben. Inside and outside. We're dropping like flies."

"Don't panic, you idiot. Go help Garcia and the others. Keep them away from this room. I want one of them captured alive. The rest you can kill. Maldonado will want to know what group they're from so he can make them pay for daring to mount a raid in his territory."

"What about the woman? Do you need help?"

"I'll take care of her. No one is taking my prize. I'll kill anyone who tries. Go. Help the others." A door slammed shut.

No locks engaged. Perfect. Made breaching the corner room that much easier. Joe holstered his Sig, grabbed his Ka-Bar, and moved into position. As soon as Jorge passed him, Joe exited the room and moved behind the soldier. He clamped a hand over the man's mouth and dispatched him with a blade to the kidney. If he could have secured the man without the chance he'd alert Flores to Joe's presence, he would have chosen to restrain Jorge. But Sam's life was at stake. To save her, he'd take out as many men as necessary without one second of regret.

Joe dragged Jorge's lifeless body into the closest room. Although he longed to storm the corner room and retrieve his woman, Joe's discipline won out and he continued to search the remaining three rooms in silence. Leaving his back exposed to an enemy combatant could get both him and Sam killed and that wasn't acceptable.

As he shifted closer to the corner room, he heard two male voices arguing. Satisfaction bloomed in his gut. Riley, the weasel, was inside this room along with Flores. Were there other people in the room? He prayed Sam was in there.

Joe palmed his Sig again. He gripped the doorknob and twisted. Joe pressed his back to the wall and opened the door a crack. His gaze connected with Sam's in the dim light of the room. She flicked her gaze to each of the two men who were cursing at each other, then she looked back at him.

He nodded. Just Flores and Riley in the room. Joe held up his hand and counted down. He kicked the door open and nailed Flores between the eyes.

At the same time, Riley raised his weapon and aimed at Joe. Sam slammed the heel of her boot into Riley's knee. A loud, sickening crack sounded in the room. The

Hollingbrook executive screamed, dropped the gun, and fell to the floor. He clutched his knee and writhed in agony.

Joe picked up the man's weapon, shoved it into the waistband of his pants, and completed a quick search to be sure Riley didn't have more weapons.

That finished, Joe glanced at Sam and froze when he got a good look at her face. Someone had beaten her. Fury exploded in his gut. "Who hit you?"

"Doesn't matter. Cut me loose so I can help."

"Sam."

"Joe, please. More of Flores's men could arrive any minute."

With a growl, he crossed to her side in two strides and used his Ka-Bar to slice through the zip ties holding her to the wooden chair. After sheathing his knife, he activated his mic. "Sam is secure."

"Copy," Nico responded. A gunshot sounded over his comm system. "Heading your way. Enemy reinforcements will arrive soon."

Joe cupped Sam's chin in the palm of his hand. They didn't have much time. "Who hit you?"

Her gaze cut to Riley.

He pressed a gentle kiss to her mouth, dropped his hand, and stalked toward Riley. The executive would be sorry he'd ever laid a hand on the woman Joe loved. He straddled the moaning man and punched Riley's face repeatedly in the same places where Sam was swollen and bruised.

A moment later, he shrugged off the hard hands attempting to drag him off Riley. Joe landed another punch, one that broke the other man's nose.

"Enough, Joe," Nico snapped. "He's down and we need to clear the area before we have to fight our way out."

The red haze clouding his mind and vision slowly faded. He drew in a deep breath, glanced at his team leader, and lifted his hands, palms out. "I'm done."

Ben whistled softly from the hallway. "Wow, buddy. That's a boatload of rage you unleashed on this clown."

"He's lucky I didn't kill him for what he did to Sam."

The EOD man swung around, his eyes narrowing when he saw the damage to her face. He strode inside and kicked Riley's injured knee, setting off another round of keening wails from the man before he slid into unconsciousness.

Nico scowled. "Haul him up and let's clear out. The feds will be interested in talking to Riley. Bravo leader, we're moving."

"Copy. On your six."

Ben used zip ties to secure Riley's hands behind his back and threw him over his shoulder in a fireman's carry. He fell in behind Nico who led the way from the room.

Joe followed with Sam at his side. "You armed?"

"Boot knife."

He handed her his backup weapon. "Aside from the bruising I see, are you hurt anywhere else?" When she was silent, an invisible band tightened around Joe's heart. What had the jerks done to her in the past two hours? "Talk to me."

"I need to see Sorenson."

Joe sucked in a breath. No. Pain speared his heart. What had his failure cost the women he loved? "What happened?"

"Flores drugged me as soon as we left the airport. I was out until a few minutes before Riley arrived and started interrogating me."

The thought of what could have happened to her while she was unconscious would haunt Sam for a long time. Joe swallowed hard against the lump in his throat. He'd royally screwed this up. Instead of protecting her like he promised, the woman he loved might have been raped because he failed. "I'm sorry, baby. If anything happened, it's on me."

"Stop," she said, her voice soft. "We couldn't have known. We took every precaution and had Bravo as backup. It's not your fault Flores threatened to kill an innocent baby. His mission was to grab Charlaine. Riley told him to grab the woman with the baby. I guess he didn't show Flores a picture of Charlaine. Riley's real name is Wade Andrews. Kirk Ferguson had a short affair with Wade's mother. Wade was Tom's half-brother."

"Z is the best at research. Why didn't he discover the connection?"

"Kirk wasn't listed as Wade's father on the birth certificate and he never acknowledged the relationship in public."

Twice on the trek through the building, Joe, Nico, and Sam dispatched more of Flores's men. Finally, the operatives from both teams met at the front of the warehouse. They covered the three blocks to the SUVs at a fast jog.

"I need to be with Andrews," Sam said. "He needs medical care."

Joe scowled. "Let him suffer."

She laid a hand on his arm. "You know I can't do that."

Yeah, he knew. Just didn't like it. He climbed into the backseat of their SUV. An unconscious Andrews slumped in the seat between Joe and Sam. If he so much as looked at Sam the wrong way much less tried to hurt her again, Joe would finish what he started.

On the return trip to the Pacific Star, Nico called Trent and put the call on speaker. Ben did the same with his call to Trace. With the rest of the team listening in, Sam reported everything she'd learned from Wade Andrews, then answered questions from the other operatives.

When they were satisfied, Nico called Maddox, reported the latest, and asked the Fortress CEO to have Torres meet them outside the terminal in Puerto Vallarta. With a glance at Sam in the rearview mirror, Nico said, "Brent, we need Sorenson down here."

Their boss was silent a moment. "Talk to me, Sam."

She flinched.

Joe cupped her jaw gently and turned her bruised face toward him. "Tell him."

Sam pressed a kiss to the center of his palm and held his gaze as she told Maddox the details she remembered and her health concerns.

When Maddox spoke again, his voice was edged with steel. "I'll have Sorenson down there in a few hours. Nico, I'll clear it for Bravo and Shadow to board the Pacific Star. Wait for Sorensen's arrival there. Once he's taken care of Sam, we'll arrange for a base of operations outside Puerto Vallarta. Fortress is taking down Maldonado and his crew. Permanently. If Sorenson says Sam isn't able to complete this operation, I'll have another medic flown in."

"Yes, sir." He ended the call soon after.

"I'm fine, Nico," Sam insisted. "I'm just bruised."

"As long as Sorenson agrees, you're good to go."

Throughout the remainder of the journey, Sam administered aid to Andrews and monitored his condition. While she focused on Andrews, Joe used chemically-activated ice packs on her face.

When the operatives walked up to Torres with Andrews slung over Ben's shoulder, the FBI agent pushed away from the terminal wall, his eyebrows soaring. "What happened to him?"

Joe tightened his grip around Sam's waist. "He ran into my fist a couple of times."

Torres gave a huff of laughter. "More than a couple from the looks of it. What did he do?"

"He's behind all the trouble on the Pacific Star, including the murders. He also made the mistake of touching Sam."

The agent pulled off his sunglasses, his gaze assessing the damage to Sam's face. His lips thinned. "I would have killed him if he'd touched my woman."

Joe shrugged. "Nico thought you might want some answers. If you don't, I'll finish the job."

The agent's lips curved. "Sorry, man. Too late now." He glanced at Nico. "Sit rep."

Shadow's leader gave him a scaled-down version of events and signaled Sam to tell him the details of Andrews's confession.

Torres growled. "Idiot. All this death and terrorism for revenge. Does he need a hospital?"

"Yes," Sam said. "He'll be hospitalized a couple days at least."

"Plenty of time for interrogation before we take him to the US and charge him." Torres held out his hand to Nico. "Appreciate the help." He grinned. "Didn't fancy crawling through the jungle to chase him down. When is your team going home?"

"Not sure yet. We still have a job to do. Maddox is flying in a doctor to treat Sam. After that, we'll clean out a viper's nest."

CHAPTER THIRTY-FIVE

In the private exam room on board the Pacific Star, Sam eyed Ted Sorenson, the Fortress physician who frequently patched up more serious operative injuries than the medics could handle. He gathered the last pieces of his medical equipment and stored them in his bag. Why wasn't he talking? The longer he remained silent, the more nervous she became. "Tell me."

"I won't have definitive information for you until I run your blood work. Based on what you told me, I think Flores gave you a sedative."

"Must have been a small dose since I was out for a short time." She swallowed hard, dreading the answer to the next question. Facing the truth was better than believing a lie. "Was I raped while I was unconscious, Doc?"

"I didn't see signs of sexual assault. I'll test the evidence I gathered for the rape kit and give you an answer as soon as I can. In the meantime, take it easy for a few days and make liberal use of ice packs. You're going to be colorful for a while." He winked at her. "Let's hope no one decides Joe put those bruises on your face and tries to teach him a lesson in how to treat a lady."

Sam's eyes burned. How would she survive until his phone call? "Thanks for coming," she choked out. "I owe you one."

"The best way to repay me is to steer clear of my clinic. Stay healthy and uninjured." Sorenson hoisted his mike bag to his shoulder. "You will be all right. I'll make sure of it. Now, I have four-legged patients who need me. I'll be in touch soon, Sam." With those parting words, he left.

Sam closed her eyes, frustrated with the lack of answers. Now the waiting began. A few tears spilled down her cheeks. Gingerly brushing them away, she grabbed tissues from the dispenser and blotted her face dry only to have more tears stream down her face. So much for being a tough cookie.

The door to the exam room opened. She knew without turning Joe had entered the room. Hard hands cupped her shoulders and turned Sam.

Joe drew her into his arms and held her tight. He said nothing, just stroked her hair with one hand and anchored her against his body with the other. When the tears finally stopped, Joe pressed more tissues in her hand.

After she dried her face for the second time, Joe captured her mouth for a series of long, drugging kisses. By the time he lifted his head, Sam's tears had complete dried up.

"Ready to talk?" His thumb brushed over her bottom lip.

Sam nodded. Although he acted as though he wasn't in a hurry to have answers, the worry in his eyes told a different story. "Sorenson took blood samples and did a rape kit. He'll let me know the results as soon as he has them. He thinks Flores gave me a sedative. Sorenson didn't see signs of rape but he won't know for sure until he has the kit results back."

He cupped her nape. "No matter what the results are, I'm in this with you. I love you, Sam. Nothing will change that."

"I love you, too." She bit her lip and glanced him through her lashes. "What if…" Sam couldn't bring herself to say the words. Would he still love her even if the worst had happened?

"We'll handle it. We'll go to counseling together and work through this as a team." He pressed a tender kiss to her mouth. "I'm so sorry. I promised you none of Maldonado's men would touch you and I broke that promise. Can you forgive me?"

She wrapped her arms around his waist and squeezed. "We took every precaution. Sometimes it's not enough. This time it wasn't."

"It's my job to protect you. How can you still trust me at your back after my colossal failure?"

"I trust you with every fiber of my being, Joe. You are the only man I will ever trust completely. We'll watch each other's backs, like always, and spend a lifetime loving each other."

"I don't know what I did to deserve you, but I'm more grateful than I can express. I adore you, Sam Coleman." Another gentle kiss, then, "As much as I would love to keep you to myself and hold you for hours, Nico and the others are waiting in the suite. We have a mission to plan." A determined glint filled his eyes.

She and Joe returned to the suite. As soon as they waked inside, the men in the living room fell silent. "I don't know anything for sure," she said. "Sorenson took blood and ran several tests. He'll tell me as soon as he knows anything. I'll let you know when I hear."

Liam stared at Joe.

He lifted his and Sam's entwined hands and kissed the back of hers. Bravo's expressions were priceless, ranging from shocked to satisfied. "If the rape kit tests positive for sexual assault, I will hunt down and kill every man who touched her."

The rigid stances of the men in the two teams relaxed at his words. "You'll have all of us at your back when you do," Cade said, a hard light in his eyes. "No one hurts one of ours and gets away with it."

Sam drew in a shaky breath, overwhelmed by the unconditional support of the finest people she'd ever worked with. To go from no family to a large group of operatives who would put their lives on the line for her left Sam shocked at their loyalty to a co-worker.

Nico eyed Sam. "Did Sorenson clear you to work?"

"He didn't tell me I couldn't. I'm taking that as a yes."

Matt Rainer, Bravo's medic, rose and walked out of the suite. He returned a moment later with a container of ice and made ice packs. "Stretch out on the couch. We need to reduce the swelling and pain. You can listen and contribute ideas to the plan while the ice works."

She complied, knowing the other medic was right. She would have insisted on the same treatment for one of her teammates. Besides, her face throbbed. When she laid down, Joe sat on the floor near her head and held the ice packs in place.

Nico called Zane and put the phone on speaker. "You're on speaker with Bravo and Shadow, Z. What do you have for me?"

"Communication is fast and furious between Maldonado and his lieutenants. The old man is threatening to gut each of his leaders himself if they can't come up with the name of the organization who sanctioned the hit on his facility. I sent information on the Maldonado compound to your email accounts. I also sent the satellite images. Latest head count is sixty men. No walls around the compound itself. However, the area is heavily patrolled, especially around Maldonado's house. Rumors abound on the Net about a shipment of women being prepped for sale in three days."

Sam's hands fisted. Prepped for sale. Mild term for the horror those women were enduring at the hands of men who sought to profit from their misery.

Nico and Trent exchanged grim glances. "If we're not fast enough or someone discovers our presence in the compound too soon, Maldonado's men might kill the women," Trent said.

Another voice came through the speaker of Nico's phone. "Do you need another team? Fifteen operatives have a better chance of getting to the women and freeing them."

"Who's available?" Nico asked Brent Maddox.

"The Texas team can be in Puerto Vallarta in four hours."

"Send them. We'll meet them at the safe house. The Pacific Star is due to leave port in ten hours."

"Copy that. Sam?"

"Yes, sir?"

"Sorenson gave me an update on you. I'm going to ask you a question and I want an honest answer."

"What's the question?"

"Can you handle dealing with this trafficking organization and the victims? I'll know if you're telling me the truth because I know you. I have to be able to trust you. If you fall apart on site, your teammates' lives could be forfeit. Since he'll refuse to leave your side if you freeze, Joe's life rests in your hands."

Her gaze locked with Joe's. His eyes were filled with trust and confidence in her and her ability to do the job. Sam searched inside herself, evaluating her physical and emotional state and her own confidence level. "I can handle it, sir." As long as she had Joe by her side, Sam could handle anything, including her worst nightmare come to life with long, sharp teeth and guns blazing.

"All right. Before you join the others on this mission, you will have a session with Marcus Lang. That's a direct order, Coleman. If you don't comply, you'll be riding a desk until further notice. Am I clear?"

"Yes, sir."

"Nico, expect contact from the Texas unit within the hour. I want an update in two hours."

"Roger that." He ended the call and glanced around the room. "Let's get started. We have plans to make and not much time to complete them."

CHAPTER THIRTY-SIX

Joe glanced back to make sure Sam was on his six. Her gaze met his and she nodded. Good. She was ready. Hopefully, the two-hour session with the Fortress counselor had shored up Sam's confidence in her ability to handle herself and the trafficking victims.

He faced the Maldonado compound again, amazed at Sam's resilience and strength. She could have been falling apart after the trauma she'd been through. Instead, she fought back. Joe admired her as much as he loved her.

Joe activated his mic. "Team 6 in position," he whispered. With 15 operatives moving in on the Maldonado compound and all using the same comm channel, the team leaders had further divided their individual units into two groups for easier identification on the comm system.

"Copy," Nico replied. "Wait for my signal."

"Roger that."

He and Sam waited in silence for the rest of the teams to take their positions and for the team leaders to give the signal to go. The night sky was cloudy, a warm breeze blowing against their grease-streaked faces. At two in the morning, the compound was silent except for the guards making their rounds of the area.

Over the next three minutes, the other five teams signaled they were in position.

"On my mark," Nico murmured. The other two unit leaders had ceded mission leadership to Nico. "Six, go. One, two, and four hold for one minute. Team five moving."

The various teams acknowledge his orders as Joe and Sam left dense tree cover and headed for the building most likely to house the women slated for sale. Footsteps ahead and to the right sent them scurrying behind bushes lined against the wall of the building. A slender soldier strode around the corner five feet from their position. Dressed in all black, he was armed with two handguns, one holstered on each side of his waist. He also carried a rifle.

Joe signaled Sam and he moved out from cover behind the enemy, Ka-Bar in hand. A quick slice with the blade and the guard was down. One more guard patrolled this area and he was due to appear in two minutes. Joe dragged the guard's body behind the bushes. He and Sam rolled him under the foliage. Not perfect but it would have to do for the moment. They didn't have much time before the second guard arrived.

He activated his mic. "Five, one tango down."

"Copy," came the whispered reply.

Sam touched his arm and inclined her head toward the left. Footsteps.

Joe frowned. The guard was early. He hadn't changed his pattern in the four hours the operatives watched the compound. Why change now? Hushed voices reached his ears.

"I'm telling you something is wrong. I swear I saw someone lurking around out here."

"Marco would have reported a problem. He hasn't. A storm is blowing in. Maybe you saw tree branches swaying."

"I don't like it."

"You're just spooked because of the attack at the warehouses. Flores's driver must have led the enemy right to them."

Two men rounded the corner, each carrying weapons in their hands. Joe signaled Sam to take the man on the left, the smaller of the two. He still outweighed her by a good 60 pounds but he was closer to her height. The second man was Joe's.

They waited until the men walked past the bushes and continued their discussion before moving from cover. Joe tackled his target from behind, deliberately drawing the attention of the smaller man to give Sam a better chance to take the thug by surprise. He trusted Sam to make sure her target didn't nail him in the back of the head with a bullet.

A swift intake of breath and a heavy thud behind him told Joe that Sam had dispatched her soldier. He grunted as his opponent managed to land a blow to his ribs. Joe slammed his fist into the enemy's throat, crushing his windpipe. Shock widened the other man's eyes as he struggled to breathe. Soon, the light in his eyes dimmed and his struggles ceased.

"Let's hide these two with their friend. Clock's ticking." Joe and Sam dragged the two men behind the bushes.

"Five, two more tangos down." Joe took the lead again as they approached the window of the room they had chosen as their entrance point. If it proved to be occupied, he and Sam would find another entry point.

He jumped, grasped the small ledge, and carefully peered over the bottom of the window. A storage room. No people. Perfect. Joe glanced at Sam and gave her a nod.

Dropping to the ground again, Joe crouched and threaded his fingers together to provide support for Sam's foot. As soon as she placed her foot in the cradle he created, Joe lifted her. She quickly unlocked and raised the window, then climbed inside.

"Clear," she whispered into the mic.

Joe hoisted himself through the window and dropped soundlessly to the floor in a crouch, weapon up and tracking. He activated his mic. "Team 6 inside target building."

"Copy," Nico acknowledged.

According to the infrared images gathered with the Fortress satellite, the women were being held in a room at the end of this hallway. He and Sam had taken care of three roaming guards on this side of the compound. Their intel suggested that four soldiers were posted inside this building to guard the women.

Joe motioned for Sam to take position on his left side. He slowly twisted the door knob and eased the door open a crack. No movement and dim lighting. The room they'd chosen to breach was just inside the entrance to the hallway.

He opened the door further. Light flickered to their left. A television. At least one of the soldiers was distracted for the moment. Joe signaled Sam to follow him. They followed the sounds of the action flick to a room with a large-screen television, leather furniture, and one snoozing guard. In less than a minute, Joe crossed the room with silent steps, clamped a hand over the man's mouth, and slit his throat. They couldn't afford to leave a threat at their backs. The lives of the women depended on them.

He and Sam returned to the hall and made their way toward the room that contained the women. Snoring could be heard through the door of one of the rooms they passed. Excellent.

The operatives entered the room in silence, killed the second guard, and returned to the hallway. At least two of the four guards were down. That left two unaccounted for.

Joe and Sam continued toward the room containing the women. They checked each room as they passed. All empty. Were the two remaining guards inside the room with their captives?

The possibility made Joe's stomach knot. Close quarters combat with civilians in the room was not his first choice of places to engage the enemy. Too easy for a stray bullet to hit an innocent victim.

Didn't have a choice, though. The guards had to be taken out before they became aware the compound was under attack.

When they arrived at their target room, Joe grasped the knob and twisted. The room beyond was dimly lit. Four women lay on mattresses, chained to grommets on the concrete floor.

One of the guards stood with his back to the room, watching out the window into the darkness. Where was the other guard?

A repositioning of booted feet clued Joe in to the other man's location. He looked at Sam and used hand signals to tell her where the guards were stationed. She nodded and indicated she'd take the guard closest to the door.

Joe counted down with his fingers. He kicked the door open, dove into the room, and shot the guard who turned from the window with a shout and a handgun pointed in his direction. The women screamed as the guard flew back against the window, breaking the glass. He slid to the floor as Sam shot the other guard.

Joe covered the distance to the man he'd shot and checked for a pulse. Nothing. He rose and started to turn toward the women when Sam shouted, "Gun!"

Joe dove to the floor away from the women. A shot rang out in the room followed a split second later by another shot. Pain exploded in Joe's thigh as he hit the ground and rolled to his stomach, weapon trained on the doorway. "Sparky?"

"I'm fine. You?"

"I'm hit."

"How bad?"

"Don't know. Don't want to look, either."

Sam scrambled to his side and tore at his pants leg, then activated her mic. "Five, my partner's down." She unbuckled her belt and cinched it around Joe's thigh to slow the bleeding. He hissed. "Sorry," she murmured.

Jesse Phelps, the Texas unit's medic broke in. "I'm on it."

"Copy," Nico acknowledged. "How bad, Sam?"

"Bullet to the thigh. I haven't been able to assess the extent of the damage yet."

"Joe?"

"Hurts like crazy. I think it's a through and through. I'm not mobile." Sam couldn't work on him, soothe the women, and protect all of them at the same time.

"One minute," Phelps whispered.

"Copy," he murmured. Joe groaned as he moved to a sitting position and leaned his back against the wall. He prayed he stayed conscious long enough to protect Sam and the other women until the other medic arrived.

He waved her toward the women. "See if you can calm them before Phelps gets here."

"You're the one who's hurt."

"I'll survive. They'll be more likely to respond to you since you're a woman. Once they're free, the women can't run into the compound with getting shot or recaptured. You have to convince them to stay in place until it's safe."

Sam spoke softly to the women as she picked the locks on the collars around their necks, telling them to remain calm and stay in place until it was safe to leave the room.

A moment later, Phelps said, "I'm down the hall and coming in soft. Tell the women I'm with you so I won't terrorize them more than they already are."

"Copy," Sam acknowledged and conveyed the information to the women.

Although his vision was starting to blur, Joe trained his weapon on the doorway. Phelps stepped into the room.

Once more, Sam reassured the captives that Phelps was there to help. Once she was assured they wouldn't panic, she motioned for him to take over freeing the women from their chains.

She ran to Joe's side, dropped to her knees, and slid off her mike bag. "Let me see." Sam pushed aside his hand, ripped the fabric of his pants further, and smoothed the ragged edges away from his wounded thigh.

Joe growled as the pain spiked. "How bad?"

"Just a scratch." She winked at him, then concentrated on examining his wound. "You're right. A through and through. I can't tell if the bullet nicked the bone without an x-ray. No weight on it until we know how bad the injury is."

"Patch me up until we get to Sorenson's clinic. I'm not letting anyone but you work on me in this country."

"That's the plan. Guess we'll have a few weeks to recuperate together."

"Can't think of a better partner to recuperate with."

Sam pulled out packets of QuikClot. Joe grimaced. Man, he hated that stuff. It did the job, though. He clenched his hands and gritted his teeth, preparing for the searing pain. Just before Sam poured, he sent a pointed glance to Phelps who knelt on his other side. The other medic acknowledged the unspoken order to protect Sam with his life.

"Ready?" she murmured.

"Do it." He prayed he wouldn't embarrass himself by passing out and becoming more of a hindrance to the operation than he already was.

Sam ripped open one packet and dumped the powder into the wound at the front of his thigh.

Joe dragged in a ragged breath and rode out the pain, beads of sweat forming on his skin. After applying a pressure bandage, Sam and Phelps eased him to his stomach and repeated the treatment on the wound at the back of his thigh. By the time she finished, Joe was weak and felt like puking his guts out. No way would he be able to maneuver from the compound under his own steam.

Sam activated her mic again. "Five, the women are free. I patched my partner for now. We need to get him out of here."

"Five minutes. Our fed friend called in a favor with a group of federales that he's familiar with and trusts. They'll be here soon. We need to be gone by the time they arrive."

"Copy." She glanced down at Joe who still rested on his stomach. "You hanging in there with me?"

"No way I'm leaving you with Tex here guarding your back. Don't want to give him a chance to make a move on my woman."

Phelps chuckled. "Like that, is it?"

"Yep. Hands off." Joe frowned. His words were slurring. Why?

A soft hand cupped his cheek. "You lost a lot of blood. Rest. We'll give you a pint of blood on the jet."

He sighed. His eyelids were so heavy he couldn't keep them open any longer. "Protect her," he murmured to Phelps.

"I've got her and you, buddy. Don't worry."

With that reassurance, Joe quit fighting the darkness.

CHAPTER THIRTY-SEVEN

Joe scowled at the taciturn world-class trauma surgeon turned veterinarian. "I want out of here, Doc. Don't tell me I'm not ready to travel yet." He'd been in Sorenson's clinic for two days. The walls were starting to close in on him. All he wanted to do was go home to Nashville to recuperate and take Sam with him. She hadn't left his side for more than ten minutes during the past 60 hours. Joe was worried about her.

Ted Sorenson snorted. "You have a medical degree in your Go bag, Gray?"

"You know I don't." He glanced toward the door to be sure Sam wasn't in sight. "Sam is wiped out. I have to get her home so she'll rest. If you release me to recuperate in Nashville, she'll relax enough to let go and sleep. She's been catnapping since I was shot."

The doctor looked thoughtful.

"Come on, Doc. The flight's only a few hours and I promise to stretch out on the bed in the back of the jet the whole time."

"I want your word you'll use the crutches I gave you for the next two weeks. Absolutely no weight on that leg until you're cleared. And you are not to go on a mission for at least a month, possibly longer."

Joe started to protest but he was worried enough about Sam to promise almost anything to get her home. "I promise."

Still Sorenson hesitated.

"Come on, man. Help me take care of the woman I love."

A deep sigh. "All right. I'll prescribe pain meds and antibiotics for you to take. Don't skip a dose. You need to see the doctor in Nashville in two weeks. You have to take time off. Your leg needs time to mend."

"No problem. As long as I have Sam with me, I won't mind the vacation time."

"You going to marry the lady?"

"I'm not letting her get away."

Sorenson gave a slow nod. "Good. She's an amazing woman."

"No argument from me."

"Well, I'll get your meds ready and let Maddox know you're cleared to leave. I understand the jet has been fueled and ready since you came out of surgery." A wry smile curved the doctor's face. "Your boss knows you well."

Sam walked into the room a few minutes later with Trace on her heels. "Hey, I hear we're going home."

"As soon as Sorenson brings my meds and Trace helps me dress." He glanced at the crutches propped against the wall. "I'm stuck hopping around on those things for the next two weeks."

"I'll see if Dr. Sorenson wants help preparing the meds while Trace works with you." A slow smile spread over her face. "The doc said the rape kit results were negative." With those words, Sam walked out and closed the door behind her.

Relief had Joe sagging against the hospital bed. Thank God.

"How did you get the doc to agree to release you?" the sniper asked as he assisted Joe in dragging on his cargoes.

Joe yanked his black t-shirt over his head before answering. "Told him Sam wasn't sleeping well and wouldn't until I got her home."

Trace chuckled. "Smart man. The doc has a soft spot for our medic." He stared at Joe a moment. "You planning to marry Sam?"

"I'm not stupid. You bet I am."

"Good."

An hour later, the Fortress jet raced down the runway of the Bayside airport in Texas and lifted into the air, bound toward Nashville. In the bedroom at the back of the plane, door open for Sam to hear if a teammate needed her, Joe held out his hand to the woman he loved. "Come here."

"You should be resting."

He motioned to the bed he was sitting on, his back pressed to the headboard. "I promised Sorenson to stretch out my leg. I'm doing that. Doesn't mean I can't hold you while I'm following his orders. Come here, Sparky. You're exhausted and so am I. I'll rest better if you're in my arms."

She looked doubtful but settled against his uninjured side.

He tugged her closer, her head resting against his shoulder. "I love you, Sam."

"I love you, too." One hand stroked over his chest.

Joe's heart raced. Would she reject him? "Enough to marry me?"

His question stilled her movements. "You want to marry me?"

"I want everything with you. A home, a family, a dog. Please say you'll marry me. I need you, Sam."

She tilted her head back to look at him. Sam smiled. "I would love to be your wife."

"Fantastic." He captured her mouth in a deep, hot kiss. When he came up for air, Joe asked, "Any objections to a Christmas wedding?"

Sam blinked. "That's six months away. Why Christmas?"

"I want the chance to romance you the right way. That means dates. Lots of dates and time for the two of us to really get to know each other as a couple. I want you to trust me with every part of your heart. Will you let me do this for us?"

"Of course. I adore you, Joe."

He dropped another kiss on her mouth. "Perfect. We're a matched pair. We're going to have a great life together, my love." He couldn't wait to get started. Joe fell asleep, holding the woman of his dreams against his heart.

ABOUT THE AUTHOR

Rebecca Deel is a preacher's kid with a black belt in karate. She teaches business classes at a private four-year college outside Nashville, Tennessee. She plays the piano at church, writes freelance articles, and runs interference for the family dogs. She's been married to her amazing husband for more than 25 years and is the proud mom of two grown sons. She delivers occasional devotions to the women's group at her church and conducts seminars in personal safety, money management, and writing. Her articles have been published in *ONE Magazine*, *Contact*, and *Co-Laborer*, and she was profiled in the June 2010 Williamson edition of *Nashville Christian Family* magazine. Rebecca completed her Doctor of Arts degree in Economics and wears her favorite Dallas Cowboys sweatshirt when life turns ugly.

For more information on Rebecca . . .

Sign up for Rebecca's newsletter: http://eepurl.com/_B6w9

Visit Rebecca's website: www.rebeccadeelbooks.com

Printed in Great Britain
by Amazon